LOOK
BEHIND YOU

Center Point
Large Print

Also by Iris Johansen and Roy Johansen and available from Center Point Large Print:

Sight Unseen
The Naked Eye
Night Watch

**This Large Print Book carries the
Seal of Approval of N.A.V.H.**

LOOK
BEHIND
YOU

IRIS JOHANSEN
AND
ROY JOHANSEN

CENTER POINT LARGE PRINT
THORNDIKE, MAINE

This Center Point Large Print edition
is published in the year 2017 by arrangement with
St. Martin's Press.

The text of this Large Print edition is unabridged.
In other aspects, this book may vary
from the original edition.
Printed in the United States of America
on permanent paper.
Set in 16-point Times New Roman type.

ISBN: 978-1-68324-496-7

Library of Congress Cataloging-in-Publication Data

Names: Johansen, Iris, author. | Johansen, Roy, author.
Title: Look behind you / Iris Johansen & Roy Johansen.
Description: Large print edition. | Thorndike, Maine : Center Point
    Large Print, 2017.
Identifiers: LCCN 2017023996 | ISBN 9781683244967
    (hardcover : alk. paper)
Subjects: LCSH: Murder—Investigation—Fiction. | Large type
    books. | BISAC: FICTION / Thrillers. | GSAFD: Suspense fiction. |
    Mystery fiction.
Classification: LCC PS3560.O275 L67 2017b | DDC 813/.54—dc23
LC record available at https://lccn.loc.gov/2017023996

LOOK
BEHIND YOU

PROLOGUE

"Another soda and lime. Easy on the lime this time."

The bartender pursed her lips and gave him a pitying look. She obviously thought he was a recovering alcoholic, desperately clinging to sobriety by his fingernails.

He was nothing of the sort. He just needed to keep his wits about him.

Zachary looked up at the bar's mirrored backdrop where he could see dozens of people shoehorned into this popular downtown watering hole. There was only one who interested him, though.

Pretty, strawberry-blond Amanda Robinson sat in a corner booth. Late twenties, medium height, and a smile that lit up the room. She was surrounded by friends, three women and two men, who obviously adored her. They were finishing their third round of drinks. As always, Amanda had an apple martini and gave her dark-haired friend the toothpick-impaled cherries.

Zachary checked the time; 9:45 P.M. The group, many of whom worked at the same insurance company as Amanda, started making noises about it being a "school night." Pretty Amanda picked up her phone and opened an app that bathed her face in a soft blue glow.

That was his cue. Zachary threw a twenty onto the bar and walked outside. The sidewalks on University Avenue were much less crowded than they'd been a couple of hours before. He rounded the corner and found his car on the lonely side street. He unlocked the trunk, pulled out a large magnetic Vroom ride-share sign, and slapped it onto the passenger-side door. He climbed inside, started the car, and circled around the block.

He smiled as he saw Pretty Amanda outside the bar. She and her friends were now talking on the sidewalk. He powered down the passenger-side window as he rolled up to the group.

"Amanda Robinson?" he shouted to the group.

"That's me!" she shouted.

After a few good-byes and quick hugs, Pretty Amanda hopped into the back seat. She pulled the door closed behind her.

"So . . ." he said, pretending to study his phone. "We're going to Rillington Drive?"

"Yes," she said absently. She was already engrossed in her own phone, scrolling through emails.

Perfect.

"This won't take long." Zachary power-locked the car doors as a shiver of excitement tore through him. "I promise, Amanda. This won't take long at all."

CHAPTER I

Kendra Michaels studied the nine-year-old boy in the wheelchair.

Just as his file had stated, Ryan Walker was unresponsive. Disengaged, borderline catatonic. He'd been that way since suffering head and spine injuries in the same boating accident that had killed his father.

It had been nine months, and although there was some hope that he might one day walk again, doctors were less sure about his cognitive ability. He hadn't spoken since the accident, and doctors disagreed whether the principal cause was psychological or physiological.

Kendra knew she was a port of last resort for Ryan's harried mother, Janice. The poor woman had been trying to find answers for her son at the same time she was grieving for her husband. She'd been advised to consult a music therapist after Ryan had supposedly shown a slight response to a few television commercial jingles. It was a phenomenon Kendra had so far been unable to reproduce in her studio.

Janice Walker was watching from behind a one-way glass on the studio's far side, and Kendra could almost feel her despair.

Kendra studied the boy's unresponsive eyes. *Let me in, Ryan. You'll be safe here.*

She walked across the room to the keyboard. Her studio was a large carpeted room twenty-five by fifteen feet, filled with an assortment of musical instruments: a keyboard, a drum set, and an array of woodwinds. She'd played some recordings and live guitar pieces for Ryan, but those elicited no response.

Maybe the keyboard would work better.

She sat down and turned on the console. "Okay, Ryan. Here's something I think you'll like. Your mom tells me you like Kiss. You're a Paul Stanley fan, right?"

No response.

Kendra started playing "I Love It Loud" using her keyboard to emulate the band's hard-driving sound.

Still nothing.

But then, there was . . . something.

A slight furrowing of the brow.

A pull on the right corner of his mouth.

But that was all.

Kendra finished the song without any further response from Ryan. "Did you like that one?"

No reaction.

She stood. "Well, that's enough for today. We'll listen to more music the next time you're here, okay?"

The door to the observation room opened, and

Janice Walker stood smiling with excitement in the doorway. "Did you see that?"

Kendra glanced down at Ryan. "Let's talk in there."

Kendra ushered Janice back into the observation room and closed the door behind them.

"That was progress, right?" Janice asked.

"Maybe. I've had clients make facial expressions like that when they pass gas. Or when they're hungry. Or for a dozen other reasons."

"I know my son. He was reacting to the music."

Kendra thought so too, but it was always better to keep parents' expectations in check. "I hope you're right."

"I am right. Where do we go from here?"

"We keep working at it. In some people, music is the crowbar that opens the outside world to them. It helps them make connections that no other kind of communication can. Those small connections can lead to bigger connections. That's the goal anyway."

"Can we come back tomorrow?"

Janice was anxious, like a starving person who had been tossed a bread crumb. Not that Kendra could blame her. Her response would have been the same if Ryan had been her son.

"We should wait a couple days. It helps to give the brain time to process between sessions."

Janice nodded, but she couldn't hide her disappointment. "I know. It's just . . . This is the first time I've seen him respond to anything since . . ." Her voice trailed off. "I want it so *much*."

Kendra reached out and squeezed Janice's arm. "I know. If this is the crowbar that will work for Ryan, I promise I'll find the right way to use it. I'll call you every day, and we'll talk and search for that way. We just need to be patient. Okay?"

She nodded, still staring at her son on the other side of the one-way glass. "It's hard to be patient." She tried to smile. "But I believe you're doing everything you can for him. And I know you have other clients. A couple of them came in here while you were working with Ryan."

Kendra wrinkled her brow. "Really?"

"Yes. They came in through the other door, the one that leads out to the hallway."

"Ryan's my last appointment of the day. Are you sure . . . ?"

"Well, they said they were here to see you. I just assumed . . . It was a man and a woman, both well-dressed. They said they'd come back later."

Kendra wasn't sure she liked this. She had an idea who it might be, but she hoped she was wrong.

"Is everything all right?" Janice asked.

"Yes. Fine. Nothing to worry about. I'm sure they'll be back soon."

• • •

"Soon" was only five minutes after Ryan and Janice left, when FBI Special Agent Roland Metcalf entered her studio. He was a tall, good-looking man in his mid-twenties and he possessed a self-effacing sense of humor that she'd always found refreshing for a man in his profession. Kendra had known him for a couple of years and today he was with a young woman she had never met. The woman was tall, attractive, fit-looking, with sleek brown hair and a completely professional demeanor.

"Sorry to barge in on you at work, Kendra." He motioned to the woman at his side. "This is Special Agent Gina Carson. She just transferred in from the Chicago office."

Kendra adjusted the stacks of sheet music she'd picked up. "Hello."

Gina nodded her greeting with obvious uneasiness. She clearly wasn't sure why they were there.

Metcalf was strolling around the studio. "You know, I've never seen this place. I've always wanted to see what you do."

"Well, it seems you did that today. I heard you let yourself in the observation room while I was working with my last client."

Metcalf nodded. "Sorry about that. The main entrance was locked."

"I didn't want to be disturbed."

Metcalf quickly caught the nuance in her tone. "We didn't want that either. That's why we left."

"But you came back," she said without expression.

"Come on, Kendra. You *have* to know why I'm here."

"I have a pretty good idea." She continued to tidy the sheet music. "Doesn't mean that I like it."

Metcalf frowned as he waited for her to finish.

She let him wait.

After another moment he said, "Three murders, Kendra. Three murders in the last eight days, all within a couple of miles of here."

She didn't look up. "Three? I thought it was just two."

"A third popped up this morning. We're on our way to the crime scene now. San Diego PD has been handling the cases, but the FBI has just joined the investigation. My boss wants you to join us."

"Fortunately, Special Agent in Charge Griffin isn't *my* boss. Therefore I get to politely decline."

Gina moved toward the exit. "Then thanks for your time."

Metcalf held his ground. "Hold on, Carson." He smiled at Kendra. "I need a few more minutes to appeal to Kendra's sense of civic duty."

Metcalf's partner was clearly annoyed as she stepped back toward him. "You didn't tell me she was a music therapist when you said you wanted to stop here."

"It wasn't relevant to our investigation."

"I'm thinking *she's* not relevant to our investigation."

Kendra's lips quirked. "You heard the lady, Metcalf. I'm not relevant."

"We're wasting time," Gina said. "You asked and she answered. She said she's not interested. Are we working this case or not?"

Kendra was getting more annoyed at this foul-tempered woman than she was at Metcalf. Her eyes narrowed on the agent's tight mouth and annoyed expression. She found herself suddenly feeling protective of Metcalf, not that he needed anyone's protection. She liked the guy and it irked her that this agent would speak to him with such a total lack of respect.

Metcalf, perhaps sensing Kendra's reaction, suddenly snapped at Gina. "Cool your jets, Carson. Griffin wants an extra set of eyes on that crime scene. *Her* eyes."

"I'm still missing something," Gina said sourly. "On our way here, didn't you tell me she used to be blind?"

"Yes," Kendra answered for him. "For the first twenty years of my life. An experimental surgical procedure gave me my sight."

Gina clicked her tongue. "So now you have super vision or something?"

15

"Not at all," Kendra said. "I'm sure my eyesight is no better than yours."

Gina turned back to Metcalf. "Then would you like to tell me why we're here groveling to a music therapist to help us on a murder investigation?"

Metcalf was obviously losing patience. "I don't grovel, Carson. I ask politely, because that's what the Bureau does when they go hat in hand trying to get help keeping a serial killer from claiming other victims. You obviously haven't spent much time reading our case files since you transferred down. If you had, you would have seen that Kendra has helped crack over a dozen cases in the past few years. Many of those would've gone unsolved if she hadn't stepped in."

Gina was slightly taken aback by the attack. "And how, exactly, has she been of—"

"I don't take anything I see for granted," Kendra interrupted. God, she got tired of going through explanations. Particularly to arrogant agents like Carson. "When I got my sight, I got into the habit of identifying and mentally cataloging everything that passed in front of my eyes, just to make my way in a world that was totally new to me."

"I guess that makes sense," Gina said skeptically.

"That isn't the half of it," Metcalf said. "Like most blind people, Kendra had already developed her other senses to help her get by. Hearing, smell, touch, taste . . . She's held onto those skills, too."

Gina still seemed unsure. "Huh. Interesting."

Kendra shrugged. "Most investigators only go by what they see. They're missing well over half the story."

She could almost see Gina's hackles rise at her words. "Have you had any law enforcement training?"

"No. It's nothing I've ever had any interest in."

"No, you'd rather play with your instruments or try to impress agents like Metcalf here. Believe it or not, we're actually trained observers," Gina said. "It's a big part of our jobs. I appreciate that you've assisted my colleagues, Dr. Michaels, but I really don't see how you could be of any help in a case that is shaping up to be—"

"You want to show her?" Metcalf was smiling at Kendra.

"Not really."

Gina was frowning as she looked from one to the other of them. "Show me what?"

"Come on, Kendra," Metcalf murmured, his eyes twinkling. "She annoyed the hell out of you, and you're no angel. You know you want to do it."

She *had* annoyed her, but she'd been trying to ignore it.

"I'd rather not."

"Please. You're not the only one who took flack."

Kendra sighed. He was right, she was definitely no angel. It had been a rough day and Gina Carson had rubbed her the wrong way. "If I do this, will you leave?"

Metcalf laughed. "We'll *think* about leaving."

"Bastard." She turned toward Gina and looked her up and down."

Gina shifted uneasily. "What the hell is going on?"

"You used to smoke," Kendra said. "But then you quit for a while. Maybe a *long* while. But you recently started again."

Gina cursed. "You can smell smoke on me?"

"No." Kendra walked toward a cabinet with her sheet music. "But it's only natural for someone who's been under the kind of stress you have been under."

"What stress?"

"Moving, for one. You've lived in Chicago for most, if not all, of your life. Your parents are from there and probably their parents before them. It's also stressful getting out of a long-term relationship. You recently broke up with your boyfriend or girlfriend. Is that what prompted the move?"

Gina stared at her for a long moment. "Boyfriend. Matt. After seven years. But that wasn't the only reason."

"In any case, you're still living out of a hotel

18

while you get your own place. You're looking to buy, not rent. For now, you're staying at the Pacific. I hear it's nice."

Gina glanced at Metcalf accusingly. "Someone told her."

"Don't look at me," he said. "And I'm sure she didn't even know you existed until five minutes ago."

"I didn't," Kendra said. "But I know you drove here from Chicago even though the FBI provides you with a company car. Maybe you did it because you wanted to bring a car of your own here, but I'm thinking it was because it was the best way to bring your pet. A parakeet?"

Gina's expression was becoming more stunned by the moment. "Cockatiel."

"A very loved and spoiled little bird," Kendra said.

"Extremely," Gina said weakly.

"You like seventies rock and Starbucks. You may cook, but you're also partial to Papa John's Pizza. And you're a tennis fan, aren't you?"

Gina appeared to be dazed. "Yes."

Kendra turned to Metcalf. "Satisfied?"

His smile was still brimming with mischief. "Come on, you're not gonna tell her who her first grade teacher was?"

"Mrs. McAlister. She had a mole on her left cheek."

His jaw dropped. "What in . . ."

"I'm joking." She turned back to Gina. "But it would've been awesome if I was right about that one, huh?"

She was silent and then said grudgingly, "It's still pretty awesome. Who the hell told you all this stuff?"

Kendra shrugged. "You did, in the first thirty seconds you were here."

"I seriously doubt that."

"Doubt all you please. It's true."

Gina was suddenly looking uncomfortable. "Okay, what about the smoking? I've been trying to hide it from my new coworkers. It shows a lack of self-discipline."

"For what it's worth, I can't smell smoke on you at all. But I can tell you've been chewing Nicorette gum. Cinnamon Surge flavor. It's on your breath."

Gina rolled her eyes. "I was trying to decide between that and Fruit Chill."

"White Ice Mint may be their least distinctive flavor."

"I'll take your word for that," Gina said grimly.

Kendra pointed to Gina's right upper arm, left bare by her sleeveless top. "There's also a slight tan line there in the exact dimensions of a nicotine patch."

Gina looked at her arm. "I quit for four years, and I started up again after my boyfriend and I broke up."

". . . which brings me to another tan line," Kendra pointed to Gina's neck. "It looks like you've been wearing a heart-shaped pendant for quite some time. Every day for years but you recently stopped wearing it. Your skin is much lighter there. With no sign of an engagement or wedding ring, that suggests a breakup. Also, your left upper arm is much more tanned than your right. That's where I got the long car trip. You drove here from Chicago."

"But you knew my parents were there. And my grandparents."

"Linguistics. You have a born-and-bred Chicago accent. Anyone who's seen *The Blues Brothers* could spot it a mile away. It's doubtful it would be quite so pronounced if your parents didn't imprint it on you. And if *their* parents didn't imprint it on *them*."

She scowled. "Right on all counts. But how the hell did you know about my bird?"

Kendra took Gina's hand and pointed to dozens of light scratches on the back of her hand and arm. "Too small and too light to be a cat or even a pet rodent. It's clearly a small bird. Those light scratches run all the way up your arm and onto your shoulder. You take him out of his cage frequently. Obviously loved and spoiled."

"But what about all those other things? Papa John's? Tennis?"

Kendra smiled. "You were holding your phone

when you walked in here. You'd probably just checked messages and your main screen was still lit up. Your app icons gave you away. Papa John's Pizza, Starbucks, and The Tennis Channel. I could see that your most recent album played from your phone was The Who's *Tommy*."

Gina looked down at her phone. "Oh, man."

"You can write a biography based on a person's main Smartphone screen."

"Pretty pathetic life story." Gina's lips twisted. "Pizza delivery and drive-through coffee."

It did sound pathetic, Kendra thought, and suddenly all the vulnerable details she'd pulled together about Gina Carson were scrolling through her mind. Her antagonism toward the woman was abruptly gone. She smiled. "For the record, I have the same apps on my phone. But I also saw you had the Pacific Guest Suites app, which lets you use your phone to unlock your room. It's a place I recommend to my colleagues and clients when they're in town for more than a few days. And you also gave the Zillow real estate app prime placement on your screen, which tells me that you're looking to buy instead of rent."

Gina nodded ruefully. "Well, I'll be more careful about who sees my phone, that's for damn sure."

Kendra turned to Metcalf. "The dog and pony show is over. Time for you to go."

"I said I'd *consider* leaving. I just did that and

I've rejected the idea. At least not until you agree to come with us to the crime scene." He coaxed, "What would it hurt? Just a quick glance around."

Kendra shook her head. "I have real work to do. My work."

"Dr. Michaels." Gina Carson's voice was hesitant. "I know I probably came on too strong with you. It's a habit I have. Maybe it's a little worse right now, because I'm the new kid in town. Everything's pretty strange here for me right now. I just want you to know that, if you're not doing what Metcalf wants because you're pissed off at me, I'm not going to give you any trouble."

Shit. Those words had been hard for Gina. All she had was a tough façade and that damn cockatiel in her life right now. This was becoming more and more difficult for Kendra. "I'm not pissed off at you." She made a face. "Not any longer. I just don't want to get involved in another case right now."

"I know you don't," Metcalf said. "Griffin told me I'd have trouble convincing you. I was hoping that you'd think I was so charming and lovable I wouldn't have to pull out the wild card Griffin gave me."

"Wild card?" Kendra repeated warily.

"Griffin told me to tell you something."

"I can hardly wait to hear what it is," she said dryly.

"He said you owed him."

Kendra cursed. "He's playing *that* card?"

"He really wants your help on this."

That was clear enough. Griffin had recently been helpful when a friend of hers was in deep trouble. He'd given her manpower and lab time when he had no official obligation to do so. She had known his help would not be without strings.

Now he was cashing in.

"Okay," she finally said. "I'll visit this one crime scene with you and take a look around. That's it."

Metcalf nodded. "That's all I'm asking."

But one thing could lead to another, and she would have to be the one to call the halt. Her last case had been both physically and emotionally draining, and she needed to step back and heal for a time. She didn't *need* this.

But evidently she was going to get it.

Just one quick look around. That was going to be her limit.

"Let's get this over with," Kendra said. She turned to Gina. "And when we're finished, you can use that Papa John's app to order me a medium Meat Lovers pizza. I'm starving."

Metcalf offered her a lift to the crime scene, but Kendra turned him down flat. She preferred to follow in her own car. She didn't want to be stuck there any longer than she needed to be.

Within minutes she turned onto Holt Street and

immediately found herself at a police road block. She saw Metcalf waving his badge at the officer, then pointing back to her. The cop waved them through.

It was a block taken up by Kimbrough Elementary School on one side and a two-story apartment building on the other. In the middle of the street was a large white tent, approximately ten by ten feet. Kendra counted no less than a dozen uniformed police officers on the scene plus several detectives and forensics personnel.

She parked behind Metcalf and walked toward the school with him and Gina. "I'm guessing the tent isn't a PTA bake sale," she said grimly.

"San Diego PD put it up to spare the kiddies from what promises to be a horrific sight."

"Great. Thanks again for the wonderful afternoon."

"Aw, come on. What would you rather be doing today?"

"Root canal. Colonoscopy. Having my fingernails removed with a pair of pliers." She stopped outside the tent. "I smell gasoline. Something's been cooking." The realization hit her. "Something . . . or someone."

"Exactly," Gina said. She grabbed the tent's door flap. "Ready for this?"

No, Kendra wanted to tell her. She wasn't like them. She could never get used to the sad, horrible stories that greeted her at these crime scenes.

She nodded. "I'm ready."

Kendra ducked through the flap and stopped cold. There in the center of the tent was a charred woman's body bound to a desk chair.

Her breath left her.

It was the work of a monster.

A police detective had entered behind them. "It happened around 11:30. The principal saw her burning out here. He ran out with an extinguisher and put it out."

Kendra still hadn't adjusted to the shock. There were wisps of strawberry blond hair and a face that was half gone.

Kendra looked away.

Detach.

Concentrate.

"Burned alive?" Gina asked.

Kendra shook her head. "No. She's been dead for a few days."

"How can you tell?" Metcalf asked.

"The odor. It's not just charred flesh, there's been decomposition."

The detective nodded. "The M.E. was just here. He backs that up. He says she's been dead a few days at least."

Kendra made herself turn back toward the corpse. Corpse. That's right, think of her as an object, a puzzle. Not as a woman who'd had a life, friends, lovers. "Do we have an ID?"

"Not yet," the detective replied. "We've just

started running her against missing persons."

Kendra studied the corpse, trying to pull anything from it she could. "If that doesn't pan out, you might canvas some of the high-end hair salons. She used a Japanese hair conditioner that isn't common around here. Tsubaki."

Gina jotted this down into her notebook. "I'm not sure I'm spelling it right. I'm a Pantene girl myself."

"I know." Kendra knelt beside the corpse, which was still dripping with extinguisher foam. "Did anyone see her deposited here?"

"Not so far," the detective replied. "We've done a preliminary canvas, but no one reports seeing her before the fire."

"Probably a truck with a ramp. The chair could have been rolled out quickly, set on fire, and the truck took off before anyone noticed." Kendra looked up. "It's my guess her body was taped to the chair at a fairly active construction site. You should start there."

"What makes you say that?" Metcalf asked.

She pointed to the casters, which were covered by a chalky powder. "That looks like silica dust, which you'll find at many building sites. The body was already in this chair when it rolled across the dust and kicked some up." She gently lifted the corpse's left pant leg. "See? It's not underneath the body."

"Very good," Metcalf said.

There was nothing good about anything connected to what had happened to this woman, Kendra thought. Certainly not the fact that Kendra was able to see what had happened to her. Why hadn't someone been able to see it before it happened?

Three more investigators entered the tent as Kendra examined the corpse's high-heeled shoes. "It's obvious she's been dragged. There's more construction dust here, too, but it's different."

"Different how?" Jennings asked.

"It's darker. Looks like residue from cut granite."

One of the investigators shone his high-powered flashlight over the shoes. "Wait!" Kendra said. "Keep that light where it is."

She squinted at the pool of extinguisher fluid beneath the chair. The mirror-like surface reflected the seat's underside. There was something there . . .

"Someone give me evidence gloves."

Four pairs were suddenly thrust in her direction. She took a pair of plastic gloves from Metcalf and slid them on. She peered underneath the chair, which was relatively unscathed from the fire.

Affixed to the chair's underside was a shiny silver pouch.

Kendra peeled it off and stood up.

"What is it?" Gina asked.

"Maybe nothing," Kendra said as she loosened the pouch's drawstrings. "But this seems like it might be made from a fire-retardant material." She pulled two items from the pouch. "A set of keys and a pair of eyeglasses."

"Hers?" the detective asked.

"Maybe, but I doubt it." She opened the glasses. "These are men's spectacles, probably for a face larger than hers was. And the keys have a tag for a supermarket loyalty program. Meijer's."

"It's a Midwestern chain," Metcalf said. "If these things aren't hers, what are they doing here?"

"Your guess is as good as mine." Kendra put the items in Metcalf's hand. "The smell is getting to me. I have to get out of here."

Kendra lifted the tent flap and slid outside.

"Wait." Metcalf was following her. "That's it?"

"Yes. That's all I got." Her nostrils still burned from that horrible stench. She didn't break stride. "Catch the beast who did this, will you?"

"It would be easier if you helped us."

"I already have."

"You know what I mean."

"Not this time, Metcalf. Tell your boss that I consider my debt repaid."

Metcalf nodded. "I'll tell him. Between you and me, we're still in the position of owing you."

Kendra finally stopped. No use running away. She was far enough away that she shouldn't be able to smell the terrible odor; it must be her imagination.

"You've never owed us a thing," Metcalf continued quietly. "Thanks for coming out here today."

"Sure. I'm certain you'll get him. Whoever it is, he's very concerned with calling attention to himself."

"You've given us a good start."

She nodded toward the tent. "Your partner's very attractive. I'm pretty sure she's interested in you."

Metcalf shook his head. "Your powers of observation have seriously let you down. She barely tolerates any of us."

"It's a defense mechanism. She's probably lonely, trying to start a new life for herself in a new town."

"You're cutting her way more slack than I am." He shook his head. "Anyway, she's really not my type."

"Don't tell me you're one of those guys who's threatened by strong women."

He smiled at her. "Not at all. It's a quality I find most attractive."

Kendra turned away slightly. Metcalf was smart, good-looking, and a nice guy. She liked him, but she couldn't return that romantic vibe she occasionally got from him.

"Then maybe you should give her a chance."

Kendra cocked her head toward her car. "I'm outta here. Good luck with your case."

Had Kendra Michaels met Pretty Amanda yet?

Hard to say.

Zachary sat on the park bench and unwrapped his sandwich. As much as he wanted to be watching the activity in front of the elementary school, he knew better. Only amateurs lingered near their crime scenes. Profilers studied behavior traits in what they assumed were people like him. It was one sure way of getting caught.

He was no amateur.

And there was no one like him in all their books and charts.

Still, he would have been thrilled to see Kendra Michaels admiring his handiwork.

If, that is, she'd even been brought into the case. He had already been disappointed twice before, and there was no guarantee she was there this time either.

Patience.

It was a plan years in the making. He could wait a little while longer.

He took a bite of his tuna-and-peppers sandwich as he watched the collegiate soccer team on the practice field. The goalie, a strapping young man named Todd Wesley, was doing well today.

Zachary smiled. A good way for the young man's teammates to remember him.

Strapping Todd was a creature of habit. After practice, he'd grab a smoothie from the little shop on the corner before going to his apartment for a quick shower. He'd eat while watching television, then spend an hour on his sofa surfing the web until his girlfriend got off work at the campus library. She'd swing by, and the two of them would go out to dinner.

Zachary shook his head. Did Strapping Todd know how monotonous his life had become? He certainly would've done things differently if he'd known this would be his last day on earth.

No matter. Tonight would be different.

Very different.

Because this *might* be the one that would catch Kendra Michaels' notice.

And when she finally gave him the attention he deserved, the game would be on. . . .

CHAPTER 2

It was dark by the time Kendra got back to her condo. She hadn't cashed in on the pizza she'd only half-jokingly extracted from Metcalf's partner, and her appetite had just started to recover from the horrible sight that had greeted her at the crime scene.

She lived on the top floor of the four-story downtown complex, and before she'd even made it to her door, it occurred to her that she might be able to corral a friend to join her for dinner. She bypassed the elevator and walked down a flight of stairs. She rounded the corner to see her friend Olivia's door was wide open.

Kendra froze. What in the hell?

There were voices inside, and a moment later three men emerged carrying tripods and camera cases.

Kendra leaned inside the open door. "Knock knock," she said.

Olivia turned from the living room. "Hi, Kendra. I'll be just a minute."

"Sure."

She smiled as she entered Olivia's two-bedroom condo. The place was the base of operations for Olivia's web destination *Outasite,* a popular site for the vision impaired featuring articles, product reviews, and discussion boards, all accessible by integrated audio screen-reading apps. The site occupied most of Olivia's waking hours and it had evolved from a simple hobby to a full-time business that generated an income well into the six figures.

Kendra watched as the last two members of the television crew left. She closed the door behind them. "Another news crew. Who was it this time?"

"The BBC in England." Olivia reached out for a chair near the large U-shaped wraparound desk that centered the room. "Nice guys, but like all camera crews, they move things and don't put them back exactly where they belong."

"Ah, the price of fame." Kendra watched her friend reach out for the chair next to her desk. "It's a little to your left."

"Thanks."

She and Olivia had known each other since they were children at a school for the visually impaired in nearby Oceanside. Olivia had lost her sight in a childhood car accident but she still harbored hope that she would one day emerge from the darkness as Kendra had done. It was no wonder why TV crews were lined up to feature her in their broadcast stories; in addition to her considerable accomplishments, Olivia was extremely attractive, with olive-toned skin and long dark hair.

Olivia moved carefully around her office restoring the furniture to its proper place. "It's good exposure for my site, but days like this really put me behind in my content. I have a half-dozen product reviews to write."

"Hey, I didn't mean to get in your way. If you'd rather I just—"

"No, stay. Please. What's been going on?"

"Well, I have a new client. Borderline catatonic. I think I might be able to reach him, though."

"Good."

"It's early going, but I think I may have a shot. I may try—"

"Enough," she interrupted.

Kendra gave her a quizzical look. "Enough what?"

"Your head isn't with that client right now, no matter what you say."

"What are you talking about?"

"You're on a murder case right now. Right?"

"How the hell did you know that?"

"You're not the only one who's pretty good at picking things up. I may not be on the FBI's speed dial, but I know my best friend pretty well. It's all in your voice. Quieter than usual, a little sad, slightly withdrawn . . . You sound like that whenever you've been consumed by a murder case. Is it one of those two killings here in downtown?"

"There are three now. And I'm not consumed."

35

"Are you sure?"

"Yes. But I'm extremely impressed by you and a little disturbed that the tone of my voice could give that much away."

"Now you have an idea how it feels for other people to hang out with you. It's incredibly hard to keep secrets when you're around."

"There's no reason for you to."

"So you say."

"Anyway, the FBI just asked me to visit the latest crime scene. I looked around, gave them my impression, and left. No big deal."

"It's always a big deal with you. You can never let these things go."

Kendra walked into the room. "This one was especially bad. I guess I'm having a tough time shaking it."

"You wouldn't be human if you could." Olivia cocked her head toward her sliding glass door. "Want to sit out on my balcony and eat a box of doughnuts?"

Kendra laughed out loud. "Doughnuts?"

"I would suggest opening a bottle of Chardonnay, but I still have to write those reviews later." Olivia motioned toward the two pastry boxes sitting on her desk. "The crew left those. There's about two dozen still there, from The Donut Bar."

Kendra smiled. "Sounds like dinner to me."

"Take 'em outside. I'll fire up the Keurig and make coffee."

In less than three minutes, Kendra and Olivia were relaxing on Olivia's balcony with their nutritionally deficient yet delicious dinner.

"Who was the agent who brought you in on the case?" Olivia asked.

"Roland Metcalf."

Olivia laughed. "Ah, your FBI admirer. Did he make eyes at you the whole time?"

"Not the *whole* time," she said dryly. "I guess the horribly disfigured corpse kind of broke the mood."

Olivia finished her sour cream doughnut and licked her fingers. "I used to think you and he would be good together. He's funny, he seems smart, and he absolutely adores you. It's not a bad foundation for a relationship."

"I don't think of him that way."

"Of course you don't. You need a man who challenges you. Keeps you on your toes. Someone you can admire because he possesses skills and aptitudes that you don't."

"I think you should know, I'm rolling my eyes now."

"You think I'm wrong?"

"It's not that, I just have a hunch you have someone specific in mind."

"Do I?" Olivia smiled mischievously. "So . . . How long has it been since you've seen Adam Lynch?"

"Six weeks, but I got a supremely sarcastic text

from him about ten days ago. If you can call that keeping me on my toes."

"He's been gone all this time?"

"Yes." Kendra leaned back in her chair. Adam Lynch was a former FBI agent who now worked freelance for whatever agency needed his particular abilities. She'd successfully partnered with him on several investigations, most recently on a case that involved Dr. Charles Waldridge, the brilliant medical researcher who had given her the gift of sight. The last time she'd seen Lynch, he was whisking Waldridge away to a secret location to continue his work in safety and solitude.

"Why was the text sarcastic?" Olivia asked. "I know you always struck sparks off each other, but the last time you were together, you were more grateful than combative. And he's always been—" She snapped her fingers. "Waldridge. I was wondering if you'd talked him into helping Waldridge disappear. That would have been a major favor on his part. Lynch didn't care much for Waldridge."

"They got along well enough." Not exactly true, but Kendra didn't want to go into details regarding Lynch and Waldridge's guarded relationship with Olivia right now. "And in the end Lynch was perfectly willing to do what he could to keep Waldridge's research safe."

"In the end," Olivia murmured. "I wonder what

it was in the beginning. And is Lynch still with Dr. Waldridge?"

"No, not for a few weeks now. He stuck around long enough to help Waldridge set up his lab, then he was off. I think he got called away to Eastern Europe and he's been tied up there ever since."

"Doing what?"

"Who knows? Quelling a revolution, or causing one, and maybe propping up a puppet dictator."

"Now that's the kind of man you need to be with."

"A bit too much of a challenge if you ask me."

"I don't think so. A challenge is what you need in *every* part of your life. Otherwise you'd get bored."

Kendra thought about it. "That's not true. I don't need *you* to challenge me."

"Sure you do. I'm doing it right now. What kind of friendship would we have if I wasn't here to bust your chops once in a while?"

Kendra laughed. "You think I want this from you?"

"Maybe not, but it's what you need. For all your amazing gifts of observation, I think you're the last person on earth to realize that Adam Lynch just might be the perfect man for you."

"He's on the other side of the world right now, so it really doesn't matter."

"He'll be back. He always comes back to you."

"No, he comes back to his home. That's very different."

"We'll see. In the meantime, it sounds like you have your hands full. How long will it take you to catch this killer?"

"The FBI and/or San Diego PD will catch this killer. I'm out of it."

"Now you're just *asking* to have your chops busted, because I don't believe you."

"Believe me, don't believe me, I don't care. Because right now, all I want is to help little Ryan Walker reconnect with the world around him."

"Well, I have no doubt that you'll do that, too."

Kendra half-smiled. "No pressure or anything."

"Sure there's pressure, but you thrive on it. We've just established that, remember? Just also remember to be careful. And if you need help with anything, remember I'm here."

"How could I forget?" she said gently. From the time they were little girls, Olivia had always been the practical one, the grounded one. There had never been a trace of jealousy when Kendra was granted the gift of sight; just happiness and love for her amazing good fortune.

"I should get to work," Olivia said. "So I'm kicking you out." She thrust the box of doughnuts in Kendra's direction. "But you have to take these with you."

"I really don't want them."

"You do. You have a sweet tooth. Once again, I

know you better than you know yourself."

Kendra reached in, grabbed a triple-nut glazed, then took the whole box. "Damn you, Olivia."

"Shh. Any time now."

Zachary stood over Strapping Todd in the dark closet. The young man was on his stomach, hog-tied with his bound hands almost pulled back to his ankles.

So far it had gone much easier than expected. He'd rapped at the door, Strapping Todd answered, and he'd quickly stabbed the young man in the stomach.

He'd further overpowered Strapping Todd with a few deft blows to the throat and kidneys, then dragged him at knifepoint to his back bedroom.

A bit disappointing for a student athlete, Zachary thought. But of course, fending off a homicidal maniac required a far different skill set than chasing a soccer ball.

Strapping Todd grunted something through his cloth gag.

"It's uncomfortable, I know." Zachary smiled. "But the gag is coming off in a minute or so. We're going to do a little experiment. Are you up to it?"

The young man squinted up at him.

Zachary leaned closer and whispered. "We're going to see how much you care for that pretty girlfriend of yours. Sweet Anissa. She'll be here any moment now, correct?"

Strapping Todd's eyes bulged and he tried to scream.

Zachary shushed him, a finger to his lips. "Here's how it's going to happen. When your girlfriend enters the apartment, I'll take your gag off. You'll be free to scream and shout as loud as you want. How's that for a deal?"

Strapping Todd's nose was running.

"But if you do that, just know I will have to kill her. And then I'll kill you, which I fully intend to do no matter what happens. But if I don't catch her, you could both survive. It's a slim chance, but a chance, nevertheless. The only chance you have. The question is, are you really willing to risk Anissa's life to save your own hide?"

Strapping Todd's nostrils flared.

"If you keep quiet, I'll wait until she leaves to kill you. You have a decision to make. What kind of a man do you want to be, Strapping Todd?"

There was a sound from the front of the apartment. The door was being unlocked.

Zachary smiled as he loosened the gag and pulled the cloth from Strapping Todd's mouth. "Right on schedule. The choice is now yours."

The front door squeaked as it opened. "Todd?"

Anissa waited for an answer. "Honey?"

She waited again, then moved through the apartment.

They listened as her footsteps pounded on the hardwood floors. "Where the hell are you?"

She stepped into the bedroom, just a few feet from where her boyfriend was trying to decide whether or not to call for help.

For the moment he was being good and noble, not even daring to breathe.

"Honey?" she called out again.

With one hand still on the knife, Zachary raised Todd's phone with the other hand. He silently snapped a photo of young Anissa through the crack in the door.

She disappeared from view.

Rustling fabric. More footsteps.

She was walking toward the closet.

Zachary raised his long blade. If she opened that door, this little test would come to a quick and violent end.

She stopped. "Todd?"

Strapping Todd was still holding his breath.

Another long moment of silence.

She finally turned and walked out of the room.

But she didn't leave the apartment. After a few seconds, her voice wafted in from the living room. She was on her phone, leaving a message for her beloved boyfriend.

"What the hell, Todd? I'm here at your place. You knew we were supposed to meet Trish and David. Why aren't you picking up your phone?"

Because I took it from him and turned off the ringer, Zachary wanted to reply.

Anissa let out an exasperated sigh. "Well, I'm

leaving. If you get this, meet me at the Black Cat. Bye."

Her footsteps moved away toward the front door . . .

Zachary smiled. Poor Strapping Todd. His last chance of survival was slipping away. But at least he'd shown a tiny shred of nobility by not endangering the life of this innocent young—

"Hel—!" He suddenly shouted, but Zachary silenced him with a deep slash in the throat. The blood gurgled from his open wound.

Zachary looked up. Had she heard?

The footsteps in the front room proceeded with their same unrushed pace. There was no urgency as she opened the door, closed it behind her, and locked it.

Zachary crouched beside the dying man. "You almost cost her everything, Strapping Todd. But there's no reason for her to suffer just because her boyfriend was a selfish pig."

Strapping Todd gasped for air through the gash in his throat.

Zachary whispered. "Should I make her acquaintance and tell her what a coward you are? Should I? Hmm, I think I may."

Todd stared at him with a look of total panic, an expression that remained even after life left his body.

CHAPTER 3

The charred face was still staring at her.

Kendra turned over in her bed. That horrible sight was there every time she closed her eyes. She'd been a fool to think she could just leave it behind.

She sat up and yanked the covers away. Her mother always urged her to leave town whenever a case preyed on her psyche, but it was no use. She knew wherever she would go, that vision would still be with her. The awful sights, smells, and excruciating details always followed her.

And the Feds knew it, she thought bitterly. Griffin had called in his favor knowing this would happen. Even if she could turn her back on that poor woman and the two other victims, it was harder to ignore the possibility of the victims to come. This murderous sicko was clearly enjoying himself and there would be more. Soon.

How in the hell could she turn her back on them?

She picked up her phone and punched Griffin's number. He answered on the second ring.

"Kendra Michaels," he said with more than a hint of annoyance. "Do you have any idea what time it is?"

"It's two-thirty in the morning. Ask me if I care. I'll be extremely disappointed if I didn't wake you from the sleep of angels."

"Oh, you did. I've just gotten very good at eliminating that groggy, half-asleep tone in my voice when pain-in-the-ass colleagues call me in the middle of the night."

She made a choking sound. "Ugh."

"Are you okay?"

"No, I almost threw up at the thought of us being colleagues."

"I believe I detect a tad of annoyance in your tone."

"More than a tad. You knew what seeing that victim would do to me."

"I didn't think you were just calling me to hash over the Padres game. What's on your mind, Kendra?"

She paused for a long moment. Was she really going to do this?

Shit.

"Griffin, I want to see the files for the other two murders."

He was ready for her. "Written reports? Crime scene photos?"

"Videos, lab results, whatever you have."

"Okay. Swing by the office tomorrow morning and we'll—"

"Now. Have somebody meet me there in half an hour."

"Nobody's there, Kendra. Just a skeleton crew."

"Get somebody there."

"At three in the morning? Be reasonable.

Come by at nine A.M. We'll give you every—"

"Do you want my help or not?"

"Come on, Kendra . . ."

"You want me to repay your damn favor. Well, I'm working tomorrow. At my real job. I have therapy sessions booked at my studio, and it's too late to reschedule."

"Then shouldn't you be getting a good night's sleep?"

"You pretty much destroyed all hope of that when you dragged me into this case."

He sighed. "And now you're going to make me pay for it."

"That's not what this is about. Call it . . . a pleasant side benefit."

"You're not hurting me. This is Metcalf and Carson's case. They're not going to be thrilled at the thought of dragging their asses to work at this time of night."

"Guess they shouldn't have signed up to work for the FBI, huh?"

"You tell them that when you see them. That'll put 'em in a *really* good mood. Meet them in the building lobby in thirty minutes."

Federal Bureau of Investigation
San Diego District Field Office

Kendra was seated in the building's main lobby for a full ten minutes before Special Agent Gina

Carson arrived looking bleary-eyed and slightly disheveled.

"This is some kind of hazing ritual, isn't it?" Gina said sourly. "The San Diego office does this to all their new people?"

"No hazing. Just the Kendra Michaels trial by fire, I guess." Kendra flipped open the lid on the box Olivia had given her. "Doughnut?"

Gina just glared at her.

Metcalf entered from the door across the lobby. He looked even more bleary-eyed than Gina. "Not cool, Kendra. I'd only been asleep for an hour and a half when Griffin called."

She looked at him with mock concern. "Up late cataloging your comic book collection?"

"Hah. That's hilarious." He shrugged. "Actually, I was playing the new Mortal Kombat Playstation game."

"Ooh, even geekier."

"Afraid so. Wanna go look at some gory crime scene photos?"

"No. But that's why I'm here."

They took the elevator upstairs to the third-floor conference room, which was centered by a long conference table. Metcalf motioned to two bulletin boards covered with printed photos. "Here are the first two crime scenes. I'd just as soon show you on the television monitor. But you know Griffin. He's old school. He insists on printing the photos and sticking them up here with pushpins like in 1985 or something."

Kendra stepped over to the bulletin boards. "I like it. It's good to be able to see everything at a glance. Sometimes it helps you make connections that are hard to see otherwise."

Metcalf turned back to Gina. "It's a rare and beautiful thing when Kendra agrees with anything Griffin does."

Gina crossed her arms and stifled a yawn. "She persuaded him to stir us from our nice warm beds, so there was bound to be some sadistic common ground there."

"Who is this?" Kendra was staring at the photo of a young woman's pale, bloated corpse. "First victim?"

"Yes." Metcalf picked up a manila file folder and opened it. "Meet Sofia Williams, age twenty-six. She was abducted outside her apartment building Sunday night. Her car door was still open and keys, purse, and phone were left on the passenger seat. San Diego PD fished her out of the bay the next morning."

Kendra nodded, trying not to dwell on the family and friends left behind, the years of joy taken from this woman. This wouldn't help now.

Detach.

Concentrate.

She pointed to a series of marks on the corpse's torso. "Stab wounds?"

Metcalf nodded. "Eleven to be exact. It was the

cause of death. The punctures were made with a large, double-serrated blade, two and a half inches at the widest point."

"The wounds are how they were able to connect the first two murders," Gina said, pointing to the other bulletin board. "It's a unique signature. The serrations on each side of the blade are remarkably different. One side is better suited for scaling fish, the other better for skinning a deer. There aren't many knives out there with that size and character. Our lab is pulling together a list."

Kendra's eyes narrowed on a photo of the corpse's feet. A short length of twine was knotted around one of them and extended out of frame.

She looked up. "Was something tied to her left ankle?"

Metcalf pointed to another photo. "This small plastic bag. It was sealed tight. There were two objects inside." He pointed to a pair of photos. "A pocket watch and a sun visor."

Kendra leaned closer for a better look. "Do you have them here in evidence?"

"Afraid not. We officially took this investigation over from San Diego PD just today. We'll be picking up all the evidence later in the morning."

"Yet another reason why you should have waited," Gina said.

"Not that you're bitter or anything." Kendra was still studying the photos. "These objects probably weren't hers. Not many twenty-something women wear watches of any kind and even less carry antique brass pocket watches. And that visor looks far too big for her."

"That's the consensus," Metcalf said. "But we don't have any idea why this was attached to her. Just like we don't know why that stuff was attached to the chair today."

She moved on to the next board, which was centered by an eleven-by-fourteen-inch print of another woman's corpse. The skin was a light shade of blue and her hair looked almost like icicles dangling in front of her face. Her eyes were wide open, but not in the thousand-yard stare she'd seen in too many dead bodies; the victim looked strangely alert, almost expectant in her bearing. Kendra abruptly turned away. "What happened to her?"

Gina picked up another file folder. "She was found thirty-six hours after the first victim. Her name was Amber McKay. She was an assistant manager at a movie theater. She was abducted late Monday after she got off work and was walking toward her car in the small lot behind the theater. Her purse, phone, and keys were found on the ground by her manager less than ninety minutes later. Amber turned up just a few hours later in a freezer behind a Chinese restaurant. It's normally padlocked, but it looks like the lock was snapped off by a pair of bolt cutters."

Kendra pointed to the corpse's left wrist which had a cord wrapped around it. "And this?"

"Bolo tie," Metcalf said. "And threaded through it is a 300 ring."

"A what?"

"The American Bowling Congress used to give away a commemorative diamond ring every time a bowler scored a perfect game during sanctioned league play."

"And they didn't go broke?"

"Perfect games used to be rarer. These days, bowling alleys oil the lanes in such a way to make it easier to score higher."

Kendra turned back to face him. "Something tells me this is knowledge you didn't just recently obtain."

He shrugged. "I grew up in St. Louis. Big bowling town."

Kendra nodded her approval. "Apparently."

"Anyway, there's a number inside the ring and we're trying to track its owner through the association that took over a few years ago." Metcalf grabbed a freestanding bulletin board from the other side of the room and rolled it closer to the others. Its surface was only partially filled with photographs of the crime scene they'd visited just hours before. "We started this after we got back here. It's not complete, but it might jog your memory about what we saw out there in front of the school."

She didn't need her memory jogged; it was too vivid at the moment. "Thank you." Kendra stepped back to look at all three boards at once. "Three murders in four days. Serial killers usually take more time between kills."

"And yet these seem just as methodical as any I've seen," Gina said.

"I agree," Kendra said. "There's nothing rushed about this. The killer is extremely methodical. He obviously chose his victims carefully and had been watching to get a sense of their schedules. He managed to abduct and murder three women, then dispose of their bodies in fairly public areas, all without getting caught or seemingly leaving a trace of himself behind. He's been planning this for weeks, then killing them quickly, one after the other, for maximum impact." She looked grimly at Metcalf. "He may have his next victims already picked out."

He nodded. "Griffin agrees. That's why he called in that favor from you. It's all hands on deck around here."

Kendra studied the crime scene photos again, trying to glean something, *anything* that could help them catch this monster before he struck again. But her eyes kept going back to the random objects that had been planted with each corpse.

Keys. Bowling ring. Bolo tie. Pocket watch. Visor.

She leaned closer and murmured under her breath, "What are you saying to us, you sick asshole . . . ?"

Metcalf bent down alongside her. "We've been asking ourselves the exact same question. Do you want us to give you a call when we get the objects from San Diego PD?"

She shook her head. "I'd rather you get these up to the lab and see if you can get DNA from them."

"Sure. The visor band is a good possibility for that. The ring, too."

"That's what I'm thinking."

"Does anything else jump out at you?"

Her eyes darted between the various photos. "I would have had a better shot if I'd been there myself. Here, all I have to go on is what I can see. I feel a little . . ."

"Handicapped?" Metcalf offered.

"At a disadvantage. I really can't see anything that—" She froze. "Wait."

"What is it?" Gina asked.

Kendra squinted at the young victims in the first two crime scenes, staring at one, then the other, then back again. "Do you have high-res photos of these victims' faces?"

Metcalf flipped up the lid of a laptop on the conference table. "San Diego PD gave us dozens. Which would you prefer? From the crime scene or the autopsy table?"

What a choice, she thought. How in the hell had she gotten to this point?

Because she'd insisted on coming here tonight over the objections of everyone. Way to go, Kendra.

"Let's start with the morgue shots. It would show us both victims under the same lighting. But I need to see pictures taken before the bodies were cleaned."

Metcalf tapped the keyboard, scrolling through the photos. He grabbed a remote control and switched on a flat panel monitor at the end of the room. "I'll put them up there side by side. Pre-autopsy morgue shots of the first two victims."

The monitor flickered, then displayed head-and-shoulders pictures of the two murder victims. Amber McKay's eyes were still open, but from this angle she appeared less expectant and more . . . *sad.*

Kendra walked toward the monitor and studied the victims' faces for a long moment. She turned back to Metcalf. "Can you zoom in on these? Tighter on the faces."

With a few keystrokes by Metcalf, the women's faces filled the monitor screen.

Kendra turned back to Metcalf and Gina. "See it?"

The agents stared at the monitor.

Metcalf shook his head. "I'm not sure what I'm supposed to be—"

"The lipstick," Gina interrupted. "That's what you're talking about, isn't it?"

"Yes." Kendra pointed to the peach-tinted lips on each photo. "The lipstick is identical. The exact same shade and level of gloss on each. And what's more, I'm pretty sure the burned corpse we saw was wearing the same lipstick."

Metcalf grimaced. "How could you tell?"

"The left corner of the corpse's mouth was reasonably intact. She was wearing lipstick. *This* lipstick."

Metcalf thought about it. "Okay. That means either we're dealing with a killer with a serious grudge against women with peach-colored lipstick . . ."

". . . or, more likely, he's putting it on them himself. Either before or after he kills them," Kendra said.

Gina glanced back and forth between the photos. "Why in the hell would someone do that?"

"Why do psychopaths do any of the things they do? Maybe he stole it from his nasty boss. Maybe it was worn by the prom queen who wouldn't give him the time of day in high school. Maybe it's what he'd like to be wearing himself, but he just can't admit it." She turned to Metcalf. "Call Kearney Mesa. Make sure they scrape a sample of the third victim's lipstick before they clean and prep her body for autopsy."

"And if they've already autopsied her?" Gina asked.

Kendra shrugged. "Then some lucky lab assistant will soon be rummaging through bags of medical waste." She looked at Metcalf and then at Gina. "Let's go there now."

"Seriously?" Metcalf said. "Just show up at the medical examiner's offices at three-thirty in the morning?"

"Why not? You know someone will be there. Death doesn't have much respect for a nine-to-five work day."

Metcalf stared at her. "You know, I think I liked Reluctant Kendra better. Gung-ho Kendra can be exhausting."

Her lips curved in a half smile. "Too bad. You opened this Pandora's box."

"My boss opened it. He just made me pick up the heavy end of the lid."

Gina took one last look at the side-by-side photos before turning around. "I'll drive."

"Really?" Metcalf said. "I was about to tell you to go home and grab a few winks while Kendra and I went over there."

Gina shook her head. "No, I'm beginning to see why the boss wants Kendra on the case so much. I want to see where this goes." She pulled her keys from her pocket. "Ready?"

San Diego Medical Examiner's Office
Kearny Mesa

They made the short drive to the M.E.'s office in a neighborhood dominated by office parks and industrial structures. After a brief confrontation with an over-zealous private security officer, they entered the office building and were escorted to the office of Dr. Christian Ross. The heavyset man was seated at a cluttered desk, about to devour a chicken parmesan sandwich.

He leaned back and regarded the three of them with a bemused expression. "A man with my abilities and experience doesn't have to work the overnight shift, you know. Everyone here thought I'd gone mad. But you know why I did it?"

Kendra smiled. "So you wouldn't have to talk to people like us?"

"Exactly. No offense."

"None taken," Metcalf said.

"Do you know how many times I've performed an autopsy with police officers pacing the halls outside, figuratively cracking the whip? Or how often I've been brow-beaten for a report, when it's all we can do to stay above water?"

Kendra sat on the edge of his desk. "A lot?"

"A lot. But it almost never happens on the overnight shift. I work in peace. I eat lunch at three A.M. and I interact only with a few like-minded souls who populate this place while the rest of the world sleeps. It's a good life."

"And it will be good again in just a few minutes." Kendra cocked her head toward the two FBI agents. "Do you know Special Agents Metcalf and Carson?"

Dr. Ross nodded toward them. "I know Metcalf. How do you do, Carson?"

"A pleasure," Gina said.

Dr. Ross took a large bite of his sandwich. "So what brings you to my door at this ungodly hour?"

"The burnt female Jane Doe that came in today," Kendra said. "Has she been autopsied yet?"

Dr. Ross sighed. "And the whip gets cracked again."

"I'm hoping the answer is no," Kendra said.

He raised an eyebrow. "That's a switch. And you're in luck. We got a new kid who called dibs on it, but he won't be in until nine A.M. What do you need?"

"Lipstick."

Dr. Ross didn't bat an eye. He'd obviously seen it all before. "I just might be able to help you with that." He stood and grabbed his white lab coat from the chair back. "Follow me."

They accompanied Dr. Ross downstairs to the morgue, and Kendra was struck by the creepy vibe the building gave off in the pre-dawn hours. They didn't see a single person during their journey, and about two-thirds of the overhead fluorescent lights were turned off, casting shadows in long stretches of the corridors. The morgue itself, by contrast, was almost blindingly bright, with white-tiled floors and chrome fixtures reflecting the light in a harsh glare.

Dr. Ross consulted a clipboard and led them to a row of refrigerated drawers. He pulled one open and before Kendra could brace herself, she once again saw the burnt corpse.

Metcalf saw her wince. "Doesn't get any easier to look at, does it?"

"No."

"At least here it doesn't smell like it did out on the street."

"I'll be damned," Gina said. "Look at the left corner of her mouth."

Kendra was already looking. As she'd remembered, it was the same peach lipstick as on the others.

Metcalf turned toward Dr. Ross. "I need to swab this. Can I have an evidence vial?"

"I'll swab it," Dr. Ross smiled. "I'm a professional."

Dr. Ross used a sponge-tipped swab to scrape the lipstick from the relatively burn-free side of the corpse's mouth. "FYI, it appears that the lipstick was applied post-mortem."

"Are you sure?" Kendra asked.

"Almost positive. Cosmetics interact differently with a corpse's epidermis than they do with a live person's. The oils and oxygenation affect the way it absorbs—or doesn't absorb—into the skin."

Kendra watched silently as he deposited the dried lipstick sample into a glass vial. As he sealed it with a screw cap, Metcalf asked the question she'd been waiting to put forth. "There were two other corpses that came through here with that same lipstick. Wouldn't the examiners have noticed that same thing on them?"

"Maybe, maybe not. The difference is less pronounced with lipstick than with other types of makeup. It's a thicker base, usually more solid than other cosmetics." He cocked an eyebrow. "Most people here aren't as good as I am."

"I believe that," Kendra said.

Dr. Ross handed Metcalf the vial. "Anything else?"

"No," Kendra said. "But I'd appreciate it if you'd close that drawer as quickly as you can."

Dr. Ross hip-checked the drawer and it quickly slid shut. He shrugged. "Like I said, I'm a professional."

It was after 4:30 A.M. by the time Kendra made it back to her condo. When she'd said good-bye to Metcalf and Gina in the FBI parking garage, they were already on their way up to the lab with the evidence vial. The agents felt confident that the lab could identify the lipstick in short order.

More information was better than less, of course, but Kendra found herself feeling more frustrated than ever. Even if they could ID the lipstick, what good could it do? It had most likely been purchased in one of the thousands of supermarkets or drugstores across the country.

There had to be something else, some other path to the monster who had murdered those people.

As she entered her building, she felt in her pocket for the USB flash drive Metcalf had given her. It contained the working files for all three murders. She'd upload them to her tablet and peruse them when she got the chance. Peruse, hell. She knew herself better than that. She'd study, memorize, and obsess over every detail.

But first she needed some sleep. She had morning appointments at her studio and she'd be worthless if she didn't get at least a few—

BUZZZZ-BUZZZZ-BUZZZZ.

Her phone vibrated in her pocket.

She pulled it out and saw that a text had come through. She squinted at her screen and saw a message from someone she hadn't heard from in a long time. Well, ten days wasn't that long, but it had seemed long to her.

Can't keep you away from a good murder, can we, Kendra?

She couldn't help but smile. It was Adam Lynch, agent-for-hire, who Olivia had tried to convince her was the challenge she needed. His main skill was infuriating her to no end. But sometimes he was just what she needed, especially on a day like this one.

She tapped out her reply: **Depends on how we define 'good' murder. Your own?**

He replied immediately. **Keep dreaming, Kendra. I'll be around to harass you for a long time.**

He was probably right about that one, she thought. She typed. **Where in the world are you?**

Guilin, China. On assignment. Impressed yet?

Nope. Sorry. Those govt. Pencil-pushers who sign your checks don't know you like I do.

Probably right about that. Keep it our secret. Okay?

She didn't know a tenth of Lynch's secrets and probably never would. But those words gave her a warm feeling of intimacy.

She stepped into the elevator, knowing her phone had only a 50-50 chance of maintaining her data connection. She typed anyway: **Will keep your secrets if you keep mine.**

His reply came quickly. **Afraid you have no secrets to keep. You're an open book. A fascinating, page-turning open book.**

And here I thought I was an alluring woman of mystery.

Alluring, yes. Mysterious, no. Only fearful people are mysterious. That isn't you.

While she was still deciding how to respond, he added: **Haven't been home since the night I saw you last. Wish I was there now.**

She was momentarily taken aback by his uncharacteristic sincerity. She instinctively tried to joke. **That makes one of us.**

She paused. Wrong. Be honest. **Not really.**

He responded. **Are you okay, Kendra?**

Still sincere.

She typed: **You're half a world away. How in the hell did you know I was on a case?**

The world is a small place. I repeat: are you okay?

She waited to answer until she finished the elevator ride and walked down the hallway to her condo. She let herself in and locked the door behind her.

She stared at the phone in her hand. Of course, Lynch knew she was on the case. He had tentacles everywhere, intelligence agency connections she could only dream about.

And he knew *her.* He knew how these cases affected her.

She finally responded: **I'm fine. Need to find this psychopath now. Real monster quality. Don't know how.**

You will. Anything I can do?

She smiled and typed back: **From China?**

Again, the world is a small place.

She sat down at her dining room table and replied: **Sometimes it feels very large and overwhelming.**

If I had a dime for every time a woman has said that about me . . .

She snorted in spite of herself. Then she typed: **Classy guy. Are you fourteen?**

Sorry. Momentary lapse. Anyway, you'll be fine. Any leads in your case?

Lipstick.

Lipstick?

Long story. Don't know what it means. Still working on it.

Gotcha. Be careful, Kendra. If you need help, I'm here.

She typed: In China.

Afraid so. For now.

Good night, Lynch.

She put down her phone. Adam Lynch always knew what she needed even before she knew it herself. Guess what she needed now was a smart-ass to reach out to her from the other side of the world.

She pushed herself up and headed for the bedroom. Time to grab a few hours of sleep before work. And, thanks to those distracting, amusing, and intimate texts from Lynch, she might be able to put those three corpses out of her mind and get it.

Anissa Scott checked her watch. 7:40 A.M. What in the hell was wrong with Todd?

She'd met their friends at the bar the night before, and the asshole hadn't even bothered to call her back. She didn't call him again on principle, but now she was wondering if he was with that blond slut who practically hung on him in their chem labs. She'd just noticed his car parked around the corner and knew he was home. What if that bitch was with him?

She didn't give a shit. Better to know and rid herself of the prick.

Anissa climbed out of her car and cut through the narrow alley that ran alongside his yellow stucco apartment building. She walked to the exterior stairway and down the corridor to Todd's apartment. She pulled out her key and took a deep breath, knowing she might be about to unravel the one thing that had made her life bearable these past few months.

Didn't matter. It was better to know.

She pushed open the door. "Todd, it's me."

No answer.

"Todd?"

She knew he was home. His wallet, phone, and keys were on the table next to the door. She imagined him in his back bedroom desperately trying to hide his slut under the bed or maybe behind the shower curtain.

"Todd?" Dammit, it was like a replay of last night.

She stopped, frozen in place. On the floor in front of her there were five sheets of paper, each with a photograph printed on it.

She picked up the papers and studied them.

The photographs were of *her*.

What in the hell . . . ?

She could see they were taken in Todd's bedroom the night before; she was wearing her new blue sweater. But how . . . ?

The pictures were taken from the closet, she realized, through the slightly-ajar door. She'd had no idea . . .

Had Todd been there the whole time, laughing as he hid and took pictures of her?

More pages in the hallway. More pictures of her.

She picked up the pages as she walked, following a trail that led into Todd's bedroom.

Three more pages there.

She stepped inside and picked them up one by one, until she found herself in the center of the room. She looked at the last page.

The printed picture was the same as all the others, but this page had large letters scrawled on the lower half.

The letters read: **LOOK BEHIND YOU.**

She spun around.

She *screamed*.

CHAPTER 4

"Nice of you to join us."

Griffin gazed at Kendra with tired eyes as he stepped out of the apartment. He nodded toward the uniformed police officer, who lifted the police tape for her to duck under and walk toward the open door.

"I was in the middle of something." Her phone hadn't stopped vibrating during the second session in her studio. When she'd finally picked it up to look, there were sixteen voicemail messages and over forty texts, all concerning the murder victim in this apartment.

"Something that couldn't wait?" Griffin asked sourly.

"No. Except to the people who needed me. They were interested in life, not death." She looked beyond him toward the back of the apartment. "Are you sure this murder is related to the others?"

"Pretty sure. The knife wounds look similar to the others and the killer left souvenirs again."

"Souvenirs?"

He motioned for her to walk with him toward the back bedroom where two forensics specialists were packing up their kits.

Griffin pointed toward the wall behind her. "There."

Kendra turned. The closet door was wide open and the shirtless corpse of a young man was propped up against a pile of laundry. Blood had run from his torso and pooled on the floor around him.

Kendra winced. He looked like a kid, maybe even a teenager just starting out in life. "Who found him?"

"His girlfriend. She let herself in at about seven-thirty this morning, and this was how he greeted her."

Kendra forced herself to move toward the corpse. "Where is she now?"

"Taking a walk with Carson and Metcalf. She was hyperventilating in here."

Kendra knew how she felt. She had never even met this young man and yet she felt the total wrongness of a life stolen, wasted. It was all she could do to hold it together in the face of such evil, such horror.

Detach.

Concentrate.

She bent closer to the bloody corpse. "Name?"

"Todd Wesley. He was a student at San Diego State."

On the floor in front of the corpse were three small items, neatly arranged in the closet doorway.

A class ring.

A sport watch.

A pair of ear plugs.

She turned back to Griffin. "Did you look at these?"

He nodded. "We were waiting to bag them until you had a chance to take a look. The class ring is from Stanford University. That's an underwater watch, and the ear plugs are the type used by swimmers."

Kendra looked at the items for a moment longer. "I know he played soccer, but was he a swimmer?"

"Not according to his girlfriend. How did you know he was a soccer player?"

She gestured behind him. "Adidas soccer cleats in the corner of the room with a pair of dirty long socks next to them. He practiced recently, maybe even yesterday." She nodded back to the closet. "Plus, there's a black and red uniform hanging in there. San Diego State Aztec colors." She glanced around. "I can't see that he played any other sport."

"He didn't." The woman's hoarse voice came from the hall.

Kendra looked up. The pretty young woman, obviously the victim's girlfriend, stood in the doorway with Metcalf and Carson. Her face was puffy and red and her eyes were swollen.

Kendra stepped toward her. "I'm Kendra," she said gently.

"Anissa," the woman replied. Her gaze was clinging frantically to Kendra's face to avoid staring at the closet. "I can't . . . look at him again. I just . . . wanted to be here. It didn't seem right to leave Todd alone with people who didn't know him." She glanced away. "Sounds kind of stupid, I guess."

"No," Kendra said. "Not at all. He was lucky to have someone who cared about him as much as you obviously did." She motioned toward the living room. "Let's talk in there, okay?"

Anissa nodded with relief and followed her to the front of the apartment. Kendra studied the open door thoughtfully for a moment before turning back to Anissa. "Did Todd mention seeing anyone watching or following him in the past couple of weeks?"

Anissa shook her head. "What? You think someone was following Todd?"

"I do. And probably you too. This wasn't just a crime of opportunity. I think this killer spent time gathering information on Todd, his schedule, and the people in his life."

Anissa frowned in bewilderment. "Why would he do that? You think it's someone Todd knew?"

"Probably not. But once the killer selected Todd as his victim, he most likely made it his business to study him and his habits, just as he did for his other victims. You haven't noticed anyone or anything out of the usual?"

"It's all crazy. Why would anyone—" Anissa drew a deep shaky breath. "Okay, give me a minute." She thought for a moment, then finally shook her head. Kendra could see she was struggling to hold it together. "I'm sorry, I wish I could, but I can't think of anything different. Everything was just . . . ordinary when we were together. No sickos lurking in the shadows. And who the hell would be stalking a great guy like—"

"Just relax," Kendra said quietly. "Maybe something will come to you."

Anissa looked at her. "I *can't* relax. I'm scared to death. Todd is dead in that closet. And I can't believe that maniac was just a few feet away from me . . . Watching, taking my picture . . ."

"What do you mean?"

Griffin stepped from the back bedroom holding a short stack of papers, each protected in their own clear plastic document protectors. "You haven't seen these yet, Kendra."

Kendra took the pages and thumbed through the printed photos.

"I came here last night," Anissa said jerkily. "Todd and I were supposed to go meet some friends. I looked around but Todd wasn't here. Or at least I didn't think he was. When I came back this morning, these pages were spread out on the floor, leading to the back bedroom like a trail of bread crumbs."

Kendra got a sudden chill when she realized what she was seeing. "These are all the same picture of you, taken from that closet."

Anissa nodded as tears rolled down her cheeks. "He was probably standing over Todd's body when he took it. I had no idea . . ."

"We're pretty sure he used the ink jet printer in the victim's bedroom," Griffin said.

"You're lucky to be alive, ma'am," Gina said.

"Yeah, sure." Anissa shot her a glance that indicated she didn't feel very lucky. She motioned toward the stack of printed photos in Kendra's hands. "They're all the same except the last one. It was in the middle of Todd's bedroom."

Kendra found the photo and read the printed scrawl aloud, "LOOK BEHIND YOU."

Shock. Another sickening chill racked Kendra.

Anissa crossed her arms in front of her almost as a block against the hideous scrawl. "That's when I turned around and saw Todd in the closet. I ran out of here as fast as I could. Everything else is a blur."

LOOK BEHIND YOU.

Kendra barely heard her as she stared at the last page. This couldn't be happening, she thought dazedly.

LOOK BEHIND YOU.

God, no.

Metcalf caught her expression. "What is it, Kendra?"

She pushed the papers back at Griffin. "I have to go to your office and research something. Can someone come with me?"

Griffin's eyes were narrowed on her face. "What did you see?"

"That message. 'Look behind you.' A killer up in Ventura County used this stunt on his victims about ten years ago."

"One of your other cases?"

She shook her head. "No, I was working another murder up there, and they presented me with details of their unsolved cases of the previous few years. This was just one of several and we quickly realized it had nothing to do with our case. But it stuck with me, the idea of the killer taunting his victims like this."

Griffin looked down at the paper in his hand. "Yeah, I have a vague recollection of this even though it wasn't our case. It made some headlines."

"As far as I know, it's never been solved. I need to access the NCIC database and get details."

Griffin nodded. "Take Metcalf with you to the office. We'll meet you there after the scene is broken down. See what you can find out."

Normally Kendra would have resented Griffin's giving her orders as if she was one of his agents, but she was already completely absorbed in the puzzle that had been placed in front of her. At the moment it was hard to tell if this was a copycat, or if the same killer had resurfaced after all this time.

Metcalf cocked his head toward the door. "Ready?"

She took one last long look at the door of Todd

Wesley's bedroom where a young man's life had been taken for no reason but bloodlust. Yesterday he'd had a future and a woman he loved, but that had all been stolen by that killer who had savagely attacked him. *I'm going to find who did this to you, Todd. I'll make him pay, I promise.*

She turned back to Metcalf. "Yes, you bet I'm ready."

A half hour later Kendra was in the FBI third-floor conference room, pacing in front of the bulletin boards while Metcalf used a laptop to connect to the National Crime Information Center.

"Just a few more seconds," he said.

Kendra pointed to the flat panel monitor at the end of the room. "Can you mirror your laptop screen over there?"

As if in response, the large screen flickered and the NCIC logo appeared.

"The database is a little sluggish tonight," he said. "It's taking me a while to log in."

"Should I call my friend Sam Zackoff? He can probably hack his way in within a few minutes."

". . . and he'll get his door kicked in by a squad of federal agents on his way to serving three to five years in prison." Metcalf grimaced. "The government isn't wild about its law enforcement databases being breached by unauthorized personnel."

"Zackoff's work is too valuable to most of the government agencies to get him into too much trouble. Besides he's pretty good at covering his tracks."

"Not necessary. I just got in."

Kendra watched the large screen as he queried the system for details on the Ventura County murders she'd remembered. Within a minute, they were looking at photos and abstracts of the case.

"Still unsolved," Metcalf said. "All three victims were men in their late teens and early twenties." He tabbed forward through more crime scene photos. "They were all stabbing victims, but there—"

"Wait!" she interrupted. "Go back one."

Metcalf displayed the previous photo and the sight made her gasp.

LOOK BEHIND YOU.

The words were scrawled on a sheet of paper found just inches from one of the victims.

Kendra's stomach tightened. "The hand-writing's the same."

"It does look similar."

"No, I mean it's *exactly* the same." She stepped toward the screen. "The curls of the letter B look as if they were drawn before the straight vertical line, which is rare. And the letter O is started and finished on the left side each time, which you almost never see. It was the same at the crime scene today. You'll want an expert to confirm it, but I'm almost positive these were written by the same person. Can I see the others?"

Metcalf displayed shots from the other crime scenes, pausing on the same scrawled message found at each one.

LOOK BEHIND YOU.

Each time the handwriting displayed the same telltale characteristics.

"They're all the same," Kendra said. "Just like the one we saw today. Even if someone had access to these, which is doubtful, it would have been tough to reproduce with such precision. Unless it was the same person."

Metcalf nodded. "I see what you mean."

Kendra's eyes narrowed on the screen. "Hold on. Let me see some more shots of this room. Are there any in this record?"

Metcalf displayed several other crime scene shots until Kendra stopped him. "There!"

It was a picture that showed more of the room and less of the bloody corpse. Kendra squinted, her eyes searching for details. "This victim was a swimmer."

"His name was Daryl Lanton." Metcalf joined her at the screen. He slowly nodded. "Swim goggles hanging from the desk lamp."

"And nose clips on the side table. Plus, look in the mirror. It's reflecting a poster from the back wall."

Metcalf stared at it for a moment. "Is that—?"

"Michael Phelps. The victim was a fan like pretty much every other swimmer in the world."

"Shit," Metcalf whispered as the realization hit him. "Those objects at the crime scene today . . ."

Kendra nodded. "The underwater sport watch and earplugs most likely belonged to a swimmer. Maybe this guy."

"This murder was six years ago. You think the killer's been sitting on the stuff all this time?"

"There's one way to find out. Contact Oxnard PD and see if we can get contact info for his next of kin. We can send pictures of the objects."

"There's a better way," Metcalf said. He checked his watch. "Flights go up there every hour."

Kendra turned toward him. "Seriously?"

"We can head out as soon as they come back with the objects. We can be back in time for dinner. Well, a late dinner. Are you up for it?"

Kendra nodded. This was something she'd always liked about Metcalf: no dawdling, no useless meetings, no wasted time.

"Yes. Let's go."

Kendra and Metcalf were waiting in the building lobby for the team when they returned from the crime scene and after a three-minute consulta-tion with Griffin, they took the class ring, earplugs, and diving watch, all encased in plastic evidence bags. A short United Airlines flight later, they landed in Ventura and rented a car. By four o'clock they were walking up the front sidewalk to a modest Oxnard home that belonged to Daryl Lanton's parents.

Metcalf rang the doorbell. A plump woman in her mid-fifties answered the door. Her red face and puffy eyes made it obvious that she'd been crying.

Metcalf spoke gently as he flashed his ID. "Monica Lanton?"

She nodded silently.

"I'm special agent Roland Metcalf with the FBI. This is Dr. Kendra Michaels. I believe my colleague called and spoke to you?"

"Yes." She gestured toward a set of wicker chairs arranged around a table on her front porch. "Would you mind if we talked out here? The house is kind of a mess."

"Sure. Whatever is comfortable for you. We appreciate you giving us your time." They moved across the porch and sat down.

"I'm sorry for our visit," Kendra said. "I know it's asking a lot for you to speak about your son, Mrs. Lanton."

"Monica." She shrugged. "Daryl's never far from my mind, even after all these years. We keep a lot of his pictures around and all of his swim trophies . . . He's always with me. Actually, it's kind of nice to talk about him."

"I'm glad you feel that way," Kendra said.

"My husband doesn't like it when I bring him up. He says it hurts too much. But the hurt is there whether you put it into words or not. I'm not about to pretend I'll ever forget him." She moistened her lips. "But I have to admit, it knocked me for a loop when that other agent called to tell me you were coming. It reminded me that Daryl's killer is still out there." She gazed at Metcalf hopefully. "Or is he? Did you catch him? Is that why you're here?"

"No," Metcalf said. "But we may be closer than we've ever been."

"Good. I thought you all had forgotten my Daryl. I've been afraid the police just gave up."

"We looked at the file," Kendra said. "The case had gone cold. When a serial killer just stops like he did, it's often a sign that he's dead or incarcerated for another crime."

"That's what the detectives told us." Monica's lips were trembling. "I've been afraid we'd never get answers. It should have never happened. But since it did, we should at least know why and who was responsible."

"We realize that." Kendra leaned forward. "Where was your son living when he died?"

"He had an apartment here in downtown Oxnard. He had just graduated from Stanford, and he wasn't sure what he wanted to do with his life. His entire existence had always been about swimming, even in college. After graduation, he was a little . . . lost." Monica's eyes suddenly went moist and dark as if she was peering into another time, another place. "Anyway, his friends started calling us when they couldn't get hold of him. He wasn't answering his phone or his door. His father and I had a key, so we went down there one morning." Monica looked down at her folded hands on the table. "I . . . found him."

"I'm very sorry," Kendra said. "I know this isn't easy for you. But can you tell us . . . Was anything missing?"

"From his apartment?"

"Or his person," Metcalf said. "Something you noticed the killer may have taken from him."

Monica thought about it. "Well . . . I was never able to find his class ring."

Kendra and Metcalf glanced at each other.

She shrugged. "I accused the medical examiner of losing it, but the police assured me it wasn't on any of his fingers. They had the pictures to prove it."

Kendra reached into the canvas satchel she'd been holding from the moment they left the FBI offices in San Diego. She pulled out a clear plastic evidence bag that contained the ring they found at the crime scene only that morning. She displayed it to Monica. "Do you recognize this?"

Monica gasped. "That's it. That's his ring." Tears ran down her cheeks again. "Can I . . . hold it?"

"I'm sorry, I can't let you do that," Metcalf said. "It's evidence in another case, and we're going to try and get DNA from it. But I'll make sure you get it soon, okay?"

Monica nodded.

Kendra pulled out two more plastic evidence bags. "How about these?"

Monica took a moment to compose herself. "Yes. That's definitely his diver's watch. He would time his workouts, and it would vibrate on his wrist when he was done. And those look like his earplugs in the other bag. He always used Aqua Sphere brand."

Kendra put away the plastic bags. "Thank you. This will help us enormously."

"Where did you get those?" Monica stared at the canvas satchel in Kendra's lap. "It's been six years and you just now found these things? If you haven't found Daryl's killer, then how—?" Monica froze as she made the connection. "He's killed someone else. Hasn't he?"

"We can't comment on an ongoing investigation," Metcalf said.

"Of course you can't. But why else would you have come all this way?" Her voice dropped to a whisper. "He's not dead. He's not in prison. He *is* still out there."

"It's possible," Kendra said. "We don't know for sure."

"You're being so careful. Neither of you want

to tell me something that's not true." She shook her head. "But you don't understand. You brought me *hope* today. Do you know how important that is?" Monica thought for a moment. When she spoke again, it was not from a place of weakness, but of strength. "I've felt completely helpless, but now I know someday you may knock on my door and tell me that you found that monster who killed my son. But before you do that, do something else for me, will you?" Her voice was uneven as she got to her feet and turned toward the door. "When you find him, make him pay. Make him *hurt*. Just like all the other people he's hurt." She headed for the door. "Remember them, remember *us*. Make him hurt . . ."

Kendra and Metcalf spent most of the trip back to the airport in silence. To Kendra's surprise Metcalf appeared to be visibly shaken after their meeting with Monica Lanton. It was a distressing change from the glib, tough young man she'd known from previous investigations.

Shortly after their plane took off, she tapped him on the arm. "Hey, what's going on, Metcalf?"

He glanced at her. "What do you mean?"

"I've seen you talk to family members of murder victims before. That lady got under your skin."

"You're right." He looked out the plane window where the sun was setting behind the ocean.

"Dealing with the survivors, giving them bad news is a terrible part of the job. I know I'm about to give them the worst day of their lives. I can't say I've ever gotten used to it, but I've found a way to deal."

"And what was the difference with her?"

Metcalf leaned back in his seat. "I've never worked a cold case before. Six years later that woman is still living in hell. And I'm not sure if it would be any better if they'd caught the guy. When we solve a murder case, I like to think I'm giving the family some peace, you know? But seeing how this has devastated her, even after all this time . . . There's not much peace to be had."

"Maybe not. But even if there isn't much we can do for her, we might save other families from going through this. Right?"

Metcalf nodded.

"That's what keeps me going." She made a face. "This investigative stuff isn't fun for me. You know that, Metcalf. It's nothing I've ever really wanted to do. But there are so many monsters out there. If I can keep one of those monsters from taking one more life, from devastating one more family, it's worth it to me."

Metcalf nodded. "I know it is. And Griffin knows it, too."

She frowned. "What do you mean?"

"When I recruited you for this case, he told me to tell you that you owed him. And if that didn't work, he told me to remind you that innocent people might die if you didn't help us."

"That son of a bitch."

"Does it really surprise you that he'd use that?"

"Not really. I guess it just annoys me that he's so up-front about being a scumbag."

"Are you kidding? He's made a career of it. But at least he's a reliable scumbag, and no one cares about the job more than he does. And he always has our backs, which you don't often see. He probably would have gone further in the Bureau if he'd been willing to grab more credit from us or occasionally throw one of us under the bus when something didn't go his way."

Kendra smiled. In an organization where bashing the boss was practically a team sport, it was refreshing to hear Metcalf come to Griffin's defense. "Why do you do it, Metcalf? It's not an occasional case, like it is for me. You've made it your entire career."

He shrugged. "Why do you think? You seem to have everyone else in the world figured out, I'd be interested in why you think I do it."

"Those are just parlor tricks. I really don't have any special insight into what makes people tick."

"Take a stab at it."

"Well, I know you're a comic book geek, and you have been for your entire life."

"I make no secret of that, which probably explains the sorry state of my social life."

"Your social life is fine. No less than three women have tried to call you in the last two hours."

"How do you know that?"

"Cindy, Beth, and Hannah. Their names popped up on your Apple Watch each time your phone vibrated."

He chuckled. "You know there's a razor-thin line between brilliantly perceptive and just plain nosy. And for the record, Beth is my sister."

"Then you're really only juggling two women." She grinned. "Gotcha."

"And just what does my interest in the fine art of visual storytelling—"

"Comic books."

"Okay, comic books. What does that have to do with my career choice?"

"We all like stories of an ordinary man who can suddenly become a superhero who catches the bad guys. I think this is your way of becoming a hero yourself."

He wrinkled his nose. "That makes me sound kind of . . . pathetic."

"I disagree." She looked out the window at the clouds below them. Metcalf was no Adam Lynch, but it wasn't fair to compare them. Lynch was rock-star unique. Metcalf wasn't faster than a speeding bullet nor did he leap tall buildings in a single bound. But he was solid and hardworking, and he genuinely cared about making a difference in this world. All of which was enough to raise him to be a superhero contender. "It makes you one of the good guys, Metcalf."

After they landed, Metcalf's phone vibrated before their plane even reached the gate. He looked at his phone and frowned.

"Let me guess," Kendra said. "Cindy or Hannah."

"Neither. It's Griffin. He'd like for us to come up to the office right away."

"Now? It'll be after eight by the time we get there."

Metcalf put away his phone. "He knows. There's something going on."

Kendra thought for a moment. "Want to bet they've matched some of the other left-behind objects with different Ventura County murders?"

Metcalf nodded. "That crossed my mind. It was going to be my next play. The killer is obviously taunting us with his trophies. In today's case, he intentionally echoed his earlier killing in Ventura County. Both student athletes, each living alone in an apartment. It wouldn't surprise me if we found echoes with the other victims." He unbuckled his seatbelt as the plane reached the jetway. "My colleagues aren't wasting time, are they?"

"I give your new partner the credit. Gina Carson is a sharp lady. It doesn't seem like she lets the grass grow beneath her feet."

"You're right. I think she'll keep us all on our toes." He smiled. "Just like you do."

With no baggage and Metcalf's car parked in the nearby short-term parking, it was a simple matter to sprint through the airport and get on the road. Less than thirty minutes later as they approached the FBI field office, Metcalf's jaw tightened. "Uh oh."

Kendra's gaze flew to his face. "What's wrong?"

He nodded toward the building. "You're the observant one. See anything unusual with this picture?"

Her gaze shifted to the building. "Most of the office lights are still blazing." She suddenly stiffened in her seat. "That's very unusual for this time of night."

"Exactly. Nobody's gone home." He glanced at her. "Something's happened. This is big. Bigger than we thought."

She couldn't take her eyes off those blazing lights. What could have driven Griffin to keep his whole department there? "How?"

"I have no idea." He pulled into the parking lot. "But we're about to find out."

CHAPTER 5

"The case has exploded!"

Gina Carson pushed Kendra and Metcalf back into the elevator before they could step out onto the third floor and punched the fourth-floor button. Her cheeks were flushed, her eyes shining, and though Kendra could see that she was trying to be cool and businesslike, she could almost feel her seething excitement.

"Exploded? And just where are we going?" Kendra said.

"The large conference room. Everyone is up there. We're turning it into our war room."

"You matched the killer's trophies with more of the Ventura County cases?" Metcalf guessed.

Gina shook her head. "No."

The elevator doors opened to reveal that the large fourth floor conference room generally used for seminars, regional meetings, receptions, and other sizable gatherings, was now a whirlwind of activity, with agents and support staff rushing between the large wheeled bulletin boards that lined the walls.

The center of the room was occupied by half a dozen computer workstations and color printers that were manned by assistants who grabbed and collated printouts as soon as they were spat out.

Griffin was holding a stack of printouts in his hand as he approached them. "This is all your fault, Kendra. I hope you're happy with yourself."

She glanced around, dazed by the activity. "I refuse to take any blame when I'm not even sure what I'm seeing here."

Gina motioned for them to follow her into the room. "A lot has happened in the last few hours. I started out trying to match our killings and trophies with other victims up in Ventura. It didn't work, not like how easily our college athlete matched with the Stanford swimmer who was killed a few years ago." She gestured to the organized chaos in the room. "So I decided to broaden the net."

Kendra's breath left her as she spun around and took in the images from the dozen bulletin boards around her.

More cities.

More victims.

More horror.

"My God . . . These are all . . . him?"

"That's what I'm trying to tell you," Gina said impatiently. "The trophies match up with objects taken from victims in at least four other cities. Twenty-six victims in all."

"Holy shit," Metcalf whispered.

"Four separate cases," Griffin added. "In addition to the one you discovered today. In each one, he adopted an entirely new MO. That's why they were never linked before now."

Gina was shepherding them on a tour of the bulletin boards, which were still being organized by the agents and assistants. "Nine years ago, he was Washington, D.C.'s Southside Strangler. Sixteen months after that he became Hartford's Roadside Slasher. Less than three years later, he was the Jacksonville Daylight Killer. Just before that one, he was your Ventura County Killer."

"This is incredible . . ." Metcalf said. "Serial killers almost never alter their methodology this way. It looks like that in some of these cases, he targeted men, in others it was women, in others it was only the elderly . . ."

"He changed how he did *everything* from town to town," Gina said. "He was a chameleon. In Washington he set his victims on fire postmortem, just as he did the woman we found yesterday. We have an ID on her, by the way. Her name was Amanda Robinson. The objects we found with her belonged to a young Washington woman who was murdered and burned almost nine years ago. Her name was Katrina Harmon."

Kendra nodded absently, staring at the photo. "I'm guessing you used the supermarket loyalty card on the keychain to track her."

"Exactly. And her former husband identified the eyeglasses as hers. We have a driver's license photo of her wearing them and the maker and prescription is a perfect match for a pair of glasses she purchased at the Connecticut Avenue

LensCrafters in D.C. a few months before she was killed."

Kendra couldn't take her eyes from the photo of the smiling, bespectacled young woman, just inches from nightmarish shots of her crispy corpse. Blue tape separated her case from the current San Diego case of Amanda Robinson. Here, too, were similarly grisly before-and-after shots.

"It's the same story with the others," Griffin said. "Each of our new killings matches the methodology of one of these old cases. He wanted to make sure we knew it was the same killer in both and not some sick copycat. So he left behind his trophies." Griffin walked over to another board. "And look at this. Each of the victims in Florida had Revlon Matte Peach Smoked Lipstick applied post mortem."

"The same brand as in our killings?" Kendra asked.

"We're still waiting for our report, but it sure looks like it."

Kendra shook her head at the sheer magnitude of what she was seeing on the boards around her. "So five of the nation's most notorious serial killers, spanning over a decade . . . were actually the work of one man."

"That's what it looks like," Griffin said. "And we're still combing the database to make sure there aren't more."

"He could point the way to more with his very next victim," Metcalf said. "This may not be the end."

Kendra looked at more of the boards as the group followed close behind. "He's gone all these years without getting caught or anyone realizing that these were all the work of a single killer," she whispered. "Why did he choose this moment, this city to tie them all together?"

Griffin shrugged. "We have our best profilers working on that question right now. But frankly, I doubt they have much to compare this to. They don't have anyone who's ever performed in this way before."

"Performed," Kendra repeated the word numbly. "Yes, that's what he's done all these years. He's set the stages and chosen the actors and then made himself both star and director. But maybe he's getting bored with no audience to applaud him or maybe he wants a grand finale."

"But that still doesn't answer the question 'why here?'" Griffin said. "He's very calculating. He has to have a plan."

"Yes, he has a plan. He chose this place for a reason." She was looking at the photo of Amanda Robinson. "Two victims. Two sets of trophies. Two clues that would link him to other cities, other revelations. It seems he's trying to tell us what it is." She moistened her lips. "No, he's tossing it in our faces."

"Conjecture, Kendra," Griffin said.

Kendra realized that was true, but it still felt right. Those photos on the bulletin boards were whirling around her. Burned, scorched victims, stabbed, sliced, bodies like Todd's, one old lady who had been tied and run over by a truck in her own driveway. So much evil, so many victims . . . And it had gone on for more than a decade.

She tried to shake off the images. "Have you been in touch with the investigators in each of these other cases?"

"Yes," Griffin said. "All except the D.C. detective, and I have a call into his department. I'm looping all of them into our investigation and some or all may join us here to assist."

Metcalf clicked his tongue. "And we're going to have to babysit a bunch of local cops while we try to catch this guy?"

"Adjust your attitude," Griffin said curtly. "These people know our killer better than anyone. There probably hasn't been a day in the past few years that they haven't thought of their cases and tossed every detail around in their heads. Whether they're here or not, they'll be a good resource for you."

Metcalf nodded, but Kendra wasn't sure if he was convinced. She turned to Griffin. "He obviously believes he can't be caught, that he's too clever. Your profilers would recognize that brand of arrogance. They just haven't run across it in this quantity before. You might throw that possibility at them."

"I already have," Griffin said bluntly. "It took a great deal of arrogance to stay in that closet taking photos with a victim bleeding out while that young woman was strolling from room to room." He paused. "Arrogance or madness."

"Or both," Metcalf said.

Griffin nodded. "I never said that wasn't possible. Aren't most serial killers designated by society as insane? It just depends on how the courts look at them."

Metcalf was looking at the Connecticut murder photos. "I think the prosecutors in these particular cities will fight very hard to get him the death penalty and not a cushy mental hospital." He glanced at Gina. "What do you think?"

"I think we'd better concentrate on catching him and not worry about extradition," she said dryly. "I've been doing my part while you've been narrowing your vision down to that one cold case in Oxnard. Don't you think you should start going through all these cases *I've* given you to work on?"

"Ouch," Metcalf murmured. He was suddenly grinning. "Point taken." He turned to Griffin. "Should I take your orders or hers, sir?"

"It better be mine, if you want to keep your job." He glanced at Gina. "But she did okay when you two left me in the lurch here with all these cases to work. It's good to know that I have a replacement available. Get busy." He turned to Kendra. "And you could make yourself valuable as well, but I don't suppose you want to volunteer for overnight duty." He scowled. "Even though you started all this."

"I believe it was the murder case you tried to involve me in that started all this," Kendra said. "And, no, I have no intention of staying here and being just one more pair of hands to put out the fires. I'm going home and get a good night's sleep. And then I'll see how I can schedule my sessions for tomorrow to give me enough time to go over the case files Metcalf and Gina are going to send to my printer tonight." She turned to Gina. "Don't email them to me. Send them directly to my printer. I want paper I can hold and compare. Okay? Every city. Every victim."

She nodded. "You've got it. Does Metcalf have your printer's IP address?"

"Yes, I do," Metcalf said. "Is this discrimination, Kendra? I'm the good guy, remember?"

"I remember," she said. "But Gina's becoming Wonder Woman. So adjust and conquer or have her drag you behind her chariot wheels."

He flinched. "Now that hurt."

"You'd be more use if you'd hit the phones with me," Griffin said. "I have to start talking to police captains in all these cities and making explanations and begging records and info."

"But I don't want to be of use to you," Kendra

said. "At least not in that way. That's not why you pulled me into this case." She turned back toward the elevator. "I'm afraid we're all going to be dealing with it very soon. But I'll handle it in my own way and not yours, Griffin." She got on the elevator and pressed the button. "Get me those case histories right away, Gina."

"No problem," Metcalf said quickly. "They'll be at your place before you know it."

"Thanks." As the door closed, she leaned back and took a deep breath. She felt smothered, sick, her chest tight.

All those victims.

The blood.

The scorched skin.

The pain.

The death.

The memory of that first killing was with her now, she could almost smell that burned flesh again.

She had barely managed to hold herself together before she could escape that FBI war room. The monumental numbers and scope of those deaths had stunned her. Serial killers were not new to her, but this one was different . . .

They were all different, she told herself. She was being foolish.

But there had been a kind of frightening intimacy about the way she had felt about these murders. It was as if she had been standing next to Todd Wesley when his life had been taken.

And her urgency to find this monster was unusual. She had even mentioned it to Lynch . . .

Instinct?

Had she felt driven because somewhere deep inside she had felt how truly deadly, what a complete threat he was, to everyone around him?

Twenty-six cases. Perhaps more.

He had been touring, skipping around the country, pausing wherever it pleased him, and then killing again and again. He'd reached out and a young man died. He'd reached out and a girl was made into a human torch.

She had to compose herself. The elevator doors were opening and she had to pretend she was as tough as these professionals like Metcalf.

The hell she did. She didn't have to pretend anything after what she had seen upstairs on the fourth floor. She was human, and she would stay that way. The minute she stopped feeling that sense of horror and outrage, she would never work another case.

Tonight she would go home and do exactly what she'd told Griffin she would do. But maybe she'd also say a prayer for all those poor men and women who had suffered so terribly at the hands of that beast.

Her front door was unlocked.

Kendra paused, automatically tensing, as she removed her key. It could be nothing. Olivia had her key. Kendra had excellent security these days since she'd been invaded a couple years ago. But it wasn't like Olivia not to call before she came—

"Well, are you going to come in or not?" Her mother threw open the door. "I've made coffee, and I picked up some of that Danish that you love from that deli across the street."

Mom. Relief fought with the surprise she felt. Of course, Mom had a key to her condo, too.

"Hey, what on earth are you doing here, Mom?" She reached out and hugged her. "I just heard from you last week. You're supposed to be in Athens, aren't you?"

"I got depressed. All that ancient glory and it's all going to hell for lack of filthy lucre and care. So I spent a few days in London and then decided I'd come back here." She tilted her head critically as she slammed the door. "You look tired. Don't you ever sleep?"

"I get a fair amount." Her mother, on the other hand, looked her usual energetic self. Dr. Deanna Michaels was vibrant, attractive, in her late fifties but looked younger. She was a brilliant and highly-regarded professor of history at UC San Diego. She was also dominant, loving, and as involved with Kendra's well-being as she'd been for all the twenty years when Kendra had been blind. "And as a matter of fact, I was planning on getting some sleep tonight." She raised her brows. "And I could have met you for coffee and

Danish tomorrow morning. Did that occur to you?"

"Yes, but my flight landed two hours ago and I decided this would be better." She moved toward the breakfast bar. "If I'd gone home, I would have dwelt on all this nonsense in which you're currently involved, and then I wouldn't sleep. Jet lag is bad enough. I wasn't about to allow anything else to interfere with my sleep time." She poured two cups of coffee. "It's bad enough that you permit it to disturb yours."

Kendra stiffened. "What nonsense?"

"The nonsense that's all over the San Diego news sites. Four intensely hideous murders." Deanna sat down on the stool beside her and lifted her cup to her lips. "Very nasty stuff. Did you really think that I wouldn't check on what's going on in my own hometown? Particularly when I know you have a passion for choosing the most worrisome possible cases on which to work."

Her mother's tone was light, but Kendra was aware of something a little feverish and tense beneath that smooth exterior. It was making her uneasy. "No, I know you keep informed." She lifted her coffee to her lips. "But I wasn't really involved until yesterday. Did Olivia text you?"

"No, though I did call her from my taxi when I was on my way here. She seemed more concerned with your sexual choices than with serial killers.

You must have downplayed exactly what you were facing."

"I don't lie to Olivia. I told her this one was a monster." She shrugged. "But she was busy trying to convince me that Lynch and I were—" She broke off. "You know Olivia. She thinks she knows me through and through."

"Maybe she does," Deanna added serenely, "but I know you better. I just seldom express opinions to keep from arguing with you."

Kendra grinned. "The hell you don't. Why else are you here?"

"Well, not about Lynch. I have mixed feelings about Lynch. Part of me wants you to jettison him because he's undoubtedly dangerous." She shrugged. "Another part of me wants you to keep him close . . . again because he's dangerous. You persist in living in a lethal environment, and he's capable of keeping your head above water."

"I'm capable of keeping my own head above water," Kendra said. "And at present, Lynch is in Guilin, China."

"Olivia told me he was off to some outlandish place." Her mother was frowning. "When is he coming back?"

"I have no idea." She was watching with alarm as the expressions flickered across her mother's face. "No, Mom," she said firmly, "I would not be pleased if you decided to casually call Lynch."

"There's no way of casually calling someone in

China," Deanna said regretfully. "It comes off as a big deal however you'd do it. But I'd feel better if he was around." She smiled. "Oh, well, I'll think of something."

"That's what I'm afraid of." She shook her ahead. "Look, Mom, you're right, this one is a monster. And I can't avoid working the case. But it's developing into something gigantic, and there will be all kinds of FBI and police after him. It's not as if it will be one on one."

"Good God, I hope not." Her smile disappeared and that smooth façade had cracked. "I couldn't *take* that, Kendra. I'd stop worrying about how you'd feel about me interfering and I'd call Lynch, the FBI, the CIA, and maybe the president. You keep away from that bastard."

"It will be okay. I told you, the case is growing out of—"

"I *know* how the case is growing." Her mother's lips were suddenly taut, her eyes glittering. "You don't have to tell me. Your damn printer has been doing that for the last thirty minutes." She slipped from the stool and strode across the room to Kendra's cubbyhole of an office that was more like a laundry room. "It kept going off while I was making the coffee. I went back to check and see if it needed paper." She threw open the door and Kendra heard the sound of the printer. "It didn't, but the tray had overflowed and there were sheets all over the floor. Do you want me to tell you what they were?"

Kendra flinched as she caught a glimpse of the gruesome body in the first photo on the floor. Metcalf had been busy but not selective. She could imagine the effect on her mother. "No." She crossed the room and took Deanna in her arms. "I know what they are. I'm sorry you had to see it."

"So am I." Deanna's arms closed tightly around Kendra. "I didn't want to see any of it. I don't want you to see it. I don't want any of it to *touch* you."

"I know. But you just saw some of what he did to those victims. He can't go on, Mom."

"Then have someone *else* catch him." She held Kendra still closer and then she released her and stepped back. "But you're not going to do that, are you?" She cleared her throat. "We've had this argument before. Someday I'm going to win it." She looked down at the photos and case histories lying on the floor. "But that's not going to be today, is it? If he did all that, then he's too hideous for me to budge you." She drew a long, shaky breath. "Then I'll have to try to find a way to help. I can do that. All your life I've helped you, haven't I?"

"All my life." All the years of care and love and understanding, of searching for a cure when everyone told her mother it was hopeless. And at every defeat never making Kendra feel that she would be loved any less if that cure was never found. No one could have been kinder or more patient to a special child, or any child, than her mother. "You're terrific."

"Yes, I am." Deanna nodded brusquely. "You're wise to realize that, Kendra. When you also realize that your mother always knows best, you will be totally perfect."

"Almost always," Kendra said gently.

"Perhaps. But not in this instance." She hugged her again and then stepped back. "We'll talk about this again and I don't promise not to try to change your mind and the outcome." She turned toward the door. "And now I believe I'll go home and take a hot bath and then start thinking about how to do that. Lock your door behind me."

"The condo is absolutely secure." She followed her mother to the door. "Except against the people I love."

"Then why did you hesitate before you came in tonight?" She looked over her shoulder. "Why, Kendra?"

A young man bleeding-out in a closet.

"I wasn't expecting you." She changed the subject. "And if you promise not to harass me, I'll ask you to dinner later in the week. What about it?"

"I'll let you know. I'm a busy woman and you're probably going to be wary of me for a little while." She opened the door. "You should be. I can be pretty formidable. Ask my students." She smiled. "Remember to eat that Danish I brought. I bet you haven't had dinner. It's not nourishing, but it will have to do. And you always did like sweets."

The door closed behind her.

But Kendra knew she was waiting until she locked the door before she moved toward the elevator.

She shook her head ruefully and then shot the lock.

Formidable, indeed. But she wouldn't have her any other way. It was just that right now she had no desire or energy to battle people she cared about. There was a bigger battle shaping up on the horizon. She just wished her mother hadn't seen the casualties that had already been inflicted.

Then she turned away, went back to her office, and started to gather up the photos and case histories scattered on the floor. There were still others pouring out of the printer onto the tray. She felt overwhelmed at the sheer volume. She felt again as if that damn murderer was standing there watching, smiling . . . waiting.

How many?

Her hands were shaking as she grabbed up the last of the photos on the floor and then whirled back to the spitting printer with fists clenched.

How *many,* you son of a bitch?

4:35 A.M.

The knot!

Kendra's eyes flew open as she woke from a sound sleep.

Yes!

She'd been studying those case histories all night and had only gotten to sleep a couple hours ago. But her mind had obviously still been working on them because she'd been jarred fully awake.

The knot!

She turned on the lamp, swung her legs to the floor, and jumped out of bed. The next moment she was rifling through the files she'd left on the chair across the room.

Oxnard. Check.

Jacksonville. Check.

Washington, D.C. Check.

She quickly went through the other cities.

Yes.

Okay. She had a key. Now what did she do about it?

She leaned back in the chair and closed her eyes.

Detach.

Concentrate.

Who could help her the most?

Lynch.

Of course she'd immediately thought of him. But not available. Dismiss him.

Griffin?

Maybe. But he was limited to official channels and might be stonewalled. With bodies falling in all directions, she didn't want that to happen.

Who else?

Qualifications. Smart. Innovative. The right background. Contacts.

Jessie Mercado.

She jumped to her feet, flew over to the nightstand, and reached for her phone. Jessie Mercado, private investigator extraordinaire, who was not only her friend, but had all the qualifications Kendra needed to explore the clue that had emerged from those files. Jessie would probably kill her for calling at this hour, but she was going to do it anyway. If she didn't, she'd be tossing and turning for the rest of the night. She'd find a way to make it up to her later.

She quickly dialed her number.

Jessie answered on the third ring. She did not sound pleased. "The last time you called me in the middle of the night I ended up on a jet to an undisclosed location, and I had to put my business on hold for weeks, Kendra. This had better not be a repeat."

"It's not; you know that was an emergency."

"And this isn't? It had better be. It's four-thirty."

"I know. And you have a right to be upset with me. Right now it's only an emergency to me. I woke up and realized I needed help and that it had to be you. I hoped you wouldn't mind if I woke you a little early."

"More than a little." She was silent. "You're in trouble?"

"Not personally. I just thought I'd see if I could hire you to work on something that—"

"It sounds personal to me. I know you, too, Kendra. You wouldn't call at this time of night if you weren't pretty upset. You're very cool and savvy. So let's cut to the chase. I'm hearing hesitation. I want to see your face while you're trying to persuade me to do this job for you. But I need a cup of coffee and a shower. I'll have time to get them if you come to my office in LA instead of me coming to you. Okay?"

"Okay." Kendra drew a deep breath. "Thanks."

"I haven't taken the job yet. You're my friend, so you've got a good chance, but I try to keep friendship and business in separate compartments." She added ruefully, "It doesn't always work out that way. But I'm relying on the fact that you'd generally not involve me in anything that would hurt me physically or financially. Okay, then I'll see you at my office in a couple hours." She ended the call.

And Kendra would have to get her own coffee from Starbucks on the road. But that was fine, she had a chance to convince Jessie to help her untangle that knot. One step closer. She got to her feet and headed for the bathroom.

Kendra drove to Santa Monica, which took her only slightly more than ninety minutes despite some momentary confusion from her phone's map app in the final blocks of her journey. It was close to dawn when she finally found herself on a pleasant, tree-lined stretch of Montana Avenue, just a couple of miles from the beach. The stores were small and charming, as was the art deco Aero Movie Theater, which seemed to specialize in classic films. Kendra walked around the theater to a side alley. She thought she was in the wrong place, until she saw a door with a small plaque that read MERCADO INVESTIGATIONS. Kendra pulled open the door and climbed a narrow staircase that ended in a tiny reception area. There was no one behind the receptionist's desk, but a red-haired young woman in faded designer jeans and a black t-shirt was curled up, sleeping on a leather couch. She didn't stir when Kendra came into the office.

"Hello?" Kendra asked.

The young woman finally opened her eyes. "Oh, hi."

"Hi."

"You're here to see Jessie?"

"Yes. Is she in?"

"I think she ran into trouble on the freeway. She called me to see if I was here about a half hour ago and told me to tell you. I guess I must have fallen back asleep. Too much wine at that party . . ." The young woman sat up and scooted to the end of the couch. "Have a seat. Want something to drink? I think there's water and juice in that fridge."

Kendra didn't sit down. "Uh, no. Thanks. Will Jessie be long?"

"No idea. I don't even know how long I was asleep."

Kendra studied her. She was even younger than she'd first thought, with a dewy complexion and gray-green eyes. "You look familiar. Have we met?"

"Don't think so, but I get that a lot." She extended her hand. "I'm Dee."

Kendra shook her hand. "Kendra Michaels. How long have you worked for Jessie?"

"Oh, I don't work for her." Dee covered a yawn. "Actually, she used to work for me."

At that moment, Jessie Mercado appeared in the doorway. "Good morning, Kendra." She was wearing black leather pants and boots and was as lean and toned as she'd been when Kendra had last seen her. She was always a study in contrasts, with that shining dark hair worn in an urchin cut surrounding her delicate features and those enormous brown eyes that belied her sleek toughness. "Sorry I kept you waiting. Construction traffic."

"No problem."

"I made her feel welcome," Dee said. "But you *really* need to get a receptionist."

Jessie made a face. "Or maybe just a bouncer to keep you out. You have a gorgeous home, Dee. Go sleep there."

"Too many people there. And what kind of talk is that?" Dee stood. "Admit it, you need me to give this place a little flair."

"I really don't."

"Sure you do. I'll convince you someday." Dee nodded to Kendra. "Nice to meet you. Don't believe the unpleasant things she's about to tell you about me. She doesn't really mean them."

Jessie took Dee by the arm and steered her to the door. "Hard as it might be to believe, we may actually have things to discuss other than you."

"As if." Dee started down the long stairway. "See you tomorrow, Jessie."

"No," she said firmly. "Don't count on it. I may not be here."

"Then the next day!" she called up.

"Dee . . ."

"I'll bring coffee!"

At the bottom of the stairs, the door opened and slammed shut.

Dee was gone.

"Is that who I think it was?" Kendra asked.

Jesse nodded. "My old boss. Delilah Winter, worldwide pop music phenomenon. Twenty years old, Grammy winner, rabid fans in every corner of the globe, and all she wants to do is hang out in these humble digs."

"You used to be her head of security, right?"

"Yep." Jesse looked down the stairway to make sure Dee had left. "The trippiest year and a half of my life. She tries to lure me back every time she comes here. One day she showed up with a knapsack stuffed with a million dollars in cash. All mine if I would agree to head up security for her year-long world tour."

"You didn't take it?"

"Nah. Not worth the aggravation. And besides, I had to teach her not to depend on me. She zoomed to the top when she was in her early teens and you can imagine the chaos of her life. She's a nice kid, though. But vulnerable and kind of lonely. I think she likes coming here because it's the one place she can go where no one wants anything from her. She kept dropping in on me at all times of the day and night, and I finally gave her a key." She sighed. "Though if I'd known she was going to be here so often, I could have used that money she was offering to get a nicer office."

Kendra glanced around their surroundings. "I like it. I've never known anybody with an office over a movie theater."

"Well, you do now. It's not a bad spot. Sometimes it gets a little noisy, especially when they're playing an old war movie downstairs. And on the weekends they run the films twenty-four hours a day." She cocked her head back toward the open door. "Come inside."

Kendra followed her through the doorway to her office, which was only slightly larger than the cramped waiting room. There was a worn mahogany desk that was a perfect match for the built-in shelves that lined the front of the room. The crown and corner molding continued the art deco design from the theater façade, and a side window offered a view of the street outside. The back wall of the room was covered with photographs depicting Jessie's colorful background: her time as a soldier in Afghanistan, a stuntwoman on a cheesy superhero movie, a contestant on *American Ninja*, and her stint as Delilah Winter's bodyguard and security chief. Kendra doubted if those photos depicted even a quarter of Jessie's experiences. Jessie was a very private person who seldom spoke of any of those events of her past nor the people who had lived them with her. Kendra regarded Jessie as a good friend, but that friendship was based on the fact that they'd gone through a multiple amount of emotions and experiences in the short time they'd known each other. She had found Jessie honest and amusing and ready to go the extra mile if a friend needed her. It wasn't often you happened on someone like that.

Jessie grimaced when she saw Kendra looking at the photos. "Sorry about those. Not very modest of me, but they're good for business. Clients like the idea that I didn't earn my detective license by taking a course on the Internet."

"You've had a lot of amazing experiences. People should know that."

"Oh, I just can't make up my mind. I think about replacing them every day." She motioned toward the two chairs in front of her desk. "But you didn't come here to give me design tips. Have a seat."

"I'll stand if you don't mind. I've been in the car all morning on the drive from San Diego, and I have to drive straight back after I leave here."

"Fine." Jessie sat on the edge of her desk. "So what's going on? You need someone followed? A background check?" She added slyly, "Another world-renowned research scientist you need hidden away?"

"No, but you did do that superbly." She made a face and then said, "Something much nastier, I'm afraid. You'll probably throw me out. I could use your help to catch a serial killer."

Jesse raised her brows. "Wow. Is that all?"

"Okay. It's asking a lot, I know."

"You think?"

"If you're not interested, I under—"

"I didn't say that," she interrupted. "It sounds a hell of a lot more interesting than busting the balls of some Beverly Hills adulterer or tailing some movie star's daughter to make sure she doesn't buy drugs. Two of my most recent jobs by the way. A serial killer kind of sounds like a breath of fresh air to me." She tilted her head. "Unless I've just disqualified myself by making such a psychotic admission."

"Not at all." Kendra suddenly chuckled. "Which is either a reflection of how much I respect you or how desperate I've become. Take your pick."

"Desperation, I like it." Jessie smiled. "And I'm curious why you came to me. So that's an added incentive to the desperation. How can I help?"

Kendra stepped away from the wall of photos. "We've had four murders in the past week. Have you heard about them?"

"In San Diego? Sure. They're all over the news. You're right, that is nasty. But your police department hasn't officially linked them, have they?"

"That's about to change. The FBI has taken over the investigation, and they've asked me to help out."

"Good. At least they've done one thing right." She paused. "And are you going to do it? The last time I saw you I thought you only wanted to get back to teaching your kids."

"I did." She shook her head. "But yes, I'm going to do it." Her lips tightened. "I *have* to do it."

"Why?" Jessie's gaze narrowed on her face. "Bored?"

"No, of course not," she said impatiently. "That's my chosen career. I always find it fascinating and challenging. It's just that those killings are . . . different."

Jessie's lips quirked. "And also fascinating and challenging?"

"No." She shuddered. "Hideous and scary."

Jessie's smile disappeared. "And that's where the nasty comes in. You don't scare easily. I take it the crime scenes are even worse than the journalists are hinting?"

"Much worse. Someone's got to stop him, Jessie."

Jessie nodded. "And you're pulling out all the tricks you can find to try to do that. It's really bothering you, isn't it?"

"It will bother you, too."

"Nah, not much does these days. I'm a tough nut, Kendra."

"Not that tough. I know you, Jessie."

She shrugged. "Maybe not. Tell me about it. Are the cases linked, or not?"

"They are linked, but in a way none of us has ever encountered before. We've uncovered something . . . unusual."

"Yeah?"

Kendra told her about the souvenirs and their links to the earlier murder cases in other cities. After she was finished, Jessie sat in thoughtful silence.

Kendra gestured for a response. "Well?"

"I'm just trying to process this. If what you're telling me is true, this guy has been at this for over a decade. He's adopted four MO's, each

116

different enough that nobody has ever put them together."

"Well, *we* put them together."

"Only because the killer wanted you to."

"Exactly. And we have no idea why he's chosen this moment to step forward and connect the dots for us."

"Okay . . . What help do you think I can be?"

Kendra hesitated before speaking. "Well, there are some potential legal ramifications in what I'm about to ask. If the answer is no, I'd appreciate it if you keep this conversation between us."

Jessie lowered her voice melodramatically. "Ooh, I do like the sound of this."

"I thought you might. The forbidden usually intrigues you. I've been looking over the case files, and in a few of the killings it was obvious that the victim had been tied up before the murder occurred. The rope was never left behind but in two cases there was a recognizable impression left on the victims' skin."

"Recognizable as *what?*" Jessie asked.

"A clove hitch."

"And what, exactly, is that?"

"It's a knot. It's one of five knots that Navy SEALs have to tie in an underwater test before they can graduate."

"How in the hell do you know what that looks like?"

"I live in San Diego, remember? Home of the SEAL training school. At any given time, there are scores of incredibly fit young adults walking around town with short lengths of rope so that they can practice whenever an opportunity presents itself. Sit in a Starbucks long enough, you're bound to see one practicing underwater test knots over their Caramel Macchiato."

"Hmm. Do Navy SEALs really drink Caramel Macchiatos?"

"Okay, bad example. But you get my point. It's a knot I've seen and can recognize. And it happens that each of the other four cities are near Navy bases: Oxnard is very close to Port Hueneme; Washington, D.C.; is near Naval Station Norfolk; Jacksonville, Florida, is a short drive to Naval Station Mayport; and Hartford, Connecticut, is near the New London Naval Submarine base."

Jessie thought about this. "Just to satisfy my own curiosity, you didn't know that off the top of your head, did you?"

"Afraid not. Google is my friend. I knew about Oxnard and Hartford, which is what made me look up the other two once I recognized that knot."

"Nobody in the FBI ever figured this out?"

"They didn't know the cases were connected, remember? And it's possible someone recognized the impression of that knot, but there's nothing in the case files about pursuing a military angle."

"Did you tell the FBI about this?"

"I will. I wanted to talk to you first."

"The million-dollar question: Why?"

Kendra paused for a moment, trying to think of a way to explain it to her. There was no way she wanted to offend her. Jessie had done two tours in Afghanistan. "Military cases can be difficult. I've been involved in a case that crossed over military lines before and it was a nightmare. There were communication problems, secrecy issues, egos, and general stonewalling. I'm sure the FBI will hit that again but we don't have time for it. Three more people could be dead by the time we cut through the red tape. You have connections everywhere, and I thought with your military background, you might be able to find out if there's any one person who has been stationed at each of those bases during these times."

Jessie bit her lip. "These are Navy bases. You *do* know I was in the Army, don't you?"

"Of course. I just thought—"

"You thought the United States Armed Forces are all just one big happy family?"

"I know better than that, but I was still hoping—"

"As it happens, I *do* have some connections I can tap. But it's far from a sure thing, and you should definitely get the FBI working on it from their end."

119

"I will as soon as I get back." Kendra reached into her pocket and produced an index card. "Here are the places and date ranges for each series of murders. If you need anything else, let me know."

Jessie took the card and looked it over. She murmured, "You know who would *love* to help you out with this, don't you?"

She stiffened. "If you say Adam Lynch . . ."

"You know it's true."

"I don't need his help. Besides, he's in China."

"Too bad." Jessie pocketed the card. "I got to know him when we were away tying up the loose ends of your last case. I was very wary of him in the beginning. But he's a pretty amazing guy."

Kendra shook her head. Jessie wasn't the type to impress easily but apparently no one was immune to Lynch's charisma.

"*He* certainly thinks he's amazing."

Jessie smiled. "You don't think so?"

Kendra shrugged. "He has his moments."

"Well, from what I can see, he'd like to spend quite a few of those moments involved in extremely carnal games with you. Though I can understand why you're hesitant to get involved with a guy like that."

Kendra said, exasperated, "Why is it that everyone has an opinion on my and Lynch's relationship, or rather, our lack of one?"

Jessie crossed to the other side of her desk and

shoved some folders into a worn leather knapsack. "Because everyone in the peanut gallery can see the sparks flying. You have to admit, there are some major sparks there."

"Then why did you say I should be hesitant? Not that I disagree with you."

"I've been involved with men like that. Well, maybe not quite as intense as Lynch, but close enough. They roar into your life with all the subtlety of a Mack truck and suck up all the oxygen in the room. Sometimes there just isn't much left for yourself. It can be fun, but it can also be intense and all-consuming."

"Which is something I definitely don't need. This case is all-consuming enough." She paused as she listened to movie music swell in the theater beneath them. "I take it we're finished? Do you need anything else from me?

"Photographs. I want the most gruesome pics you have from murder scenes in each of the cities."

"You're joking."

"No. Trust me, it isn't for my own sick pleasure. But it will be helpful to me."

"Okay. I'll email you some before I get on the road. Anything else?"

Jessie was pushing her out the door. "I'd like shots of the rope impressions you were telling me about."

"Done. They'll be in your inbox within the next

few minutes." She watched Jessie lock the office door. "Any idea when I'll hear back from you?"

Jessie slung the knapsack over her shoulder. "No idea. I'm going to see someone about it right now. I'll let you know." She pointed her finger at her. "Remember. The most gruesome crime scene pics you have. It's important."

"I told you that I'd—"

But Jessie held up her hand and was answering her phone. "Dee's home, Colin? Good. Talk to you later. I'll be in touch." She cut the connection. "What were you saying, Kendra?"

"Nothing important." She was smiling. "Do you always check up on people who aren't even your clients?"

She shrugged. "What can I say? I set up Dee's security with Colin Parks when I quit my job with her. She likes to feel like she can slip away and have her personal time. God knows, she has precious little freedom. So I told Colin to let her think she was getting away with it." Her lips twisted wryly. "She doesn't, of course; security with a celebrity has to be 24/7. But what she doesn't know makes her happy. Nothing wrong with that. Whenever she comes here, I just have Colin make certain to tell me when she gets home safely."

"No, nothing wrong with that," Kendra said solemnly. "Even to a tough nut like you, Jessie."

"Knock it off." Jessie was heading down the stairs. "And send me those photos."

She had already roared off on her motorcycle by the time Kendra reached her car. Typical Jessie reaction and response, she thought as she got back on the road. Once the decision was made and that sharp brain in high gear, she'd waste no time in starting the search. And evidently she already had a few ideas about how that search should go.

Relief. After all the frustration and fear that Kendra had been experiencing, it was good to know that she had Jessie in her corner. It was all very well to have Griffin and all those other agents to tap, but Jessie was a friend. She could talk to her, she didn't have to pretend that she was invulnerable. Jessie understood people and would always help without judging.

Well, almost, she qualified. Jessie had certainly inserted her opinion about bringing Lynch into the picture to help. But so had everyone else in her circle, she thought sourly. Lynch might be thousands of miles away, but he was clearly sending out vibes to one and all. It was disturbing that the minute she'd been pulled into the search for this monster everyone around her had tried to get her to contact Lynch. Disturbing and upsetting. She was fully capable of taking care of her own business without him. Why couldn't everyone see that? Particularly Jessie, who was the most independent woman Kendra knew.

But then Jessie had been arguing principally

about sex, not that Lynch was absolutely essential to the investigation. And she had dropped the argument immediately when she had become interested in taking on the investigation herself.

Kendra doubted if Jessie would even mention Lynch from now on. They both would be too busy working leads and trying to find out where they would take them.

She felt again that rush of warmth at the thought. It was going to be good to have Jessie on the case. It would be comforting to have a friend to help ward off the terrible coldness this killer exuded and keep it from smothering them.

Was there anything in the world more important than a good friend?

Nice place, Zachary thought.

He stood in the center of the downtown condominium, glancing around at the living room that had been repurposed as a home office. Sad how work had been allowed to intrude on the sanctity of the home these days.

So much had changed in the years since he'd begun his dangerous and fascinating hobby. Now there were WiFi-connected security cameras all over the place, mounted on the underside of roofs, on windowsills, on automobile dashboards. Traffic and ATM cams were everywhere. DNA evidence retrieval had gotten so refined that he could get a death sentence for breathing on a window. It was almost impossible to move through any densely-populated urban area without leaving behind some type of incriminating footprint.

Which made this game more exciting than ever.

He flexed his gloved fingers as he paced around the condo. Everything was impeccably neat and well-organized here, just as he expected it to be. After all, it was the home of a blind person.

He'd done his research on Olivia Moore, and although time constraints had curtailed his penchant for in-depth study, he felt he knew whom he was dealing with. She was somewhat of a public figure with her remarkable Web site and its worldwide following. He'd watched over a dozen interviews with her on YouTube, most of them recorded in this very room.

Impressive young lady.

He glanced at the modernist paintings on the walls. Strange. Why were they even here? For visitors, he guessed. Maybe her best friend had chosen them for her. If so, Kendra Michaels had excellent taste.

Enough sightseeing. It was time to—

He froze.

Footsteps.

In the hall coming toward the door.

Surely it was just a passing neighbor. Olivia wasn't due back for hours.

The footsteps drew closer.

It couldn't be . . .

Olivia had two appointments today and she shouldn't be back for hours. Unless . . .

A key slid into the lock.

. . . unless there had been a change in plans.

In one lightning-fast motion, he unsnapped the leather sheath beneath his jacket and slid out his long blade.

The deadbolt lock clicked and the knob turned . . .

He held up his knife. He hadn't planned to kill today, but he might have to improvise.

Just like in Connecticut. Just like in Oxnard.

He could do it again.

The door swung open. It was Olivia and she was alone. She moved toward her oval wraparound desk and opened a drawer.

Zachary didn't breathe.

He stood only five feet from her. One rustle of fabric, one bone creak, one stomach growl, and it was all over. She'd know he was there and he'd have to kill her.

But what if she smelled him? His knowledge of Kendra Michaels had taught him how hyper-aware blind people could be of their surroundings. He hadn't wanted to leave any trace of himself for Olivia to pick up, so he had bathed only with water, no shampoo or soap. He'd used no detergent when he washed his clothes.

His precautions might not be enough.

He watched her. She seemed to be in a rush as she pulled a USB flash drive and a telephone

126

headset from the drawer. She was obviously still going to her second appointment of the day, a speech at a school for the blind in Oceanside. Maybe she'd forgotten something.

She stopped.

Uh oh.

She slowly lifted her head and turned around. She kept turning until she faced him.

He wanted to grip the knife tighter, but he knew he couldn't, not as long as he wanted to make this work.

Not a sound. Not a breath.

She looked as if she was staring deep into his eyes.

The effect unnerved him, although almost nothing ever made him feel that way. He felt a sudden urge to lunge across the desk and slice her throat, if only to stop the stare-down that wasn't.

Her head turned. She faced a different direction before finally picking up her items and moving away from the desk.

Good girl.

She walked across the room and pulled open the front door. She stopped and turned around. Once again she turned toward him. After a long moment, she stepped away and locked the door behind her.

Zachary finally let out the breath he'd been holding. He was relieved . . . and disappointed.

Relieved he could now move forward with his plan, but disappointed he hadn't been able to execute this bit of improvisation that had already quickened his pulse and given him a jolt that made life worth living.

No matter. There were bigger jolts to come.

He walked to Olivia's desk, sat in the chair, and oriented himself with her computer system.

He leaned forward and began to type.

Kendra turned toward the assembled group of FBI agents and assistants. Were they buying it?

She was in front of one of the massive bulletin boards in the FBI fourth floor war room. She'd begun by speaking only with Griffin, Metcalf, and Gina about her theory concerning the knot and the murders' proximity to Naval bases, but as she spoke and moved between the push-pinned photos, her group of listeners grew until she was addressing everyone in the room.

Now that she was finished, everyone seemed to be waiting for Griffin to respond before they weighed in.

He finally nodded. "Interesting. It's definitely worth exploring. I'll reach out to NAB Coronado." He glanced back at the group. "Though I'm disappointed someone here hadn't come up with this yet."

With the boss's stamp of approval in place, the rest of the group responded with enthusiasm.

Kendra spoke with a few of them and answered questions before Metcalf approached her.

He smiled. "Admit it, you like this work. At least a little, right?"

The politics? The knowledge that there were beasts waiting around every corner? "I'll like it when we catch this guy."

Griffin stepped up to her. "Good work. We'll run this by the dream team."

"Who?"

"All the investigators who were on the different cases are coming here from their respective cities. Two police detectives, an FBI agent, and a federal marshal."

"And a partridge in a pear tree," Metcalf quipped.

It didn't seem to bother him that no one except Gina laughed.

"Anyway," Griffin continued after giving Metcalf a cold glance, "we all know how it feels to be haunted by a case we could never crack. For each of these people, this killer was one of those. They all want a piece of this investigation."

Kendra frowned. "It sounds a little cannibalistic. Couldn't that get a bit . . ."

"Unwieldly?" Griffin said. "Absolutely. But these are the best and brightest serial killer investigators in the country. They could give us real insight into this guy."

Insight into the soul of a monster? "We may get

more than we bargain for. When do they arrive?" Kendra asked.

"A couple of them are already on their way. I expect to see them all here by tonight or early tomorrow." Griffin lowered his voice. "I know one of them. Richard Gale. He works for the Bureau out of NYC. Not what you'd call a people person. A real son of a bitch, actually. But in the last twenty years, he's helped catch some of the Northeast's most high-profile serial killers. It's almost spooky how good he is."

Metcalf and Gina looked at each other and nodded. "Gale is the real deal," Metcalf said. "His cases are on the study list at Quantico."

"The others are just as impressive," Griffin said. "You'll meet them all soon enough."

Kendra's phone blared from her pocket with a ringtone of the "Ooga-Chaka" intro from Blue Suede's "Hooked on a Feeling."

Metcalf's brows rose. *"Really?"*

Kendra reached into her pocket. "That's Olivia's ringtone. I let her pick her own and that's just her way of driving me crazy." Kendra answered the phone. "Olivia, I'll call you back. I'm in the middle of—"

"Kendra, don't you hang up."

Kendra stiffened. Something was wrong. She had never heard Olivia's voice that hollow and frightened.

"Olivia . . . ?"

"He was here."

"Who?"

A long moment of silence, then jagged breathing.

"Olivia? Are you okay?"

"Yes. I'm just . . . a little freaked."

"Who was there, Olivia?"

"That . . . killer. The one you're looking for. You need to get over here right now. He left you a message."

CHAPTER 6

Kendra, Metcalf, and Gina bolted out of the FBI office and raced to Olivia's condo, paying only passing deference to the rules of the road. Kendra frantically rapped on the door before using her own key to unlock it and enter.

"Olivia?"

"Over here." Olivia was in her kitchen, leaning against the counter. She was pale and shaken as she turned to face Kendra. "God, I'm glad you're here."

Kendra ran toward her. "We broke every speed limit. This is crazy." She grabbed Olivia's arms. "I'm so sorry. Are you sure you're okay?"

"Well, I'm no longer freaked," she said unsteadily. "I've made a graceful transition to royally pissed off."

Kendra felt a surge of relief. "That's the Olivia I know."

"That's perfectly natural, ma'am. Shock can do that to you." Gina was already in full investigative mode as she moved into the condo and glanced around. "I'm FBI Special Agent Gina Carson and I'm here with Special Agent Roland Metcalf."

"Hi. And yes, I recognized his footsteps. Hi, Metcalf."

Gina paused for a moment as she realized that

Olivia was blind. Kendra hadn't mentioned it to her.

Metcalf smiled. "Hi, Olivia. You've created quite a stir. Do you want to tell us what happened?"

"Sure." Olivia took a deep breath as she stepped from the kitchen into the living area. "I was out during the morning and early afternoon, but when I got home, I noticed that my desk chair was slightly out of place."

Gina moved toward the U-shaped desk. "Like how?"

"I always slide it in when I walk away from the desk. Otherwise it gets in the way if I want to look for something in one of the drawers. When I came home, the chair was pulled out and angled slightly to the right. Then I noticed my keyboard was tilted in a way I would never use it. I realized someone had moved it."

"You said he left you a message?" Kendra said.

"I said he left *you* a message." Olivia moved closer to her monitor and keyboard. "There was a Word file open. I knew it wasn't one of mine. So I used a text-to-speech app to read it to me. It sounded like . . . *this*.

Kendra pressed her keyboard's spacebar and the vaguely robotic voice spoke.

"Hello, Sweet Capable Olivia . . . Please pass this along to your friend Kendra. My name is Zachary and I'm under the distinct impression that she would very much like to meet me . . ."

Kendra couldn't breathe. Although the text-to-speech app did a decent job bringing words to life, the slight mechanized quality was making the message even creepier than it already was.

It continued, *"All in good time, dear Kendra. But you're no doubt wondering what brought me to your fair city. The answer is you, my dear. I've spent years weaving yards of beautiful ribbon and I needed the right person to help me pull it all together in a perfect bow. And that person is you. Flattered? You should be. It's been a long search . . ."*

Kendra mouth went dry. This couldn't be happening . . .

"To celebrate our new partnership, please accept these few tokens of my esteem . . . Good luck, Kendra. I look forward to meeting you."

The message ended.

Kendra looked down to Olivia's desk. Neatly lined up along the top edge of her keyboard were four driver's licenses.

Metcalf leaned over to examine them. "One from Connecticut, one from California, one from Virginia, one from Florida."

"More souvenirs from the victims?" Gina asked.

"Yes," Kendra said with a shudder. "I recognize the faces from your crime scene photos."

Olivia crossed her arms in front of her. "He was *here*."

Kendra put a hand on Olivia's forearm and felt her trembling. "Olivia . . ."

"Sitting on my chair, typing on my keyboard," Olivia said shakily. "I feel . . . violated. This is my place, my world. I can't believe it."

"At least *you* weren't here," Metcalf said quietly.

"No? That's just it," Olivia said. "I think I was."

Shock on shock. Kendra looked at her. "What?"

"I'm pretty sure I was here when he was." Olivia didn't look quite as defiant as she had before. Fear had clearly returned. "I stopped by to get some materials for a presentation. Something didn't feel right." She turned to Kendra. "You know how it is in a place you're really familiar with, like your own home? When something—or somebody—is out of place, or there when they shouldn't be, you can feel it. The acoustics are different, the air moves differently. I had a strange feeling when I was in here before, but I talked myself into believing that the TV crew had rearranged something I didn't catch, and that's what it was." Olivia shook her head. "But now I don't think so. He was here, watching me. He could have killed me just as easily as he killed those three other people . . ."

Kendra decided not to tell her that the count was now at least twenty-six. "That's not what he wanted to do," she said. "He wanted to make *me* afraid. Afraid for you and all the other people in my life. I'm the one he's targeted."

"No," Olivia said harshly. "He needs you alive to play his sick game. Everyone else is expendable."

Kendra couldn't argue with that. She was too confused and terrified to be able to analyze anything to do with what had happened today. She was terribly afraid that Olivia might be right.

"We need to clear out of here," Metcalf said. "I have an Evidence Response Team on the way."

Kendra shook her head. "The ERT won't find anything. He's too careful. He didn't leave a single fingerprint or DNA sample at any of his murder scenes."

"We have to make sure," Gina said. "He only has to slip up once."

"Of course." Kendra turned toward Olivia. "You're staying with me tonight. Pack a bag, grab your laptop and anything else you might need to work."

"No way." Olivia had bounced back and was wearing her defiant face again. "I'm not going anywhere. I won't let him chase me out of my home."

Kendra knew exactly how she felt. She adjusted her appeal. "You won't get a moment's peace or any work done with the FBI agents who will be powdering and photographing this place in the next few hours. Trust me, you'll be happier at my place. And you'll be close enough that they can talk to you if they need you for anything."

Olivia thought about this for a long moment. "Okay, but just for a few hours."

"We'll see."

"I'm sleeping here tonight," she said firmly.

Gina looked up from the desk. "I don't think that's a good idea. He got in here without any sign of forced entry. He can do it again."

"I know. Do you think I haven't thought about that? Nothing like a serial killer to make you feel vulnerable." She made a face. "I'm calling Kendra's security guy right away. I laughed at her when she had her place buttoned down, but now I think it's a good idea. Well, really I thought it was a good idea for her, just not for me," she amended. "Kendra deals with killers and I deal with bill collectors. But now I believe I'd feel more secure with new locks, steel-reinforced doorframe, maybe a few motion sensors to send reports to my phone when there's a breach . . ."

"We can make that happen," Kendra said. "We'll call him from my place. He owes me a favor. I bet he can do it today."

Metcalf pointed to the door. "Only after the Evidence Response Team gives it the once-over."

Kendra nodded. "Well, then, you'd better have them do the door first. We'll be one flight up if you need anything." She turned to Olivia. "Come on, let's go. I don't know about you, but I need a drink."

● ● ●

"Drink this." Kendra handed Olivia her martini and took her own vodka and tonic to the couch and pulled out her phone. "I'll catch up with you as soon as I call to arrange for your security. I'm scared to death you'll get stubborn and want to chance sleeping at your own place even if you have trouble getting it monster-proofed."

"No worries," Olivia said. "All I have to do is remind myself of the moment when I stood there in my office with your murderer staring at me, trying to decide if it was necessary to kill me." She took a sip of her martini. "You know he has to have had a thought like that, Kendra."

"Yes." That had been the most chilling vision that Olivia's story had brought to mind. Because Kendra could relate to standing there in darkness, sure that someone was there, every instinct screaming, but having to tell herself there was no proof. It was the stuff of madness and nightmares. And she knew that the feeling of being helpless before a threat like that was the worst part of the experience. "But if he'd moved, you might have heard him and been able to defend yourself. You wouldn't have let him have it all his own way."

She smiled. "Your confidence in me is amazing."

"*You're* amazing," she said lightly. "Now hush while I finish making this phone call."

"You'd better be quick." She drained her glass.

"I'm going to have another drink. You didn't make this one strong enough."

Thirty minutes later after much coaxing and a significant bribe, Kendra hung up with the promise of a crew that would show up no later than nine that night to make the security changes. "Done." She got to her feet and headed for the kitchen. "Now I'm going to put a frozen lasagna into the oven for dinner. You need something in your stomach after those last three martinis I saw you downing."

"Whatever," Olivia said. "I'm feeling no pain, but our Zachary is still with me." She stood up and followed Kendra to the kitchen. "That message keeps playing over and over in my head."

"Mine, too." Kendra pulled out the casserole and took it out of the box. "Zachary. We didn't know his name was Zachary before today. So at least we learned something new." She put the lasagna on the rack and turned on the oven. "Though I'm fairly confident that isn't his real name. He's very clever, I can't see him giving anything away." She turned from the oven. "I guess we'll find out eventually, and Zachary is as good a name as any to call him until we're sure." She added, "And maybe the ERT will find something in your condo that will give us even more of a lead. No one is perfect."

She smiled crookedly. "And he'll rue the day

when he tried to use the amazing Olivia Moore?"

"Why not?"

"No reason. I agree with you, but I believe you're trying to put a positive spin on a very bad experience. I appreciate the effort, but I'm over the first trauma. So cut off the alcohol and make me some coffee. I might have to think clearly when your buddies at the FBI want to take a statement."

"Good idea," Kendra said ruefully. "I wasn't trying to get you drunk, that phone call lasted longer than I thought it would." She put dark magic blend into the automatic coffee maker. "I wanted to take the edge off, not blur it completely."

"Well, I did," Olivia said. "I almost fell apart when I first heard that message. I was ashamed of being such a coward. I'm sorry, Kendra, you didn't need me to behave like that when you must have been as scared as I was."

"Sorry?" She came around the bar and took Olivia in her arms. "You were awesome. I'm the one who should be sorry to involve you. I *am* sorry." She cleared her throat. "You didn't ask for any of this. I almost got you killed." She took a step back. "Please, believe me. I had no idea that bastard even knew who I was, much less had some kind of fixation on me. I certainly didn't have any idea my friends would be targeted. I still can't believe it's true."

"I think you'd better start assuming that he meant every word he said," Olivia said dryly. "And if I was targeted, it was only in a minor way . . . for him. You're the one who is getting his attention. So please don't get all emotional and weepy on me. You're going to embarrass me."

"Heaven forbid," Kendra said unevenly. "Am I allowed to say Zachary chose very well? He probably researched and found out how much I care about you and how scared I'd be if anything happened to you."

"Yeah, you can say that. Because it's all past tense now. I'm going to have steel doors and motion sensors and I'll be on my guard. He made a mistake, didn't he?"

"A big mistake," Kendra said fiercely. "He won't be able to touch you again."

"Right." She turned and started toward the couch. "Then get me my coffee, and we'll sit and relax and wait for the lasagna to cook. If I remember correctly, it takes about forty-five minutes. By that time, with luck, I'll no longer be blurred and you'll no longer be stressed."

"You have a better chance than I do," Kendra said. "Forgive me, Olivia."

"Forgive? We don't use that word between us." She took the coffee cup Kendra was handing her and curled up on the couch. "It wasn't your fault that Zachary knew what good taste you had in friends. Now get your coffee and come and sit beside me. I'm hoping we'll have a little time to ourselves before Metcalf comes running up from my condo. He and Gina let me off easy, but they're going to want a statement with details, aren't they?"

"Absolutely. It's their job and Griffin is going to be a hard-ass over every single aspect of this case. But they're lucky it's you they're interviewing. You're trained to observe details no one else might."

She shook her head. "Not like you."

"Still very, very good." She sat down with her own cup of coffee. "And just the questions might trigger a memory or two."

"I'll have to see what happens." Olivia reached out and squeezed her hand. "You okay now, Kendra?"

It was like Olivia to be concerned about Kendra after all she'd been through herself today. "As long as you are. No problem." She leaned back on the cushions. Like Olivia, she was trying to block the vision she was seeing of a shadowy man standing looking at her friend and deciding whether or not he'd let her live. "I only hope we'll get a chance to eat that lasagna before Metcalf comes bounding up those stairs."

But her hope was not fulfilled. Kendra had just set the table and put the lasagna on a platter when Metcalf and Gina arrived at the door.

"Lord, that smells good." Gina was sniffing the air. "Garlic bread?"

"What else goes as well with lasagna?" Kendra asked as she let them in the condo. "I was hoping you'd take a little longer before you came to take her statement. Did you find anything?"

"Nothing suspicious," Metcalf said. "Everything appears to belong to Olivia and is in perfect order."

"Duh," Olivia said. "I'm blind, Metcalf. If it wasn't in order my life would be chaos."

"Sarcasm doesn't become you," Metcalf said. "But then you're gorgeous, and you don't need anything to become you. Evidence Response is still looking, but we're not hopeful."

"I'm bringing out a security team at nine tonight. Are you going to let them do their work?"

"More than likely. As I said, we're not finding much. But I need a statement from Olivia, and Griffin's not going to take any excuses. I knew she was upset, and I wanted to give her time to settle down, but I have to—"

"Oh, for heaven's sake," Olivia said. "Stop waffling. Ask me your questions. But both of you sit down and have dinner first. I refuse to let good food get cold. There's plenty, isn't there, Kendra?"

Kendra shrugged. "More than enough."

"Well, if you insist—" Metcalf said, his gaze

on the lasagna. "And after dinner you should call Griffin, Kendra. He didn't like the way we bolted out of the office after we got Olivia's call. And when I called him back about Zachary's message, he nearly blew a gasket."

"I imagine he did." She hadn't thought about Griffin and didn't want to do so now. But she knew Metcalf had probably covered for her to keep Griffin from bothering Olivia and her during a very stressful time. The longer she waited to call him, the longer Metcalf would be under the gun. "I'll call him now. You all go on and eat."

Metcalf frowned. "You could wait until—"

"Eat." She took out her phone and headed for the living room. "This may not take long."

Or then again, it might.

"It's about time you called me," Griffin said sourly when he picked up. "Metcalf said you were busy, but after all, I do head this investigation."

"I wasn't concerned about protocol or whether I was offending you. My old friend had just been exposed to a serial killer, and she was my number one priority. It's a wonder she came out of this alive."

"Yes, it is," he said bluntly. "Reports have been coming in from the profilers in D.C., and they see no clemency in this killer's behavior. He was far more likely to butcher Olivia to make a statement than to let her go. We're generating this report to the investigators who are coming here to help work this case. We need her input."

"Yeah, I'm sure Olivia will be only too glad to be a guinea pig for them to study. You'll be lucky if she doesn't take them apart one by one."

"Then it's your responsibility to make her see that she has to be helpful if she wants this man captured."

She tried to hold onto her temper. "I have no responsibility as far as your dream team is concerned, Griffin. Your responsibility is to keep Olivia alive and well. That's my responsibility also. Don't drown her in red tape or do anything that threatens her in any way just to give your team a project."

"We're trying to do just the opposite, Kendra," he said soothingly. "I know she's very close to you. But there's something intrinsically valuable in a team effort."

Maybe he actually believed that, she thought wearily. "Then have your team find a way to tell us what he's going to do next. Because I would never have called this one in a hundred years."

"Neither would I," Griffin said. "It blew us out of the water."

"We just have to keep Olivia safe. And my mother, have you arranged protection for my mother?"

"The minute Metcalf told me that Olivia's

threat was real and credible. Your mother's fine, we'll keep her that way."

"Good. Keeping everyone safe is the primary thing we have to do now."

Silence. "That's not exactly true, Kendra. It's important, but it's not primary."

She stiffened. "What are you saying?"

"You're not thinking of anyone but Olivia. It's very natural but you have to consider why Zachary came to Olivia. He wanted to get to you, Kendra. He made that very clear. Why do you think he did that?"

"I have no idea. How could I? The man is insane and I know nothing about him. Maybe he picked my name out of the phone book."

"That's not what he said. He said he'd been searching. Perhaps we should investigate just what he meant. It could either be a threat . . . or an opportunity."

"You investigate it. Right now, I'm not thinking about me, I'm thinking about ways to keep him away from the people I care about."

"And you're fighting desperately not to realize that I'm right and you're wrong. You don't want to see it. The importance of the entire scenario is the fact that you're right in the middle and Zachary wants to keep you there." He went on quickly. "You're upset, and I'll cut you some slack, but I'll keep coming back to you. I have to do it, Kendra." He cut the connection.

Damn him, he was right. She didn't want to think about how Zachary's message was going to affect her, because he'd already shown her how vulnerable she was, how vulnerable everyone who touched her was going to be. But she had to think about it, because Zachary had made a move she couldn't ignore.

But not right now. She had to take a little time to make certain he couldn't damage the people she cared about. It was not going to be easy, because she suddenly realized that she was not an island. Her first thought had been for Olivia and her mother, but Zachary might not choose them. She had other friends whom it would hurt her to lose. He might go farther afield because he'd think she wouldn't expect it.

Perhaps that was what he'd intended, keep her busy and frantic while he made his next move. And he was succeeding, just thinking about what he *might* do was causing her heart to pound and her palms to sweat.

She couldn't allow him to do that to her.

All right, one step at a time.

Protect her assets and then use her mind instead of her emotions. Circle the wagons and keep the savage away. Don't let her mother and Olivia realize how scared she was or they'd insist on trying to rush to guard her.

Circle the wagons . . .

She stuffed her phone in her pocket and pasted

a smile on her face as she strolled back into the kitchen. "For once Griffin seems to be working at high speed," she said lightly. "He already has a few leads. Things are looking up . . . Did you save me any lasagna?"

12:35 A.M.

A ping signaled a text on Kendra's phone on the nightstand.

Lynch.

She hesitated before she reached for the phone. She'd just crawled into bed after making sure Olivia had drifted off to sleep in the guest bedroom. She was tired and on edge and didn't want to have to spar with Lynch when she felt as if she'd already been on stage all evening.

But if she didn't answer, there was no telling what effect that would have on Lynch. He was so smart and intuitive that she didn't want to risk alerting him that things weren't proceeding as she'd like them to be.

Hell, what an understatement.

She grabbed the phone and read the text.

A multi-city serial killer? Really? Were you bored with the ordinary garden variety?

Is that all he knew? she wondered, relieved. It must be or he would have instantly mentioned the message from Zachary. Something like that. Don't you have anything better to do but tap your sources about my business? Talk about being bored. If you know that, then you must know that there will be so many experts running around here that I'll have nothing to do.

He shot back: You'll find something. Probably intensely troublesome in nature.

Nonsense. She paused. Did Griffin tell you?

A slight hesitation. Does it matter?

No, just curious. She typed on quickly. What are you doing in Guilin that you have all this time to harass me?

Another hesitation. Why, trying to get their star olympic gymnast Yun Shuli to defect. What else could be more important?

Maybe their entire diving team? she asked.

That's next month's assignment. One star project at a time. But maybe I'll be able to squeeze you in after the gymnast. I'm almost there with her. Another week should do it.

And who invited you? I told you that neither one of us is going to be of much importance in this case.

You did, didn't you? Then maybe I'll just concentrate on snatching that dim but magnificent athlete and forget about bothering about you. Goodnight, Kendra.

He was gone.

She put her phone back on the nightstand. She was uneasy, but it might be for nothing. She had attempted to make the text completely normal, but she had been nervous, and she might have blown it. She had never been able to tell how well Lynch could read her. She had an uncomfortable feeling it was far too well.

But so far he had learned only the basics, and she needed to keep what had happened today from him at all costs. That would be the tipping point that could send him here to try to help her. Everyone close to her seemed to think that would be the best possible thing that could happen. She might have thought that herself a few days ago.

Not now.

Because she had been going over the list of people she cared about and checking it twice.

And Adam Lynch was very high on that list.

This was her battle. Face it alone. Keep him away.

She began to dial Griffin's number.

Circle the wagons . . .

Guilin, China

Lynch gazed down at his phone as he leaned back in his chair.

Kendra had never before asked him about one of his missions. She knew they were confidential and he didn't talk about them. The question had come out of nowhere. A deterrent?

And she had stressed that she was not going to have an active role in this investigation—that was causing him to be increasingly uneasy.

And she had asked him if Griffin was his source. Why?

Put them all together and he didn't like the result.

What wasn't she telling him?

He started to punch in the number of his contact at the State Department. He hadn't used Griffin because he had a tendency to ask for favors that were pricey in both his time and efforts. State and Justice had their own moles that were more easily controlled and usually knowledgeable.

Maybe not this time.

He hung up after checking with both contacts. He knew no more than they'd told him previously.

He had no choice.

Griffin.

He punched in Griffin's number.

He answered in two rings. "It's after one in the morning here, Lynch. In case you've forgotten, I don't take kindly to having my sleep disturbed."

"But you sound so wide awake. Almost as if I'm not the only one who's called you tonight. Could that be true?"

Silence. "I get a lot of calls. I'm an important guy. That's why they call me Special Agent in

Charge. But I don't get many calls like yours that I wouldn't choose to accept if asked."

"But I'm certain that you took Kendra's call with no argument. Did she tell you I might phone you?"

"I believe it's time I hung up. We have nothing to discuss."

"Wrong. Can you tell I'm a bit irate? Kendra is trying to shut me out and that annoys me. You're aiding and abetting and that makes me angry. I don't think you've ever seen me really angry, Griffin. I don't believe you ever want to."

"Then I suggest you go back and talk to Kendra."

"Maybe. But right now I have to know what I'm going to be facing. We both know how difficult Kendra can be." He paused. "Or you wouldn't be giving me such a hard time. But I won't give up until I know what she's keeping from me."

"Why are you so certain that she's keeping anything from you?"

"She doesn't want me there. For some reason she doesn't want me to work this case. She didn't even want to talk about it. Now when I texted her before I didn't get that response. That means something happened that was more than what I could find out from my other sources. Whatever it was, you're keeping it undercover and top secret to such an extent that the info can't be accessed in the usual ways. And it seemed so bad to Kendra that it closed her down."

"Imagination."

"Don't tell me that. I know how she thinks, how she feels. Now you tell me what happened to her."

Griffin was silent.

Lynch knew he could keep pushing, but his impatience was growing by the minute. He needed to *know*. "Okay. What do you want?"

"If I did know anything, it would be something that I wouldn't want leaked to anyone," Griffin said warily. "Particularly not to the press. This case is proving to be a real hot potato. We're dealing in very sensitive issues."

"What do you want?" Lynch repeated.

"Only your cooperation when I ask for it. At my discretion, of course. What else?"

"One job, that's all."

"I realize how valuable your time is, Lynch. Would I ask anything more?"

"If you thought you could get away with it. You can't. I'm coming to you because it's quicker. Otherwise, I'd go through Metcalf or one of your other agents."

"And they'd end up without a job."

"But you know I'd get my answers and no price for me to pay. So don't try to squeeze me, Griffin."

"I've already agreed to terms." He paused. "But

only because I believe it's best for Kendra. Honestly. I even tried to tell her that she should accept any help anyone wants to give her."

"She must have really appreciated that advice," he said sarcastically. "Do you even know her?"

"Yes, but this time I had to say it," Griffin said soberly. "I like her, Lynch. She's a pain in my ass, but I don't want anything to happen to her."

And that scared Lynch more than anything he'd heard since the conversation had begun. "Nothing's going to happen to her," he said roughly. "I won't let it. And I'll make sure you don't let it happen. Now tell me what I need to know."

8:40 A.M.

"They did a good job." Kendra gazed critically at the motion sensor the security company had attached to the frame of Olivia's painting. "Hardly noticeable, but it works with every movement."

"Providing it doesn't drive me crazy," Olivia said as she felt her watch that was monitoring the movement. "But I think I can live with it." Then she grinned. "Play on words. Get it?"

"Oh, I get it," Kendra said. "But I'm not amused. That's what all this security gear is all about. Make certain that you use it."

"I will." She went over to the desk. "In fact, I feel like burrowing down here and not coming out until you get this guy." She sat down in the chair. "But that's not going to happen. I won't let him do that to me. Screw him. I'm going to keep on living my life exactly as I have in the past."

"Well, maybe not exactly," Kendra said. She'd known that would be Olivia's reaction, but it still scared her. "I've arranged to have one of Griffin's agents maintain surveillance on you while you're not in the condo, but it still might be smart to rein in a little. Look before you leap."

"Now that's a truly ridiculous statement when addressed to me." Her smile faded. "Hey, I realize that you're really freaked out about all this. You're blaming yourself and I can feel you hovering, but back off, Kendra. It's my life, and it's Zachary who invaded it. You've done everything you can to keep me safe. Anything else is up to me."

"Bullshit." She sighed. "Okay, okay. I'll try to restrain myself or at least try a more subtle approach."

"Subtle?" Olivia repeated warily. "I don't like the sound of that. Totally out of character."

"Maybe I'm trying to change."

"I don't think so."

"Give me a break," she said quietly. "You're my friend and I love you. Work with me."

"We'll see," Olivia said as she turned on her computer. "It might be amusing to see you trying to be subtle."

"I'm glad you think that this situation has any entertainment value." She turned to leave. "Want to have dinner with me at my place tonight?"

"Again? So you can keep your eye on me?" She grimaced. "Be real. Once you get pulled into all that high-powered FBI stuff today, there's no way that you'll be home before midnight. Get out of here."

"Rude. Very rude." She headed for the door. "If you need anything, if something's not right, call Metcalf. I put his number on your speed dial, and I've told him to expect it. Then call me."

"Kendra."

"Not subtle enough?" She opened the door. "Guess you're right. But I feel better about it. I promise we'll find a middle ground." She closed the door behind her and drew a deep breath. Olivia clearly thought she was overreacting, but how could you overreact to something this frightening?

But she couldn't push too hard or Olivia would rebel and that would be counterproductive. And a middle ground that would satisfy both Kendra and Olivia? Where the hell was she going to find that?

Don't think about it right now.

Instead, concentrate on what was waiting for her at the FBI office this morning. Oh, and check in with Jessie about anything she might have learned from her military contacts since yesterday. She could phone her while she was in her car driving to the FBI office.

But she didn't start her car when she got into the driver's seat. She sat there, frozen, because something had suddenly occurred to her. By hiring Jessie Mercado to dig out information about Zachary, she had placed a bullseye squarely on her forehead. It had not immediately struck her because Jessie was tough and smart and thoroughly capable. But for all those same reasons Zachary might regard her as a threat to be eliminated. And if his research was at its usual high standard, he would also know Jessie was Kendra's friend, another reason to make her a target.

Take her off the case.

It was her immediate impulse, but Jessie would never accept that as an option. Besides, the harm had probably been done now. But what she could do was to tell Jessie exactly what had happened and warn her. Then hope that Jessie would back out on her own.

Not likely.

She quickly punched in Jessie's number. Jessie answered in two rings but her tone was rueful. "Come on, Kendra. I know you want this guy, but I'm not a miracle worker. Give me a chance."

"I take it you haven't come up with anything?" Kendra asked.

"Nothing very helpful, I'm afraid. At least not yet. But I did hear back from my source, and he says there was no single member of the armed forces who was stationed in these places during the time span of these murders."

Kendra's heart sank. "Of course not. It would have been too easy. Are you sure?"

"I trust my source. It doesn't mean that he wasn't doing something else connected with the bases, like maybe a contractor. It'll take a lot more digging to see if that's the case. You're probably better off cross-checking names through the IRS or the Postal Service."

"Yeah, we already have requests in for that." Kendra was sure Jessie could hear the disappointment in her voice. "Thanks for checking, Jessie. I appreciate it."

"Hey, I haven't given up yet. This is only the opening play. I'll think about it and see what else I can come up with. I don't like to lose."

And because she didn't like to lose, Jessie would be continually in danger, Kendra thought. It was time she let her know what to expect. "Neither does this maniac we're dealing with, Jessie. He's beginning to strike close to home." She quickly related everything that had occurred since she had received Olivia's call yesterday. "It scared me, Jessie."

"It should have scared you," Jessie said soberly. "You'd be nuts if it hadn't. And that poor Olivia must be a basket case, blind and not able to even see that creep in the same room with her."

"Well, not exactly a basket case." Kendra had forgotten Jessie had never met Olivia and didn't realize how strong she was. "But naturally she was terribly upset. She's trying to work her way through it."

"Good luck to her," Jessie said. "Someone should castrate that bastard . . . scaring a helpless woman like that. She might be scarred for a long time."

Jessie's protective instincts were obviously flying high and Kendra was remembering she'd had the same response to her former employer Delilah Winter. "I hope castration is the least of what we manage to do to him. But he's very dangerous, Jessie. Keep that in mind."

"You keep it in mind," Jessie said. "You're the one who seems to be in his crosshairs. Does Lynch know?"

She should have known that was coming, she thought in exasperation. "No." She changed the subject. "But I'll have more help than I need or want with Griffin's posse coming to town."

"In Afghanistan I always found that posses tended to get in the way." She shrugged. "But that's only my experience. Anyway, it may be a while before I manage to find out the info you hired me to unearth. Anything else I can do to help?"

Kendra started to shake her head and then went still. Maybe . . .

It was risky on several levels, but it might work.

Go for it.

"Actually, there may be something."

"Name it."

"Oh, I will," she said and then quickly began to speak.

And to circle the wagons . . .

"Good to see you, Kendra," Metcalf said quietly. "We were taking bets on whether you'd really show up today." He held her visitor badge out to her as she walked across the lobby of the FBI field office.

"Why?" Kendra took the badge and clipped it on. "Just because a psychopathic mass murderer broke into the apartment of my best friend? Okay, you saw how shaken I was yesterday. But after that, nothing could keep me away."

"I just thought when the shock faded, it would sink home that our killer is obviously fixated on you. You were already reluctant to join the case. There was some thought that you might want to distance yourself."

Yes, distance herself and everyone she cared about, but she couldn't do it. Not possible. Kendra walked with him to the elevator. "Is that what the FBI wants?"

"No way. Like Griffin keeps telling us, it's all hands on deck."

She'd thought she'd read Griffin right when she'd talked to him on the phone last night. Opportunity, he'd said. He might be regarding her as a weapon to be wielded. "Speaking of which, is your 'dream team' here?"

"Yep. The last of them arrived late last night. They're up in the war room right now getting briefed on our case here in San Diego. After that, each of them will give presentations on their cases." Metcalf shook his head as he and Kendra entered the elevator and the doors closed. "They're an interesting bunch. I've been reading up on them and they're brilliant guys. You can't take that away from them."

"But . . . ?"

Metcalf paused to choose his words with care. "I met them all this morning. Law enforcement is a collaborative profession. We work with each other, we sometimes team up with police detectives, and on big cases like this one, we join together on task forces. Teamwork, you know? But these guys, the one thing they have in common is that they all seem to be loners. I thought there was even a bit of tension when they were introduced to each other."

"But aren't they good at what they do?"

"The best. Maybe that's why they're so good. They look at things differently than everyone else."

Kendra shrugged. "I don't have any right to

criticize. I don't always work and play well with others."

"That occurred to me. In any case, they've each spent *years* wanting to catch this guy. Some of them have been in almost constant touch with the victims' families, promising that the case hasn't dropped off their radar. It's personal to them."

"Good. It should be."

"Oh, and there's another thing they have in common."

"What's that?"

"They're extremely interested in meeting you."

The elevator doors opened on the fourth floor.

She frowned. "Me?"

Metcalf followed her into the corridor. "Of course. You've become a key part of this case. The minute Griffin told them about Zachary's message to Olivia, you could see their eyes light up and their heads lift as if sniffing prey. Something about you attracted the attention of this killer. Those investigators want to know everything about you." Metcalf pointed to a freestanding bulletin board near the entrance of the war room where two assistants were working.

To her horror Kendra realized that the assistants were in the process of putting up photos of her and her previous cases.

Metcalf nodded. "Griffin gave you your own bulletin board. If that doesn't make you feel important, nothing will."

"It doesn't make me feel important," she said tightly. "It makes me feel like a piece of meat at the butcher shop. Or maybe one of the victims in their case histories."

"Oops." Metcalf added soothingly, "It's just a way to efficiently display a potential asset, Kendra. If it wasn't you he'd targeted, you know you'd want to have the most thorough information available."

She realized he was right, but it didn't make her feel any better about Griffin using her more as a piece of evidence than an investigator.

Shake it off. Today was going to be difficult enough and she didn't need to start out with a chip on her shoulder.

Kendra stopped as she spotted Griffin across the room, waving a remote in his hand as he delivered projected PowerPoint slides to a small group. "That's the dream team?"

"Yep."

"Tell me about them."

"Now?"

"Yes. I'd like to know something about them before we meet. Fill me in."

"Well, Griffin already told you about Richard Gale. That's the tall guy with the bushy eyebrows. He's with the Bureau in New York City. Griffin wasn't kidding when he said Gale wasn't a people person. He's managed to insult just about everyone here already."

"Including you?"

Metcalf ran his hands through his thick, somewhat unruly hair. "Oh, yeah. He thought my hair style showed a flaw in my character, a lack of precision."

"Hmm. He may have a point there."

"Nice. The guy standing next to him, the thin one with the curly hair? That's Edward Roscoe, he's a homicide detective with the LAPD. He's laid-back and kind of quiet. He cracked the Echo Park murders in LA a few years back."

Kendra nodded. "I remember that . . . Wasn't there a movie?"

"Yeah, a really crappy one. Roscoe was played by Matthew McConaughey."

"Interesting."

"Not to McConaughey. He still trash-talks the movie on talk shows."

"Yeah? And who's the older man with the buzz cut?"

"That's Arnold Huston, Washington, D.C., homicide. Old school all the way. I offered him a desk with an Ethernet port, and he told me he hates computers. But he's great at witness interviews. Huston can pull more out of a witness than just about anyone. People like and trust him."

"Good skill to have." Kendra looked at the one remaining person, an impossibly youthful man with tortoise-shell spectacles and thick brown hair. "And why is the junior high kid here?"

Metcalf smiled. "That's Trey Suber. He's with the FDLE. Florida Department of Law Enforcement. He's young, but by all accounts, he's one of the best criminal profilers in the world. He's a total serial killer geek. He knows serial killers the way hardcore baseball fans know player stats."

"Or the way you know Star Wars trivia?"

"Better. He probably knows details about your own cases that you've forgotten long ago."

"Impressive . . . and a little creepy."

"Sometimes impressive and creepy is exactly what we need around here."

She could see what he meant. There was no one more creepy than Zachary, and someday they might have to fight fire with fire . . . or ice with ice. "Agreed."

Griffin had spotted Kendra and Metcalf and was waving them over. Metcalf turned to her. "Ready for this?"

She braced herself. "Absolutely. Time to meet the dream team."

They walked toward the assembled group. Griffin motioned toward Kendra. "Gentlemen, Kendra Michaels. Some of you are familiar with her work as I suspect she may be of yours."

Griffin made the introductions. As Kendra spoke with each of the men, she was amazed at how spot-on-the-money Metcalf's impressions had been.

NYC FBI Agent Richard Gale was every bit as unpleasant as his reputation suggested. His salt and pepper hair was slicked back, and his face was carved by deep creases in his forehead. He wordlessly shook her hand, barely making eye contact as his attention went to an attractive young assistant on the other side of the room.

"Pleasure to meet you," Kendra said.

"Uh huh," he grunted, "I might have to talk to you later." He turned and walked away.

Definitely not a people person.

But Washington, D.C., homicide detective Arnold Huston had people skills in spades. He was probably one of the oldest cops she'd ever met, close to seventy, with a warm handshake, twinkling eyes, and a deep, mellifluous voice. "How's your friend today?" he asked. "Is there anything we can do for her?"

"She's fine. Olivia's a strong person."

"She must be. Look, I know we're each presenting on our cases this morning, but if there's anything I can tell you about my experiences in Virginia with this guy, I'm available. Any time. Don't hesitate to call, okay?"

"Thanks. I appreciate the offer." She could see why he was so good in witness interviews.

LAPD detective Edward Roscoe also shook her hand. "Call me Eddie," he said. "We're practically neighbors. Funny we haven't run into each other. Of course, this is more of a sideline to you, isn't it?"

His laid-back charm made it easy to see why Matthew McConaughey had been tapped to play him even though they really didn't look much alike.

"A sideline," Kendra repeated. "You might call it that."

"But I've heard about you. I'm almost afraid to ask . . . But how much do you know about me?"

"Just the little bit that Metcalf told me. I never saw the movie if that's what you mean."

"That's not what I mean. The movie got almost everything wrong. I'm talking about that thing you do."

Uh oh. He'd obviously heard about her parlor tricks.

She smiled. "I know everything about you that I think I *need* to know."

"Are you gonna let me in on it?"

"Maybe later."

"It could be the stories about you aren't true," he said speculatively.

"Maybe not. Guess you'll have to stick around and find out for yourself."

He leaned close and flashed a sly smile. "Guess I will."

Hmm. Metcalf hadn't told her that he was such an accomplished flirt.

FDLE profiler Trey Suber looked older than he had from across the room, but not much. He was probably twenty-three or twenty-four, but he still could have passed for a high school kid. He dispensed with the pleasantries in order to ask about what really interested him. "Dr. Michaels, I'd really like to talk to you about Eric Colby. Would that be possible?"

Hearing that name aloud literally gave her chills even after all the time that had passed. "I'm surprised you— I don't see how that has any bearing on this case."

"No, of course not. It's just that there hasn't been a lot written on Colby yet, and first-hand information is hard to come by." Suber pushed up his glasses. "You knew him better than anyone. He was one of the most notorious serial killers of the last decade and you beat him twice."

Serial killer geek, indeed.

"Sure, we'll talk." But not anytime soon, she mentally qualified. One monster at a time.

He smiled and raised his right hand as if to give her a high-five. She patted his arm instead and pointed to Griffin, who was motioning for all of the investigators to take their seats at the front of the room.

Within a minute the presentations began, accompanied by larger-than-life PowerPoint slides. One by one, the investigators took them on a graphic tour of some of the most brutal and depressing murders she'd ever seen, all apparently the work of one sick man.

Four and a half hours later, she felt drained of body and spirit. In addition to her sheer revulsion, she was most struck by the difference between the cases. No wonder they hadn't been linked until now. The placement and character of knife wounds were similar in the stabbing cases, but there were almost no other similarities.

After the last presentation Griffin called a break and said the session would resume with individual discussions in the war room. That probably meant she'd be subject to questions and not-so-subtle examinations from the other investigators.

And she'd be surrounded by all those hideous photos.

Kendra stood up and hurried from the room. She couldn't take it right now. It would be like having Zachary gazing mockingly down at her, laughing as he had on Olivia's computer. She'd thought she was only going to the bathroom, but she realized that wasn't far enough away. She had to get the hell out of that building for a while. Just a couple hours and she'd come back and finish the day.

Just a couple hours to brace herself for more horror.

She took the elevator down to the garage, where she climbed into her car, started it up, and roared away.

But she only got four blocks before she pulled

over to the curb. She sat there for a moment staring blindly out the window. She was running away like a panic-stricken child, she thought, shocked. And with the self-contempt that realization brought came the anger and the determination.

You're not going to win, Zachary. Not one hour, not one minute. I can take anything you throw at me.

She turned the car around and started to drive back toward the FBI office.

It was 9:30 P.M. before Kendra arrived back at her condo. The phone rang five minutes after she let herself inside.

Olivia.

She had been expecting the call. In fact, she had expected Olivia to call earlier in the day, possibly in a rage. If she hadn't been swamped, she would have phoned Olivia herself to see if she still had a friend. Kendra had tossed out the dice and heaven only knew whether they had come up snake eyes.

She braced herself and answered. "Hi, how much trouble am I in?"

"Big time," Olivia said grimly. "Get down here and face the music."

"I'll be at your door in three minutes."

She was actually ringing the bell in two minutes.

Olivia swung open the door and stepped aside.

"Come in." Her expression was stern. "What the hell made you think you could get away with this?" She gestured to Jessie, who was curled up on the couch. "Manipulation all the way, Kendra. We aren't pleased."

"I didn't think you would be." But she noticed Olivia had said we and not I. It brought a tiny ray of hope. "But I couldn't think of anything else to do. Two is always better than one. It wasn't really safe for you to be with me, so I thought maybe if Jessie moved in with you . . ."

"And you didn't remember how angry you were when Lynch hired me to guard you several weeks ago?" Jessie asked. "You were ready to throw me off the nearest balcony."

"I remembered. But I thought perhaps the two of you could work it out. And you don't have to guard her nonstop. Neither of you would tolerate that. I thought just having you as her roommate might deter Zachary."

"And you told Jessie I was this weak-kneed wimp who needed her to take care of me?" Olivia asked. "I could feel all that slimy sympathy oozing over me when she walked in the door."

"I didn't say that," Kendra said quickly. "I didn't really—I tried to describe—but you're fairly indescribable, Olivia."

"But you didn't push it," Jessie said. "You didn't want me to know what I was walking into when I showed up with a suitcase and my

171

'oozing' sympathy. I'm lucky she didn't karate chop me and toss me out in the street."

"I think you could have handled that," Olivia told her. "I'm no wimp, but I'm no ninja either."

Jessie grinned at her. "I could try to teach you. You have potential."

"Yes I do. For all kinds of talents." She turned back to Kendra. "And my friend here knows it, and yet she did this to us."

"Your friend wanted both of you to be safe," Kendra said. "And I handled it clumsily but an opportunity presented itself with Jessie and I took it. You told me forgiveness wasn't necessary, but I think it is in this case. Forgive me." She looked at Jessie. "I sent you in blind because I was desperate. I had confidence that you could make it work once you took Olivia's measure."

"We did make it work." Jessie got to her feet. "But we had a bad thirty minutes before we decided you were the bad guy, and we were golden. Olivia figured it out that I was on your protect list, too. I couldn't believe it. Me? The humiliation gave us an instant bond." She came toward her. "So you're going to get your way, Kendra. We're going to be roommates and keep each other safe. Because we find we like each other and respect each other and for one other reason. We'll be living one floor below you and we'll be able to take care of *you*. We'll not pay any more attention to your precious independence than you did for ours. How do you like them apples?"

"You expect me to argue? I think I got off easy," Kendra said unevenly. "After looking at those crime photos all day, I'm just grateful that you're not going to punish me by telling me that no way would you stay in the same condo. I'm grateful, period."

Olivia was listening, head tilted. "Rough day, Kendra?"

"You might say that."

"Did you have dinner?"

"A burger. Don't coddle me, Olivia. I'm feeling too guilty."

"Good." Olivia swept toward the kitchen. "Mission accomplished, Jessie. We can let her up for air. I'll make the salad, you get a drink for all of us."

"I'd prefer a tad more punishment," Jessie said regretfully. "She insulted my professionalism." She lifted her shoulder in a half shrug. "But if you insist. Sit down, Kendra. You can see Olivia is making a virtual slave of me. What do you want to drink?"

"Anything." She dropped down on the couch. She was relieved and just as monumentally grateful as she'd told them. It was obvious that the two women had already formed a strong bond and Kendra couldn't have wished for anything more. "Just not too strong. I'm so tired I'm a little dizzy now anyway."

"Well, you're off the hook for the time being. Just don't do it again." Jessie was at Olivia's small, elegant bar. "I don't know what on earth you were thinking."

"Neither do I." She wearily rubbed her temple. "Something about circling the wagons . . ."

The gang was all here.

Zachary smiled as he walked down Fifth Street. He had spent an exhilarating half hour watching the dream team arriving at their digs at the San Diego Hilton. They'd each arrived in their own rental cars, looking oh-so-impressive as they'd strutted toward the tall glass doors. The men didn't look as if they'd aged a day. Except Gale, whose lines had grown deeper and skin had gotten grayer. Those New York winters hadn't been kind to him.

But it was good to see them all.

He was quite sure they'd spent their day trying to get to know him, desperately attempting to slot him into their ridiculous psychological profiles. Didn't they know what a unique animal he was? He'd beaten each of them all on their own turf, although Detective Rosco had gotten closer to catching him than anyone ever realized.

He'd created his own unique profile for each

city and the know-nothing investigators had fallen for each one.

He knew each of them better than they would ever know him, he was certain of that. He even knew how they would spend their evenings. Richard Gale would order in room service and watch some kind of sporting event, probably the New York Knicks if they were playing. Arnold Huston, the oldest man in the bunch, would have a sandwich in the hotel coffee shop before going to his room, calling his wife, and turning in. Young Trey Suber, the serial killer enthusiast, would type up his impressions of the day before cross-referencing them with his own database of killers that he kept in his trusty laptop. Ed Rosco would have dinner in the hotel bar before enjoying a few drinks. He'd hit on the young women who might be impressed that he'd once been portrayed by a big movie star, even if the film was one they hadn't actually seen.

Did their years of experience give them any idea what he'd planned for them? Doubtful.

And are you sensing the storm that's coming, Kendra? If anyone could guess what he had in store for those fools who thought they were so clever it would be you.

His pace slowed as he felt himself being drawn away from those egotistical detectives he had just left. As much as he enjoyed thinking about his old sparring partners, his heart was a few blocks away, with Kendra Michaels. He wanted to go to her with a yearning that was almost hunger. She was so close after all this time of preparation. He had reached out and touched her when he'd sent that message through her friend Olivia.

He wanted to touch her again. He wanted to reach out and stroke her and let her feel his power.

But he didn't dare go near her building, he realized with frustration. The authorities were on high alert after his drop-in at her friend's unit, and he needed to keep his distance for the time being. And letting Kendra and all those idiots who were gathered here to trap him know that she was the target of choice put additional heat on the situation.

It didn't matter; he could wait. Now that the game had started and Kendra realized that his every move was aimed at her, every moment was going to be exciting.

Are you feeling it now, Kendra? Are your palms sweating? Did you feel sick when you knew that your Olivia was mine to kill?

Yes, Kendra was a worthy addition to this so-called dream team, and there were many things about her that he found especially intriguing. Was it the allure of the shiny and new, especially since he had already outsmarted the rest of these world-class investigators?

Partially.

And, of course, it was also her famous reluctance. She was different from these others, who seemed to live for their work. Kendra was on his trail *despite* herself, drawn only by her intense desire to do good. It would be easy to dismiss her attitude as arrogance, as if she was the only person in the world who could crack these cases.

Good and Evil. Life and Death.

The eternal battles that she should realize she could never win. Darkness always overcame light in the end.

But she did win them.

And the more he'd researched her, the more he was convinced she was right; she had undoubtedly saved dozens of lives and jailed several killers who would still be walking the streets. She had gone through hell and torment to meet the challenges she had encountered, but she had triumphed.

Was that why he'd chosen this woman, in this city, for the grand finale of his master plan?

Sometimes he thought that challenge was the reason. But at other times he was aware of something so dark and malevolent that he could see hovering over Kendra that he knew it might be something else. It might be the sheer pleasure of planning the depth of suffering that would bring her to her knees.

The excitement was growing within him as he thought about her. He had to control it. Think about the plan in its entirety. That would calm him.

He'd done his homework. It's what separated him from the pathetic amateurs who would grow old and die behind bars, he thought scornfully.

He was no amateur.

If they were the dream team, he was about to become their worst nightmare.

CHAPTER 7

"Wake up, Kendra."

Even in the depths of sleep, she could hear the hardness and biting anger that edged that deep voice.

She could also recognize that voice.

Her eyes flew open.

Lynch was standing in the doorway of her bedroom. Even in the dimness of the light streaming in the window she was able to read his body language. It echoed the harshness of that first sentence.

Excitement. Electricity. Desire. Joy. These first emotions she was feeling made no sense, she realized dazedly. They were all wrong in this situation. It must be because she was still half asleep. "Lynch?"

"Shut up." He was across the room and pulling her out of bed. "I need this. We'll deal with everything else later." He was kissing her. Passion. Hard and hot and breathtaking. His hand was on her butt, pushing up her night shirt. Touching. Squeezing. Bringing her into his body and rubbing her against him.

It was like some crazy, bewildering, erotic dream . . . but she was *awake,* she realized. Lynch was somehow here, in her bedroom.

179

How in the hell . . . ?

Then sensation after sensation was searing through her and it didn't matter how. It was only important that he didn't stop.

Her head fell back as she arched and cried out. Her arms clutched blindly at him.

The scent of him . . .

The *feel* of him . . .

Oh, my God . . .

Then he was dropping her back on the bed. "Get up and get dressed," he said hoarsely, gazing down at her. "I'm too angry with you right now. I might hurt you. We have enough problems, and I'm not going to let you add to them."

She was still hot and shaking. "I don't believe I was adding to anything in this situation."

"The hell you weren't. You know better."

"What are you doing here?" she asked dazedly.

He turned and said over his shoulder, "I'll go make coffee. You get dressed and join me in five minutes. If you're not out here by then, I'll consider it an invitation and I'll be back here and inside you."

She lay there for a moment, trying to get her breath. Everything had happened so fast that she hadn't been able to think, only react, but that wasn't unusual with Lynch. They had been walking a tightrope between being partners and lovers for the past months, and the sexual tension was white-hot at times. This was clearly one of those times, and if she didn't want to have the decision made for her, she'd better take control of the situation.

But she clearly *did* want it decided for her. She wanted *him*. Her breasts were taut, swollen, the muscles of her stomach clenched. She wanted to lie here and wait for him to be inside her.

But that would mean that she had no choice and she couldn't accept it. It was too dangerous to allow anyone that close to her right now.

Move.

Go to him.

Don't let him come back.

She swung her legs to the floor and got to her feet. The next moment she was in the bathroom and reaching for her toothbrush.

It was ten minutes, not five, by the time she was dressed and walked into the kitchen.

"You're late," Lynch said as he handed her a cup of coffee. "But I cut you some slack when I heard you in the bathroom. Though I had to think about it. Shower sex can be damn good, too."

"Cut me slack?" She was trying not to stare at him. He might see what she was still feeling. It had been dim in the bedroom and this was her first real glimpse of him in weeks. He was wearing a black leather jacket and, as usual, he was overwhelming. Those blue eyes, the movie star good looks, the sheer charisma . . .

"You've got a hell of a lot of nerve." She sat

181

down at the table and lifted her coffee to her lips. "No way, Lynch. You come busting into my condo without invitation." She glanced at the clock on the wall. "At five in the morning. And tell me how angry you are with me. I should be the one to be pissed off."

"Because I invaded your space? I still have a key from when I occupied your spare room, remember?"

"I never invited you then, either."

"You have a habit of attracting death and mayhem. It was either the spare room or your bed. You were backing away from me. So I didn't push it."

"Like this morning?"

"No, it was very close this time. I've been extraordinarily patient for a long time. You wanted a partner, I've been a partner and friend. What you've wanted, I've given you. I've even spent weeks setting up a safe haven for the doctor who gave you your sight because you thought he might be in danger." His lips twisted. "Though I'm still not sure that he doesn't feel more for you than I'll permit. But I did it anyway because you asked me." He met her eyes. "Because you're worth it. I think you'll always be worth it. And that's why I'm willing to put up with all this bullshit you're causing me. But you can't expect there not to be repercussions."

She looked down into the coffee in her cup.

"I don't want anyone having to put up with me. Maybe it's time you stepped away, Lynch."

"Stop it," he said curtly. "I didn't travel for twenty hours to have you give me this crap. You don't get rid of me, Kendra."

"What if I don't want you?"

He smiled. "Then I'll make you want me. You're halfway there already."

More than halfway. Any way and all ways. She took another sip of coffee. "Twenty hours. That must mean you took a flight almost immediately after you texted me. Who told you what was happening?" She remembered how Griffin had avoided speaking directly to her at the session. "It was Griffin?"

"Yes. Though he did hold out until I bribed him."

"Bribed him? With what?"

"What it always is. A favor whenever he needs one."

"You shouldn't have done that. He'll take his pound of flesh."

"I was in a hurry. I knew something was wrong. You weren't yourself."

"I'm glad you think so," she said wryly. "Because everything I've said and done lately has been clumsy and verging on stupidity."

"So I've heard," Lynch said. "You're lucky Jessie and Olivia have forgiving natures. I'm still not sure Jessie has given you a pass."

"You've *heard?*" She frowned. "How the hell did you know anything about that?"

He shrugged. "I woke them up and spent an hour hearing it all before I came up to see you. I wanted to know what Olivia knew about this Zachary and her take on how you were handling it. I only expected to see Olivia, but Jessie was an interesting surprise."

"You woke them up in the middle of the night?"

"My flight had just landed and I wasn't cool enough to go to you yet, and it was information I needed." He leaned back in his chair. "They appeared much happier to see me than you do right now. Though your initial response was just what I thought it would be. Olivia was right, you're definitely off-balance and not thinking straight."

"I won't deny that I'm not quite up to par. I got a tremendous shock, and I'm working on bouncing back. I'll get there."

"By trying to spread protective wings over your entire world?"

"Why not?" She smiled with an effort. "First things first."

"Because you're showing Zachary how valuable they are to you. The more you concentrate on protecting them, the more reason he'll have to take them down. You know that, Kendra. You've done all you can do. Now we have to go after him."

"We?" She shook her head. "I have plenty of

184

help. I never asked you to leave your Olympic star and come back here. You told me you couldn't leave China for another week or so. Go back there. I don't need you."

"Too late. I wrapped up things early and hitched a ride on a transport plane four hours later." He grimaced. "Though I'm going to have to make adjustments and find a way to keep anyone from knowing Ling Po has left his village for at least a week."

"Your gymnast? I thought her name was Yun Shuli."

"No, that was a lie. You didn't expect anything else from me when you asked that question. You were just trying to distract me. You surely wouldn't believe I'd be wasted on a gymnast? With all due respect for the sports world, none of my clients are willing to pay my fee to acquire their services."

"I found it a little strange. Then who is this Ling Po?"

"A fifteen-year-old genius who is on his way to being the most brilliant computer hacker in the world. He likes the idea of the American way and I managed to persuade him to hop on that plane with me."

"Just like that?"

"I had him primed and ready. His parents were whisked out of the country to be resettled twelve hours after we boarded our flight."

"I don't doubt it." Lynch was known in the U.S. intelligence community as the "Puppetmaster" due to his powers of manipulation. "And what adjustment do you have to make now that you've pulled him out early?"

"Give him time to get used to heightened security until he becomes familiar with the lifestyle. I'll settle him with someone who might be as brilliant as he is so that he won't feel lonely. I thought I'd have you call your friend, Sam Zackoff, and ask him if he'd take him under his wing."

"Ask him yourself. I'm not reaching out to any friends right now."

He nodded. "Okay, no problem. It just means a little more time than I wanted to spend on Ling Po at the moment. We'll be pretty busy."

"I don't need you. Back away, Lynch."

"It's not going to happen. You're not going to get rid of me." He looked her directly in the eyes. "I can see that you wouldn't want Zachary to know that you cared for me as a friend. And it would probably terrify you for him to know that I might be a lover. But you're just going to have to live with it."

"No, I don't." The idea was already terrifying her. "It's my choice."

"Not this time." He smiled and said coaxingly, "It will be fine. We've played this game before. We're such good friends that sometimes you even forget what else is there waiting for us. It's possible Zachary will think the same thing." He shrugged. "Though I'd prefer that he didn't. I'd enjoy sharing your spotlight. I'm beginning to really want this son of a bitch."

"And I don't want you anywhere near him. He's after *me,* Lynch. This is my battle." She could see she wasn't getting through to him. "You won't give up?"

"You know the answer." He finished his coffee. "And now we'll go downstairs and have breakfast with Olivia and Jessie. Olivia promised me French toast. Then we'll be on our way to the FBI war room, where I'm sure you've been spending entirely too much time."

She made a last attempt. "I don't *want* this, Lynch."

He stood up. "And I don't want you in this without me." He held out his hand to her. His voice was suddenly soft and infinitely persuasive. "This is a battle you can't win, Kendra. So give it up and concentrate on winning the battle we *can* win against Zachary. You know we can do it together."

She stared down at his outstretched hand for a long moment and then slowly reached out and took it. His hand felt warm and strong and alive and the touch filled her with fear . . . and hope.

"Lynch, this isn't a good—"

"Shh." He pulled her to her feet. "Let's go get Zachary. Okay?"

"Okay." Her hand tightened on his as she took a deep breath. "But don't think it's all going to be your way, Lynch. You just stay out of my spotlight, do you hear me?"

"I hear you." He pulled her toward the door. "Maybe we'll talk about it . . . ."

Kendra pushed open the main door of her complex and then shook her head at the sight of Lynch's Ferrari idling on the street. He had left her at Olivia's condo after breakfast to go down and get his car.

"Get in," he called out to her through the open passenger-side door. "What are you waiting for?"

"Principally, for you to grow up." She shook her head and climbed in. "You're still driving this ridiculous car?"

"I wondered how long it would take you to disparage my ride. It took you all of four seconds."

"I must be slipping."

"FYI, this car comes in handy when you need to get someplace in a hurry."

"But perhaps not quite as handy when you're trying to remain somewhat inconspicuous while on the trail of a psychopathic killer."

He flashed his patented high-wattage smile. "Remember, I do have a boring car at home for when the occasion demands it."

"The occasion has demanded it quite a bit in

the last couple of years, but I still haven't seen you driving it."

"Maybe someday. Buckle up. There's coffee for you in the cup holder, just the way you like it. I picked it up at the deli. You didn't seem to want to wait for a second cup at Olivia's."

No, she had been too on edge about this decision Lynch had talked her into and that she knew she'd probably regret.

Lynch gunned the engine and headed north toward the freeway.

Kendra picked up the cup and took a swig. She did want that coffee. It was hot and good and just the way she liked it as Lynch had said. But then he always knew what pleased her, which was one of his most dangerous qualities. "Thanks for the coffee. And the ride. If you hadn't left so quickly, I would have told you we should take my car. We're not going straight to the FBI office. I guess I can give you directions to the—"

"I know where we're going."

"Oh. I didn't know you were on the task force email."

"I wasn't, but I will be from now on. I had a talk with Griffin last night."

Kendra slowly turned to face him. "What kind of talk?"

He slanted a grin at her. "I stressed that you were a precious resource that needed to be protected."

"*Protected?* You really said that?"

"I just pushed the buttons that needed to be pushed."

"Or pulled the strings that needed to be pulled. That's more like it, isn't it, Puppetmaster?"

"How many times do I have to tell you? I'm not crazy about that name."

"Too bad. It's the price you pay for having such an unsavory reputation."

"Unsavory? That's a little harsh, isn't it?"

"You forget that I've spoken to your colleagues."

"True."

Kendra smiled. "The Puppetmaster" was a name given to Lynch for his uncanny ability to manipulate people and events to his own ends. He generally employed subtle psychological approaches, but when those failed, she knew he wasn't above more brutal methods to get what he needed. "Why in the hell did you tell Griffin that I needed to be protected?"

"I wanted in on this case, and I needed to give him a reason to include me."

"You couldn't have just said, 'please'?"

"No. Surely you jest? After my last phone conversation with him where blackmail and intimidation were the rules of the day, it would have been ludicrous. At least I allowed him the courtesy of consenting to what I was going to do anyway. The guy isn't terribly fond of me. We didn't even get along when I worked for him."

"So I've heard. But you've sure helped him out enough since then."

"On a freelance basis. Usually at the behest of someone else higher up in the chain. I had to give him a compelling reason to include me in this investigation and your safety and well-being fit the bill." He shrugged. "You're a valuable resource to him. He has a strong reason to see that you're protected. Since Zachary is fixated on you, it became clear that some protection is needed. Griffin saves on manpower if I'm here volunteering for the job."

"Did you think to ask how I felt about this?"

"Of course. And then I thought better of the idea. Wiser to tell you this after everything had been arranged."

Kendra's first instinct was to resist his plan, to pull back. But when she responded, it was with a simple "Fine."

"What?"

"Yeah, fine."

"Could it be that I've finally worn you down?"

She took another large swallow of coffee. "I'm used to working these cases pretty much on my own, but this one has gotten complicated in a hurry. Three murders have become twenty-six, in five different cities. And now we have four investigators in town, trying not to trip over each other."

"And you figured, what's one more nuisance thrown into the mix?"

She smiled. "Something like that. You made it pretty plain you weren't giving me a choice. I'm saving my objections for the big fights."

"I guess I should be grateful." His smile faded. "I don't believe I am. You're much too subdued. It's not like you. I knew you were upset. I didn't realize it was this bad."

"I was scared about Olivia," she said simply. "He made me feel vulnerable. It's going to take a little while for me to get over it." She made a face. "But don't get comfortable. I *will* get over it, Lynch."

"Yeah, I know." He was silent a moment. "That son of a *bitch*."

She nodded. "And he's damn good at it. With almost every victim it involved making them feel helpless and without power. I told you he was a monster; once you read the case histories you'll see what I mean."

"I'll read them," he said grimly. "I'm going to know everything there is to know about our Zachary."

"*My* Zachary," she said. "I told you to stay out of my spotlight. No focus on you. I meant it, Lynch. If he made me feel less than I am, it's only another reason why I have to be the one to confront him."

"I said we'd talk about it."

"We're talking about it. Back off."

He was silent. "I'll see. I didn't realize exactly

what he did to you. That would be worse for you than almost anything. I think I'm going to have to slit his throat."

"Back off."

"I'm thinking about it. Not very hard, but the process is there." He smiled. "In the meantime, I'm open for persuasion. Maybe Zachary will give you time enough to save him. And just think how much we can accomplish while you try to change my mind. We're so good together we might wrap this up before slaughter even comes into play." He added coaxingly, "Come on, you're not going to let a little homicide interfere with a great working relationship."

His determination was only lightly veiled by that familiar charisma, and she wasn't going to be able to budge him right now. And she was too tired and edgy to devote the energy to it at the moment. She'd just have to deal with Lynch as the case progressed. "I've told you how I feel and I'm not going to change. I'll get my way. Remember that, Lynch."

His brows rose. "Is there a 'but' to follow?"

"But actually we always worked well together. I think I can use your help on this one."

"I'm not sure, but I think I've just been relegated to the role of a . . ." He made a sour face. ". . . sidekick."

"If the shoe fits . . ."

"Nice," he said edgily.

"Relax. You'll never be anybody's sidekick. You're not wired for it. But I think I can use some extra help with Zachary. I already have Jessie working on an angle. We'll see where it takes us."

"Hmm, whatever you say, but it still sounds like we're working in the Kendra Michaels unit. Not that I'm complaining."

She smiled faintly, "Could've fooled me."

"So what's today's itinerary?" he asked. "All I got was the address for the meetup."

"It's a field trip. We're piling into a van and visiting the locations where the victims' bodies were found. It's really for the benefit of our visitors. I was at the last two crime scenes while they were still active, and I've already seen thousands of pictures of the others. Still, nothing's the same as being there."

Lynch looked ahead and nodded. "That *has* to be your dream team."

Kendra glanced up. They had arrived at the parking lot of the Edward Schwartz Federal Building on Front Street and the four visiting investigators were standing with Griffin, Metcalf, and Gina next to the large black van. Lynch parked, and he and Kendra climbed out.

Metcalf didn't look happy to see Lynch. "I didn't realize you were joining us."

"Problem?"

"Of course not." He turned to Gina. "This is Adam Lynch. He helps us out here once in a while. As an added bonus, he's really good at getting under the boss's skin."

Gina's face lit up in a way Kendra hadn't seen yet. Typical Lynch response. She smiled and shook Lynch's hand. "Sounds entertaining. Hope I get to see that."

Lynch smiled back. "Stay close. It won't take long."

One by one, the visiting investigators stepped forward for their introductions to Lynch. NYC FBI Agent Richard Gale seemed more interested in Lynch's car than anything else. Arnold Huston gave him a warm and respectful greeting, and Ed Roscoe puffed his chest out slightly when confronted with a man who threatened his "sexiest guy on the case" status. Kendra was pretty sure he caught her rolling her eyes.

Trey Suber was the most excited to meet Lynch. Before their handshake was even concluded, Trey began pumping him for details on the same case for which he'd queried Kendra. "You spoke to Colby on his second-to-last day at San Quentin, didn't you? Face to face?"

Lynch seemed amused by the young man's ghoulish enthusiasm. "Yeah, I guess I did."

"Would you, by any chance, have a recording of that conversation?"

Lynch turned to Kendra. "Is this guy for real?"

"I'm afraid so." She motioned to Suber. "He's waiting for an answer."

Lynch turned back toward him. "Uh, no. No recording. Griffin was there too. He may have—"

"He doesn't. Too bad. It would have been nice for my collection."

"Your collection," Lynch repeated.

"My database. It's more complete than anything the FBI has. It's helped me bring down four serial killers in the past three years." He raised his smart phone. "I can forward you press clippings of those cases, if you'd like. What's your email address?"

"That's okay. I believe you."

Suber seemed disappointed as he lowered his phone. "Anyway, it'll be a pleasure to work together. I hope we can sit down sometime and talk about your experiences with the Colby case. Maybe the same time I talk to Kendra."

Lynch looked at him in blank disbelief.

At that moment, Griffin walked over to the van and slid open the door. "Okay, everybody. Ready for your murder tour of San Diego?"

Lynch took Kendra by the arm. "This is gonna be one weird day."

The close proximity of the downtown locations made the tour a reasonably quick one and there were no major revelations to Kendra that she hadn't already picked up from the crime scene photographs. They visited the harborside last, alongside a large supertanker being repaired just south of the Coronado Bridge.

"This was where the first victim was found?" Lynch said.

Kendra nodded. "The corpse was recovered from the water by the tanker repair crew."

They stepped a few feet away from the others. "So, has our morning given you any special insights?" Lynch asked.

"Nothing new. It has been interesting watching how everyone works, though."

"What do you mean?"

Kendra pointed to Gale, the sour-looking FBI agent from New York. "Look at Special Agent Gale. Every site we visited seemed to make him angrier and angrier. I don't know if he learned much, but this little excursion lit a fire in him. He looks like he's ready to do whatever it takes to find this guy."

"I see what you mean. The killer had better hope Gale isn't the first one to find him." Lynch looked around. "What about the others? That guy looks more like a mellow grandpa."

"Arnold Huston, the D.C. police detective. Not mellow. Sad. He's taking this personally. I wouldn't be surprised if he's one of those cops whom the victims' families still keep in touch with and invite to their pool parties, weddings, and Bar Mitzvahs. This killer might be why he hasn't retired yet. He wants this guy just as bad as Gale, maybe even more."

"Interesting. What about the movie star over there?"

"Ed Roscoe. I'm actually a little surprised. He seemed a little superficial to me, but he's really done his homework. He already knows the San Diego dossier backward and forward. He went right to the spot where the body was found at each location, and he knows the times, dates, and other stats. I'm impressed."

"So am I." Lynch shook his head as he watched Trey Suber furiously scribbling on his tablet computer with a stylus. "But the serial killer fanboy is setting the bar pretty high. He's actually been taking measurements at every stop."

"I noticed. I think he has an app in that tablet that combines his photographs into a 3D model of each crime scene."

Lynch craned his neck to try to see Suber's screen. "Okay, I have to admit that's pretty bad-ass."

"I thought that would appeal to your inner tech geek. The models will become part of his collection, no doubt. If there's a pattern to be found, I'd count on Trey Suber to find it first."

"Without a doubt." He pointed to Gina Carson, who was sketching in a large Moleskine notebook. "She's doing something similar, but in a low-tech sort of way."

"Exactly. She's a pretty good artist. I caught a glimpse of her sketch at the last stop. She probably does that to cement each crime scene in her mind."

"She's been sticking pretty close to Metcalf. Are they a thing now?"

"I don't think so, but she may be interested. She was the only one who laughed at a lame joke he made yesterday."

"Oh, then she's definitely interested. I've heard Metcalf's jokes."

Kendra looked out at the bay for a long moment.

Beautiful waters. Bright sunlight. Intelligent men, voicing intelligent opinions.

It was all wrong.

"This isn't working for me," she said flatly.

"Really?" Lynch said mildly. "Would you like to tell me *what* isn't working?"

"This. I can't work this way." She whirled toward him and lowered her voice. "The killer is still out there and we're moving at a crawl. We're sitting here talking about Metcalf's love life? A *field* trip? Everyone is overwhelmed by the sheer magnitude of these killings, and we're stuck just trying to get a handle on it."

"Griffin says that San Diego PD is coming to brief us after lunch," Lynch said solemnly. "Won't that be interesting?"

"Stop being sarcastic. It's a reasonable thing to do. For them, not for me."

"Then what do you propose we do?"

He wanted her to be the one to say it. He'd probably been watching and expecting this reaction since they'd arrived here, but he wasn't going to give her an excuse to argue. "When we break for lunch, I'm splintering off on my own. Are you with me?"

Lynch smiled. "Well, I'm not hanging out with *them*. Trey Suber might corner me again. Where are we going?"

"I don't need to crack twenty-six cases. I just need to solve *one* to get this guy. I need to narrow my focus."

"On what?"

Kendra watched the group as they started back toward the van. "The case that brought me in. Amanda Robinson. Her body was set on fire in front of an elementary school. I picked up a few things at the scene, but I don't know how far it's taken them yet. I'll start with her."

"Okay." He made a grandiose gesture for her to precede him. "I hear and obey. You see how meek and accommodating I'm being? Where you go, I go."

"Until you decide you won't. Let's go tell Griffin."

Griffin, as it turned out, didn't need to be told. He stood next to the van's open door. "Need a lift back to your car?"

Kendra frowned. "How did you know?"

"We've worked enough cases together that I know when you're ready to go your own way. I could see you shifting and pawing your foot all morning."

"You make me sound like a pony."

"No, just a very distinguished and intelligent high-bred mare. Do me a favor, though. Keep us in the loop. I really want this dream team idea to work. The media possibilities are enormous and a real career booster. But I need to keep you people from tripping over each other." He lowered his voice. "I don't want this investigation to turn into a Marx Brothers routine."

Lynch slapped the van with the palm of his hand. "Or a clown car?"

"Too late for that." He climbed into the van. "Climb aboard. The Barnum & Bailey Express is departing."

Minutes later, Kendra and Lynch were back in his Ferrari. After he started it, he turned toward her. "Where are we headed?"

Kendra was perusing the FBI report on her tablet. "Amanda Robinson was at the Excite Bar on University Avenue with some coworkers. She sent for a Vroom car and her friends saw her picked up outside the bar. But she never made it home."

"Did they find the driver?"

"Yes. He reported a no-show for her and we've confirmed another fare for him four minutes later. He was cleared. Somebody else intercepted her."

"Did her friends get a make and model on the car?"

"There's some dispute. They agree it was a dark midsize sedan and it had a Vroom magnetic decal on the passenger side door."

"Okay. Any video of the car from traffic or security cams?"

"Not yet. They're still working on it."

"Then what's your play? Interview her coworkers? The staff at the bar?"

"Neither."

He gave her a questioning look.

She turned off the tablet computer and rested it on her lap. "The San Diego Development Services Department. It's just down the street."

Minutes after arriving at the single-story building on First Street, Kendra and Lynch were shown into the offices of City Development Manager Gareth Zane.

The large office was lined with tall shelves packed with cloth-bound survey maps. A large framed map of San Diego County, obviously decades old, dominated the wall behind the desk.

Zane crossed in front of his desk to shake hands with them. "My assistant just told me you need help with a murder investigation . . ." His brows lifted. "Did I hear that correctly?"

"I'm afraid so," she said. "I'm Kendra Michaels and this is Adam Lynch. We're consulting with the FBI on this case."

Zane motioned for them to sit down. "This is a first for me. How can I help?"

"Your office issues permits for new construction and structural renovations, is that right?"

"Yes. We make sure the plans conform to code, then afterward we inspect and sign off on the finished projects."

"And does that mean you have a current file on all in-progress construction projects in the county?"

He nodded. "Theoretically."

"What does that mean?" Lynch asked.

"Well, at any given time there are dozens, maybe even hundreds, of unpermitted construction projects underway in the county."

"Do-it-yourselfers?" Kendra said.

"That, unlicensed contractors, plus additions and renovations the property owners know won't be approved. We're always on the lookout for violators, but we can only do so much."

"But what if we're looking for projects falling within certain parameters?" Kendra said.

"Depends on the parameters. Geographic? Within a certain time span?" Zane motioned toward the computer keyboard on his desk. "We have that information in our database."

Kendra leaned toward him. "I'm looking for a new home construction site that involved gypsum paving and an in-ground pool. It's incomplete and it's not easily visible from nearby structures or streets."

Zane pursed his lips. "Hmm. I'm afraid our records won't give you that kind of detail."

"Then what can you give us?" Lynch said.

Zane thought about it. "Well, I can generate a list of unfinished construction properties that applied for pre-construction permits, but were still listed as unfinished after their target completion date. We usually don't have materials in the plan and in any case, it's not a searchable component. But I can include a pool in the search parameters."

"Do it," Kendra said. "Please."

Zane sat behind his desk. After a few minutes of typing, the printer behind him whirred and spat out dozens of printed pages.

He looked up. "Okay, that gives us nineteen properties."

"Now I need to know their proximity to other buildings. And it would be helpful to see how close they are to a power substation."

Lynch shot her an incredulous glance. "A power substation? Really?"

Kendra nodded. "I'll explain later."

Zane pointed to the large bound volumes on his shelves. "We have neighborhood survey maps, but to be honest I usually just use Google Earth. That will give you an idea what's nearby."

Kendra unzipped her folio case and pulled out her tablet computer. "Mind if I do that here? If I need anything else, I'd like to be nearby."

"No problem. Set up on the table in the corner."

"Thanks."

With Lynch holding up the printouts in front of her, Kendra's fingers flew over her tablet screen. One by one, she looked at a satellite view of each of the property sites. She discounted most immediately since they sat in heavily-trafficked areas with high visibility from the road and neighboring lots. Four seemed to fit the bill fairly well.

On the last property, she pulled up the satellite image. "Think we can count this one as a possible hit. There's the outline of a pool, but there doesn't even appear to be a paved driveway."

Lynch studied the printout. "It's a motel, but it looks like they didn't have the funds to finish it. Construction started over six years ago."

Kendra ran her fingers over a dark object immediately adjacent to the lot. "Could this be . . . ?"

"Wow." Lynch smiled. "I'd say that's a power substation. How in the hell . . . ?"

"Let's go." She jumped to her feet. "I'll explain on the way there."

CHAPTER 8

"Mineral oil?" Lynch pulled onto the I-8 freeway and accelerated.

"There was a slight residue on the chair with Amanda Robinson's burned corpse. I was pretty sure it was mineral oil, but I had no idea what it meant. So I did a little online research. Mineral oil is used as a coolant in power transformers, but only for outdoor installations. Fire codes prevent it from being used indoors in case of leakage. That's what made me think to look for a nearby outdoor transformer substation."

"Hmm. Did it occur to you that the mineral oil just may have been there to lubricate the casters of that chair?"

"It did. I guess we'll find out soon enough."

A few minutes later, they pulled up to the construction site and parked on a shadowy street in the Jamul neighborhood. The two-story motel was little more than a shell and the property had been overrun by weeds and vegetation.

"Except for the vines, it looks exactly as it did in the Google Earth satellite image," Lynch said.

"Exactly. This place hasn't been touched in years." Kendra looked down at the gravel and dirt path. "But I think a vehicle has been here recently. Looks like the rocks have been freshly punched into the earth."

Lynch glanced at the humming transformer and nearby power lines. "Poor placement for a motel. No wonder it's sat here unfinished all this time."

Kendra pointed to the dirty stucco that faced the transformer substation. "Probably some leakage from the transformer. There's a light film of oil on that wall."

"Looks like you were right," he murmured.

Kendra glanced up at the two-story structure, which had no doors or windows. It consisted of thirty-two guest rooms, sixteen on each floor, each facing what would have been the parking lot. Beyond the stucco exteriors, the guest rooms were littered with trash and construction debris, separated from each other only by thin wooden framing.

"See anything?"

Kendra squinted into the building. The sun had set over the adjacent hillside, casting long shadows over the abandoned structure. She pointed toward the dark front office. "Let's go in here."

Lynch followed her as she moved through the wood-and-stucco opening. A stale odor permeated the room.

Something rustled in the corner.

Lynch instinctively stepped in front of her. His gun was suddenly in his hand and his entire body was in attack mode.

More rustling, moving among discarded bags of cement mix.

Three rats emerged and scampered into the darkness.

Lynch lowered his gun.

Kendra took the lead again, moving through a back doorway. She pulled out her phone, flipped on the light and held it over her head. "A hallway. Looks like it runs the entire length of the building."

Her nose tingled with a familiar odor.

Death.

"She was here."

"What?"

Kendra's stomach tightened. "I think Amanda Robinson was here. She'd been decomposing for a few days before she was dropped in front of the school. That same stench is coming from this hallway."

"How do you know it's from her?"

"I don't. That means there could be another body back there right now." She turned toward him and cocked her head toward the dark hallway. "One way to find out."

He raised his gun again. "What if I told you to hang back here while I go down by myself and clear the scene?"

She gazed at him in disbelief. "I'd tell you to go to hell."

"Of course you would. Just checking."

They stepped over a pile of lumber scraps and moved down the dark hallway. The shadows swallowed them whole, even with her phone's flashlight showing the way.

The hallway was just wide enough to allow them to walk side-by-side. More rats skittered in front of them. The scent of death grew stronger.

"See that?" Lynch's grip tightened on his gun. He nodded toward the end of the hallway where something glistened in the shadows.

Crack.

Crack.

Crack.

Kendra stopped.

"We're stepping on something." She aimed her phone at the floor. The light reflected hundreds of pieces of broken glass, surrounded by dozens of intact clear capsules. The capsules were littered over the hallway, strewn into the darkness.

Kendra knelt to examine the glass pieces. They were each about two inches long and perhaps a half-inch thick.

"What are these?" she asked, puzzled. "Something a construction crew would use?"

"No crew I've ever seen." Lynch looked down the hallway. "Let's see what's down there."

Kendra stood and continued down the hall-way, breaking even more of the glass capsules as they walked.

Crack.

Crack.

Crack.

Another rat scampered across the floor in front of them.

"Hold the light up," Lynch said.

She did and what they saw made them both stop.

There, at the end of the hallway, was something she hadn't expected to see.

A car.

"A black Toyota Camry," Lynch said. "The victim was picked up by a dark-colored car, right?"

"Yes." Kendra slowly walked around and shone her light on the vehicle's passenger side.

Oh, shit.

An icy chill crept over her neck and scalp.

On the door was a magnetic Vroom sign.

"This was it," she whispered. "This was the car. How did he get it in here?"

Lynch inspected the wall at the end of the corridor. "This plywood is new. This was open until just recently. He just drove the car in and boarded it up."

Kendra shone her light into the car's interior. What terror, what horrible sadness, poor Amanda Robinson must have felt here.

Lynch joined her at the car window as she peered into the interior. "Anything?"

"Looks like it's been wiped clean. I don't think you'll find any fingerprints."

"All it takes is a spot of blood or a drop of saliva. In a few hours, the team at the FBI garage will have this car in about a thousand pieces. If there's something here, they'll find it."

"If there's something here." Kendra circled around and looked in the driver's side window. "Unfortunately, we're dealing with a killer who's shown himself to be very good at covering his tracks."

Kendra knelt beside the trunk and examined it. It was slightly ajar. She pulled her sleeve over her hand, then pulled the trunk lid open and up.

Whoa.

Lynch rushed toward her. "What's in there?"

She covered her nose and mouth with her sleeve. "Nothing. Just that awful odor."

"Yeah. I smell it too."

"He killed her, then left her in here until he was ready to dump her body. Then he—"

Kendra's nose was still burning. She felt nauseous and light-headed. What in the hell . . . ?"

There was a different scent in the air. Stronger and more bitter than the sickly-sweet odor wafting up from the car trunk.

"Lynch?"

He staggered toward her, struggling to maintain his balance. "Go. *Now*."

She turned her light back toward the hallway.

Dizzy.

She was vaguely aware of Lynch in back of her, pushing her forward. The hall was now littered with rats, dead or dying on the floor. Some were still, others trembled on their backs as if arrested by seizures.

The capsules.

Liquid from the broken glass capsules was now all over the hallway. It had combined to form something that now burned her nose and lungs.

Something dangerous. Something toxic . . .

Another wave of nausea rolled over her. This time she felt as if she might pass out.

Oh, God.

Whatever was in those capsules on that floor just might kill them.

She stumbled down the hallway.

Don't fall.

Stay conscious.

Stay alive.

How much farther?

She was hardly moving at all, she realized. What in the hell was this stuff?

"Hurry. Faster." Lynch slurred his words. "Gotta . . . get out."

Her eyes watered.

Her hands shook.

She dropped her phone, plunging them into almost total darkness.

"Lynch?"

"Right behind you. Don't stop."

She reached out, grabbed his arm, and pulled him toward her.

But now, in the darkness, she felt strangely at home. Just like old times.

She pushed forward, sliding her feet to avoid stepping on the squealing, trembling rats.

Keep moving.

She extended her right arm and used her palm to steady herself against the wall. She forced herself to take bigger steps, even as her legs turned to rubber.

She tried to hold her breath, but her eyes and nose still stung. Hot tears welled in her eyes.

Was this hallway actually getting *longer?*

Her face was numb. Her tongue felt as if it was three times too big for her mouth.

Hurts to breathe.

Hurts to move.

Her legs buckled.

"No!" Lynch was shouting at her like a drill sergeant. "Move! Now!"

She threw herself forward, letting the momentum carry her for the next few feet.

She reached behind her. Lynch wasn't there.

"Lynch?"

"Go!" He coughed. "I'll be okay."

"For God's sake, stop trying to be heroic. I can't deal with it now." Using his voice to zero in on him, she reached back, grabbed his arm, and pulled.

He coughed again. "Can't . . . get my bearings."

She half-dragged him behind her. "I can. Twenty years in the dark gave me lots of practice. Just hang on."

Finally there was a pale glow ahead. "Almost there!" she called back. "Still with me?"

More coughing from Lynch.

"We can do this." She pulled harder, and together they stumbled over the construction debris toward the office shell.

Just another few feet.

But her head buzzed and her lungs were exploding.

Daylight!

They hurtled through the office and ran outside, gulping the fresh air. They collapsed on the ground.

It was more than a minute before either of them could speak. Lynch caught his breath first. "You okay?"

Kendra nodded. "Yeah. I think so." She couldn't force enough air into her lungs. She was panting. "Still . . . hurts."

"Me, too . . ." he gasped. "And . . . for your information . . . I never *try* to be heroic . . . I'm the genuine article."

"Genuine . . . egotist." Even her throat was throbbing. "What happened to us? What in the hell was that?"

Lynch fumbled for his phone. His hands were still trembling. "Some kind of nerve agent. Just stay still. It's about to get crazy around here."

"Ma'am, how many fingers am I holding up?"

Kendra stared at the young paramedic. "Three."

"Can you tell me what day it is?"

She adjusted her oxygen mask. "Thursday."

"Good. Now I'm going to ask you to count backwards from a hundred . . ."

Kendra glanced over at Lynch, who was getting the same treatment just a few feet away.

Three police cruisers were already in the lot, and as she looked at Lynch, a pair of city Metropolitan Medical Strike Team vans arrived on the scene.

The paramedic snapped his fingers. "Ma'am, I need your full attention. Are you still with me?"

"Sorry. One hundred, ninety-nine, ninety-eight . . ."

As she counted, a second paramedic began cutting the clothes from her body.

"That was my second-favorite sweater," she said. "You could have asked me to take it off, you know."

"Sorry. We need to minimize contact."

A few more cuts and he pulled her pants off.

"Really?" She tried to cover herself.

Lynch was laughing through his mask. "If I'd known it was *that* easy . . ."

He stopped laughing when he realized his own clothes were being cut away.

Within seconds, their shredded clothes were in sealed plastic bags, and they were wearing paper gowns.

The next several hours were a blur. Kendra found herself transported to Sharp Memorial Hospital, where a waiting trauma team was oddly well-prepared to deal with her symptoms. It was all in keeping with the incredible nature of everything that had happened to them today.

"Get many nerve gas patients around here?" she cracked to the pair of doctors administering diazepam and midazolam to her.

"You're our first," the younger doctor said absently. "After years of Homeland Security drills, it's nice to finally put our knowledge to good use."

"Always glad to help." She had to joke. She was having trouble keeping control of her emotions. Nerve gas? What the hell? It brought up so many questions and frightening implications that she didn't want to think about yet. She wasn't like Lynch, who lived in this world. All she could do was just let them prod her and give her drugs and test her for damage while she tried to recover her equilibrium. Somehow that innocuous, helpful, pampering steadied her.

Her next stop was a shower followed by her placement in a hospital room for overnight observation.

This was all wrong, she thought after the nurse left her. She was fine now and there was too much to do. Why was she lying here when she had to figure out what had happened to them? And where was Lynch? He had seemed okay, but how did she know how nerve gas would affect him down the road? In spite of all that machismo bullshit, women had more endurance than men. Ask any pregnant woman on the planet. Lynch could be—

A man in scrubs and a surgeon's mask entered her room. He closed the door and stepped toward her.

She automatically tensed.

But even before he pulled off the mask, she knew who it was.

"Lynch?" she said incredulously; immediately followed by relief.

"At your service."

She jumped out of bed. "What in the hell are you doing here?" she whispered.

"It's obvious, isn't it? I'm here to bust you out."

"You think we're prisoners here?"

"Not in so many words. But those doctors are really into this guinea pig thing. And it won't be long before Homeland Security has to take a peek and swamp us with questions. I expect them to be lined up at the door tonight. Nerve gas is a favorite weapon of choice for terrorists. Those doctors must have pulled rank once they got their hands on a real live specimen to practice on. But I bet Homeland is scrambling to inundate us with paperwork. Trust me, they'll pay us a visit before breakfast."

Kendra nodded. "Then we're not prisoners, but they all clearly want us to stay?"

"Yes, but they feel comfortable about not causing a fuss about it. We're not likely to go anywhere without clothes." He looked her up and down. "Though I must say, you're abso-lutely *rocking* that hospital gown." He smiled puckishly. "Wanna turn around?"

"Go to hell. Where'd you get the scrubs?"

"Same place I got yours." He tossed a thin packet on her bed. "Linen cart. Put 'em on and let's go."

"Go where?"

"Where I know you're just dying to go. Back to the building site. By now they'll have it cleaned up and Griffin and the dream team are crawling all over the place, picking up leads that we found for them."

She grimaced. "That thought had occurred to me. I was getting a little frustrated."

"I thought you would be. Why else did I decide to forgo the traditional hospital Jell-O to immediately start making a plan to break us out of here? You wouldn't have lasted more than a few hours. I'd have roused in the middle of the night to see you in my room jerking me from my slumber and pushing me toward the nearest exit."

"Like you were pushing me out of that motel?"

His smile faded. "I believe that particular 'pushing' was cooperative and consenting on both our parts. I'm not certain that either one of us would have made it out of there if we hadn't been fighting our way together." He took a step closer and his hands gently cupped her throat. "But I can't imagine anyone I'd rather be with if I ever had to go through that again." His thumbs moved caressingly in the hollow of her throat. "You okay? You weren't just pretending with those jokers?"

The flesh of her throat was tingling beneath his fingers and she felt the same breathlessness she'd experienced earlier. No, not the same. That had been terror, this was the other spectrum of sensation.

"I'm okay." She took a deep breath. "You?"

"At the moment, just fine." He smiled. "You haven't accused me of being an egotist or a grandstander since I came in the room. And I have my hands on you." His voice lowered as his thumbs stroked gently back and forth. "I can feel your heart beat . . ." He sighed and stepped back. "But I'd better skip that, I'm afraid. Otherwise we'll end up in that hospital bed and you'd not appreciate the lack of privacy." His hands fell away from her throat. "But I could be wrong?"

He was wrong. A minute before she hadn't given a damn about privacy. She'd just wanted him to keep touching her. They had gone through too much together today. Hell, they had almost died together. Nothing else seemed as important as the fact that they were still alive. But she should care, she should be glad he wasn't touching her any longer. Sex was always the final searing element that defined life. If Zachary was watching them, he would pick up on those signals that were so obvious to Kendra. No, their relationship was chaotic enough without throwing sex into the mix right now.

"Privacy is important to me." But she'd been too obvious and she wouldn't try to fool him. "But I'm glad that you're doing well. I was scared for you. I was scared for me. Nothing like a close shave and a zillion dead rats to make you appreciate being alive." She hesitated and then said, "I'm . . . blurred, Lynch. This thing threw me for a loop. Nerve gas? It's totally bizarre. Those doctors said we're going to be fine, but I don't feel fine. I don't know what I feel."

"You will," he said gently. "It's gathering like a storm and just waiting to break free. When it does, we'll all duck for cover. I could see all this was upsetting you. It's a little outside your comfort zone. That's why I decided not to wait. The best thing for you is to get busy and just let it come to you. So let's go do it."

"Therapy according to Lynch?"

"Absolutely. It's foolproof."

"I doubt it. But it's always interesting." And oddly comforting that he was this certain he was right about her at this particular time. It was always disconcerting to her when anyone thought they were close enough to read her. Somehow today was . . . different. She'd analyze and decide why later. She'd just accept it for now. She turned away and picked up the scrubs on the bed. "I'll be with you in a couple minutes."

"I'm not going anywhere." He suddenly chuckled. "I've decided I need your protection. I was blundering around like a blind bear before you took my hand in the dark. So you're stuck with me." He nodded at the bathroom. "Get going. I'll stand guard in case a nurse pops in, but you only get that couple minutes. After that, I get to come in and help. Which might mean a significant change in agenda."

Kendra and Lynch took the elevator downstairs and made their way to the hospital's large circular driveway. Two cabs were waiting at the taxi stand. They jumped into the first one and directed the driver to take them back to the construction site.

Kendra looked back as they drove away. "A nurse was giving us a funny look. You probably should have swiped a couple ID badges, too."

"I could have, but we're not fugitives from justice, remember?"

"At least we weren't until we walked out wearing hospital property."

"Point taken. I'll make sure the hospital gets their scrubs back."

Lynch smiled at the odd looks the cab driver was giving them in the rearview mirror. He told him, "Don't worry. We didn't just escape from the Psych Ward."

Kendra jerked her thumb at Lynch. "Well, *he* may have. But I'll keep him in line."

"Nice," Lynch said.

She leaned back in her seat. "Did the doctors give you any idea exactly what we were exposed to?"

"They're still not sure. They treated us as if we'd been exposed to fentanyl or a derivative and that seems to have done the trick. It can be deadly in its purest form. I guess we can consider ourselves lucky."

"If you say so. Why in the hell would Zachary line the hallway with that stuff?"

Lynch shrugged. "Crude security system?"

"Maybe. Or maybe it was a trap."

"A trap for you?"

"Me or anyone else unlucky enough to find the trail back there." Kendra bit her lip. "It's all a sick game to him. He might not have wanted to kill us. It might just be his way of toying with us."

Lynch grimaced. "You have more experience with this brand of psychopath than I do, but that seemed plenty lethal to me."

"Well, it did one thing for us." Kendra looked outside her window. "The chemical gave us one more way to try and track this guy. If it helps us find him before he kills again, it will have been worth it."

"How self-sacrificing of you. Personally I'd prefer to spare myself that extreme discomfort, but it did rouse my killer instincts." He added grimly, "And that might make Zachary tossing out his poison seeds like Johnny Appleseed an even greater mistake."

CHAPTER 9

They knew they were approaching the construction site a full block away due to the blinding white light which now lit up the entire scene. There were over a dozen vehicles in the unfinished parking lot, including several police cruisers, a pair of Hazardous Materials trucks, FBI crime scene vans, and a fire engine. Kendra counted at least twenty people moving around the structure.

Lynch leaned toward the driver and pointed to Griffin, who was talking to one of the uniformed cops. "Pull alongside him. He'll be happy to see us."

The driver stopped next to Griffin, and Kendra and Lynch hopped out.

Griffin looked their scrubs up and down. "Interesting fashion statement."

"Thank you." Lynch motioned back toward the cab driver. "Pay the man, Griffin."

"Why me?"

"They took my wallet at the hospital. It will probably be thrown away and if I'm lucky, the cash, credit cards, and driver's license will be returned to me after they've been given a nice soapy bath." Lynch leaned back to glance at the meter. "By the way, that explanation just cost you another fifty-five cents. I recommend you pay him before it costs you any more."

Griffin paid the driver, who was obviously curious about the work lights and activity at the half-completed motel.

"Please tip him better than that," Lynch said. "He earned it."

Griffin shook his head as he shoved a few more dollars into the cab driver's hand. "Just when I start to forget what a complete pain in the ass you are . . ."

Kendra stepped toward the structure. "What have you found?"

"Nothing yet. The hazmat team just gave us the all-clear a few minutes ago. The floor has been scrubbed clean, and they aired the place out. Our evidence team is giving the car a once-over before we tow it to the garage."

Kendra nodded. "The car's interior looked as if it had been wiped. I doubt you'll find prints, but there may be something else there. Let's go inside."

She started for the entrance, but she found herself slowing almost involuntarily before she reached the doorway. She stopped.

Lynch placed his hand on the small of her back and whispered, "You don't need to do this. We can look at the car at the FBI garage."

He was trying to be supportive, but the gesture only annoyed her. It only pointed out this moment of weakness and the fact that it should be herself at which that annoyance should be aimed. "No. It's fine. Let's go in."

She moved through the wood-framed entranceway and made her way to the rear corridor, which was now brilliantly illuminated by work lights on tall stands. The floor was wet and the dead rats and most of the construction debris had been removed.

As they walked down the hallway, she saw that the boards had been removed from the opening at the far end, exposing the hallway to the night air. The car was now flooded with light and the doors were open. Crime scene techs leaned inside, inspecting the seats and floors.

The dream team stood a few feet away.

Agent Gale stepped toward them. "We didn't expect to see you here." He gave their scrubs only a cursory glance and then returned to what was important to him. "Good work finding this place."

Kendra peered into the open car door. "Have they found anything?"

"Nah. No prints. They swabbed for skin oil on the door handle, but they're not optimistic."

Kendra pointed at the magnetic Vroom sign on the car door. "What about the sign? Any way we can narrow down to where it came from?

Ed Roscoe turned and approached with a pseudo-sexy strut that made Kendra slightly ill. Was that something he developed before his movie or after?

"No such luck," Roscoe said. "Amazon and dozens of other online retailers have been selling 'em for years for seven bucks a pop. Anyone can order one."

Kendra looked down at a green cardboard disc at her feet. She glanced around and saw that there were half a dozen more placed around the car. "These weren't here before."

"They're mine," Trey Suber said from the other side of the car. He held his tablet computer in front of him, snapping photos of the scene from various vantage points. "I use them for reference. I link up the dots between pictures taken from different angles, then my software creates a 3D model I can rotate and examine any way I want." He showed Kendra his tablet, which displayed a view of the car. As he ran his finger over the glass screen, the room twirled left and right as if the camera were flying over and around it.

"I saw you doing that at the harbor this morning," Kendra said. "It's amazing. You do this for all the cases you work?"

Suber nodded. "And for locations in old cases I study. I can show you some of your old crime scene locales, if you'd like."

Kendra slapped her hand over his screen. "Don't."

"I just thought—"

"Not interested. I have no desire to even think about those cases ever again, you understand?"

He backed away. "Sure."

Agent Gale's sour expression softened slightly and for a moment Kendra thought he might smile. "The kid tried to show me some of my old scenes during lunch and I almost decked him. You think he would've learned his lesson."

Suber lowered his tablet. "I thought you people might have more curiosity about your own cases."

"Kid, we lived them," Gale said. "No need to rehash unpleasant memories. Haven't we been doing that enough this week?"

Suber shrugged. "I just don't feel that way."

"No, you wouldn't," Lynch said. "That's because you live, breathe, and eat this stuff. It's why you're such a good profiler."

"Exactly," Suber said.

Kendra smiled. "Modest, too."

"I know I'm good at what I do. Just like you're good at what you do."

"Okay, then tell me something new about our killer. Something we didn't know before," she said.

Suber pushed up his glasses. "When I was on the case in Florida, I actually thought the killer might have been of lower intelligence with difficulty holding onto jobs and relationships. I think I was wrong. The killer was playing a part for us there. I now think we're dealing with a highly-organized man, mid-to-late thirties, with high intelligence. He's planned this for a long time, and he's extremely interested in news accounts of his killings. He's probably obsessive about it. When we get a suspect, we have to check online activity or computer access at nearby libraries. Or to see if he's suddenly buying copies of every local paper at a neighborhood newsstand. I'm positive he'll be doing this, like an actor in a play reading his reviews."

"A few of mine were bedwetters," Gale said.

Suber nodded. "Possibly. Six out of ten serial killers habitually wet the bed after the age of twelve, though most outgrow it sometime during adolescence. Psychologists think it reflects a lack of control or might just be a symptom of psychological stress. This won't do us much good to find him though. We need to focus on his attention to the media."

"Interesting," Kendra said absently. She was glancing around at the construction debris.

"What are you looking for?" Lynch said.

Kendra's eyes flicked around the area. "This whole car was wiped clean. Not just the inside. I'm thinking that the towel or rags may have been tossed away among the debris here."

Gale smiled, turned, and picked up a clear gallon-size zip lock evidence bag. Inside was a crumpled hand towel. "I thought the same thing, Dr. Michaels. I found this in the corner."

She nodded with approval. "If I didn't know

better, I'd say you were a cop. Maybe one with a little experience."

"Well, we'll see if it gets us anywhere."

"You never can tell." Her eyes went to the overgrown lot where the squad cars and support vehicles were parked. There, leaning against a fire truck, Detective Arnold Huston sipped coffee with an elderly man in dirty clothes.

She nodded toward Huston. "What's happening over there?"

Roscoe shrugged. "Huston walked the neighborhood right after we got here and chatted up some of the locals. He found that homeless guy and brought him back here. Not sure what he's finding out."

"Never mind that," Gale said. "Where in the hell did they get coffee?"

"There's a dispenser in one of the hazmat vans," Kendra said, still staring at Huston.

Just then, Huston pointed in their direction and led the homeless man through the large opening. He introduced his new acquaintance to the group. "Friends, this is John Sheffield. He spends a lot of time in the neighborhood. I thought he might be kind enough to share anything he might have observed with us."

"Nice to meet you," Kendra said. "We're grateful for anything you can remember.

Sheffield nodded in response. He was probably in his late fifties though he would have looked younger without the large gray beard that covered his face. Despite his dirty clothing, he looked and smelled clean, with no unpleasant odor that she might have expected from her first glance.

Huston patted Sheffield's arm. "Tell them what you told me. About what you saw here."

Sheffield seemed hesitant as he eyed the group converging around him.

"It's okay," Huston said. "Go ahead."

Sheffield nodded, then spoke in a light rasp. "Well, things have been quiet here for a long time. A few years ago, people used to do drugs here, but the cops ran 'em off. I tried sleeping in here when it rained, but that really isn't much of a roof. And I didn't like the rats. Kinda freaked me out."

Kendra grimaced. "I didn't care for them, either."

"But I cut through this lot a few times a week. It's a shortcut to the next street. And a couple times lately I've seen a car pulled around back."

Kendra pointed to the Toyota behind them. "*This* car?"

"Nah, it was a white one. Kinda boxy, with tinted windows."

"Any idea of the make or model?" Lynch said.

Sheffield shook his head.

"I'm going to take him to the office and show him some pictures," Huston said.

"I have the entire auto flipbook collection in my

tablet," Suber said. "We can go through it here."

"Good," Huston said. "We'll do that." He turned back to Sheffield. "But first tell them about the boards."

Sheffield turned back to the open-ended hallway. "This has always been open, just like this. But around the same time I started seeing the car, I saw that it had been all boarded up."

"Sounds like it could be our guy," Gale said. "Did you ever see anybody in that car or maybe getting in or out of it?"

"Nah. It was just sitting over there behind the building. It couldn't be seen from the street. But I never saw anybody around here."

By this time, Metcalf and Gina had joined the group. Kendra turned toward Metcalf. "Have you run ownership on this Toyota yet?"

He produced his phone, which had only recently become his note-taking instrument of choice. "Yes. It belongs to a Lucinda Harris in San Ysidro. Reported stolen three days before Amanda Robinson was abducted."

"We already started working with local police on that," Gina said. "Seeing if maybe neighbors have security cameras or if there are traffic cams in the area we can use to track it."

"Good," Kendra said.

"Not good," Griffin said as he stepped through the opening. "Kendra and Lynch, you're off this case."

Kendra turned toward him. "What?"

"I just got a call from Sharp Memorial Hospital." He added grimly, "They were displeased with your unexpected departure from their facility."

"*That's* why you're pulling us off the case?" Lynch said.

"No, I'm pulling you off the case because it just might save your lives. You were exposed to a dangerous toxin, then given some medication that could cause some nasty side-effects. Your highly-skilled doctors want you both in the hospital overnight in case treatment is necessary." He added sourly, "I believe this was explained to you?"

Lynch shrugged. "When I cross-examined them on it, they admitted that the threat was miniscule. It was pretty clear they just wanted to make sure that we were available for Homeland Security when they came knocking in the morning."

And Kendra said impatiently, "Don't be crazy. Lynch would never let anything bad happen to me. I vaguely remember somebody might have said something about that to—"

"Hell yes, they did," Griffin said curtly. "I don't give a damn if Lynch wants to risk his own neck, but I'm responsible for bringing you on board. You're not working this case until you're discharged. *Officially* discharged."

"When will that be?" Kendra said.

"Tomorrow morning at the earliest."

"Forget it." As usual, Kendra was not pleased by Griffin's arbitrary attitude. "I feel fine and it's my decision what I will or will not do. I don't take my orders from—"

"Drop it, Kendra," Lynch said. "We've been busted."

He held up his hand as she whirled on him. "Don't attack me. I hate to admit it, but Griffin is right. As long as there was any threat at all, I had no right to persuade you to come back here to play with me and the rest of these guys. It just seemed better for you at the time."

"You didn't persuade me. It was my decision."

"True. It's always your decision. I was just an enabler. So is it okay if we go back and face the music? It would be my worst nightmare to have Griffin all smug and holier than thou if you happened to croak on me."

There was an element of seriousness beneath the lightness in his tone, she realized. She hesitated. "Oh, what the hell? I can't imagine anything worse. Okay, I'll save you if you promise to run interference for me with Homeland in the morning. I'm sure you have someone high up there in your pocket who could get us sprung quickly."

He smiled. "There's a possibility."

"More than a possibility," Griffin said. "Then it's settled. I'll have someone take you back there now."

"Not necessary," Lynch said. "My ride's still here." He pointed to his Ferrari parked a few yards away. "Hopefully its finish hasn't been ravaged by your wide-body emergency vehicles."

Kendra rolled her eyes. "Every time I start to think that you might be the tiniest bit reasonable and courageous, I remember what a wuss you are where this car is concerned."

"That car and I have been through a lot together."

"It's a sad, sick affectation."

"It's every man's dream."

"I don't believe that." Kendra turned to the dream team. "That can't be true, is it?"

Each member of the dream team nodded without hesitation.

Sheffield toasted Lynch with his coffee. "Pretty much."

She sighed. "Unbelievable. See you guys tomorrow."

She and Lynch walked back to his car. "Okay. Tell me . . . does that dream include paying $3,500 for cup holders?"

"What are you talking about?"

"I saw an article online that Ferrari charges over $3,500 for those rather ordinary carbon fiber cup holders of yours. I thought of you immediately."

"Good thoughts I'm sure."

"Don't you wish."

"Hmm. I may have to take a closer look at the factory invoice from now on. Would you like some coffee? It would be a shame to let these pricy cup holders go to waste."

"No thanks."

Lynch leaned down and swept his hand across the underside of his car. He pulled out a small magnetized box and showed it to Kendra.

"You keep a spare key under your car? I'm sure no one would ever think to look there," she said sarcastically.

He slid a small black panel from the box and pressed his thumb against it. The car beeped with approval and unlocked.

"Fingerprint reader," he said. "It really cost only a little bit more than the cup holder. Nobody but me is getting in here."

They climbed in the car and Lynch started it. He slowly navigated past the personnel and vehicles on the site. He nodded toward the other investigators still gathered around the Toyota. "I have to say, I believe they're starting to gel."

"What do you mean?"

"The dream team is finding a rhythm. And you're part of it. You found the car, Detective Huston pounded the pavement until he found a witness, and that creepy kid sounds like he's building a good profile. As afraid as Griffin was of too many cooks in the kitchen, I've found that when you get a group of extremely competent people together, good things can happen. They bend toward each other's strengths, and if they're lucky, they pull the best from each other."

"Sounds funny coming from such a notorious loner."

He smiled as they turned onto the street. "I'm capable of working with people when the situation demands it. I wouldn't last very long if I couldn't. And you pride yourself on being a loner yourself, but together you and I have kicked some serious ass over the last couple of years. I'm just saying it's not bad we have these guys on the case. They're the ones who know Zachary best."

Kendra settled back in the leather seat. "You may have a point there. And that creepy kid is sharp as a tack. Trey Suber . . . I'll be interested in seeing in what else he comes up with . . ."

"Me too." Lynch gave her a sideways glance. "Are we really going back to the hospital now?"

"What?" She gazed at him in surprise. "After that impassioned plea you gave me to save you from Griffin? You even said that you were wrong. Now that's the only thing that made me give in. You never admit to being wrong. You were conning me?"

"I never con you. Well, almost never, and it's always for your own good." He grimaced. "And, unfortunately, Griffin might have been a *little* bit right. It's humiliating to even give him that much. It must have been the poison gas that allowed me to tumble even that far from grace."

"I'm sure that must have been it," she said solemnly. "But now that you've recovered you've changed your mind about going back?"

"Not entirely. I'm just thinking about delaying it for a bit."

"And what else are we going to do?"

"I can think of a few things that might remind us of how lucky we are that Zachary blundered this time." His gaze moved from her face to her throat and then down to linger on her breasts. "You know, you're almost as fetching in those scrubs as you were in that hospital gown."

She felt the muscles of her stomach clench and her breath become shallow. That crazy, erotic moment when he'd come into her bedroom this morning. The *feel* of his hardness, his hands on her buttocks, lifting. His mouth, taking, giving . . .

The heat.

The dizzying need that was like no other hunger.

Had it only been this morning?

"You know that you want to do it." His voice was softly coaxing. "Why not? Because you're set on not showing Zachary that I mean anything to you?" He suddenly chuckled. "Hell, if we spend enough time in bed there's a chance that he'll only think I'm your boy-toy. No importance at all in the scheme of things. I assure you that I wouldn't mind that. I can think of all kinds of ways to keep you amused. I think we should start right away."

"You're being ridiculous."

"Well, only that I'm no boy. I think you'll prefer the man I am. But the rest of the concept would work fine." His smile was warm, amused, and infinitely seductive. "It's going to happen sometime, Kendra. It might as well be today. You're going to get very tired of Zachary controlling what you do and who you do it with."

"We discussed this before. I thought you'd accepted that I wasn't going to change my mind."

"You thought no such thing." His smile faded. "You just hoped you'd find a way to save me from the bogeyman. I was trying to take it slow, but that was blown to hell when I saw you lying on the floor gasping for air."

"I wasn't the only one gasping, dammit. That should have taught you something."

He was silent. Then his smile was back, along with that charisma that was nearly irresistible. "It taught me not to waste the good times when the bad times might be right around the corner. And that's what I intend to teach you, Kendra." He paused. "How about it?"

Tempting.

Too tempting.

She looked away from him and cleared her throat. "I'm not into lessons at the moment. I think we should go right back to the hospital."

His grip tensed on the steering wheel and then relaxed. "I was afraid of that," he said. "Even if only temporary, that winnows our options quite a bit."

That intensity had been damped down, she realized with relief. "You know it's probably for the best. For a multitude of reasons."

"Is it? I disagree." He turned at the light. "But as you wish. Back to square one. No, I refuse to admit that much of a setback. You're not running from me and that puts me very much in the game . . ."

They'd found the car.

Zachary smiled from his hilltop vantage point on Torrance Street where he could see the lights and activity around the abandoned construction site that had served him wonderfully well. It was now after midnight, and most of the police and FBI agents had left hours before. The black Toyota Camry had just been rolled into the covered flatbed truck for its journey to the FBI garage in North County.

They would find nothing, he thought with satisfaction. He'd been at this for years, and he knew how the game was played.

But there was still that one-in-a-million chance that he'd missed something during his cleanup after depositing Pretty Amanda in front of that elementary school. That tiny sliver of doubt was just enough to make the game exciting.

Zachary climbed into the white Dodge Durango SUV and drove the short few blocks to the U-Stor-It storage complex on West Valley Parkway. He parked a couple of blocks away to keep his vehicle from being seen by the three security cameras monitoring the complex's common areas. It was a small facility, with fifty garage-style units surrounding a large concrete plaza. As far as he could tell, most of the units contained boats and RVs.

Zachary pulled on a pair of latex gloves and climbed out of the Durango. He wrapped a scarf around his nose and mouth in case someone should ever try to scrutinize security video to get a glimpse of the owner of storage unit 132. He walked to the storage facility's main gate and waved his key card over the sensor. The gate groaned and rattled as it slid open. He walked across the paved lot to his unit, where he unlocked the door and raised it a few feet. He ducked under and pulled it closed behind him.

He felt for the switch and flipped on the overhead fluorescent lights. The room was almost empty, save for a few plastic storage containers, a stool, and a makeshift desk consisting of a thick piece of plywood resting on two sawhorses.

His own private artist's studio. He'd had one in almost every city and they'd each served as a sparse base of operations for his increasingly ambitious projects.

He opened one of the storage containers and rummaged through his souvenir collection. He'd once carefully organized it with each item neatly filed away with tags marking the names, places, and dates to which the objects belonged. It was no longer necessary; he easily remembered all the information for each souvenir.

He pulled out a bright red baseball cap that had belonged to David Schneer of Connecticut. The poor fool had hardly put up a fight, not that it would have done him any good. Apparently Schneer wore the cap often, based on the fact that he was wearing it in almost all of the photos of him that appeared in the media in the years since his death.

Perfect, Zachary thought. He wanted the cap to be quickly and easily recognized when it made its dramatic reappearance on the head of his next victim here in San Diego.

Because this wasn't going to be just any victim.

Zachary smiled. No, this one would shake Kendra Michaels to her very core.

CHAPTER 10

No sooner had the words "clean bill of health" been spoken by the doctor than Kendra saw a petite, well-dressed blond woman standing in the doorway of her hospital room. She assumed it was a staff member, but when the doctor left, the woman entered the room with a chrome foldable cart adorned with the Nordstrom department store logo.

"Good morning, Dr. Michaels. May I come in?"

"Uh, sure." Kendra eyed the cart. "Unless you're here to try and sell me something."

The woman laughed and handed Kendra her card. "Oh, no. I'm Darlene Wagner, personal shopping representative with Nordstorm University City. How are you today?"

Kendra stared at the card, then back up at Darlene's smiling face. "Fine, according to the doctor."

Darlene bent over and unloaded several pieces of clothing from her cart. There were at least half a dozen blouses, three pairs of slacks, and several boxes of shoes.

Kendra wrinkled her brow. "I don't know if you heard me, but I'm really not interested in buying anything."

Darlene was still smiling. "Oh, it's already bought and paid for. No need to worry about that."

"*Who* bought and paid for it?"

"Mr. Lynch, of course." Darlene held up a dark blue sweater. "This one will be wonderful with your coloring."

Kendra looked at her in disbelief. "It's 7:20 A.M. When did all this happen?"

"I received a text from Mr. Lynch at a little after 5 A.M. He wanted clothes for both of you brought here as soon as possible. He gave me your sizes."

"You picked these up from Nordstrom . . . at 5 A.M.?"

"More like 5:30 by the time I dressed and got over there." Darlene draped the clothes across the foot of the bed and on a tray table. "I've been Mr. Lynch's Nordstrom personal shopping assistant for years. He's a very good customer. We try to be accommodating. I've already been up to his room, and he was very happy with what I brought for him."

"Nice to hear," she said dryly. "We wouldn't want Lynch to be unhappy."

Darlene picked up a tee shirt. "It'll be a bit cool today, you might want to consider wearing the sweater over this white tee shirt. I think it'll look smart with this pair of khakis." She frowned consideringly. "And how would you feel about a pair of Kate Spade tennis shoes?"

• • •

Twenty minutes later, Kendra walked across the hospital lobby to where Lynch stood in the waiting area. He wore a smart tweed jacket and gray slacks that looked as if they had been custom-tailored for him.

Kendra nodded in approval. "Darlene did well for you."

"She knows what I like. I hope you don't mind me taking the liberty of getting a few things for you."

She raised the two stuffed bags of new clothes she was carrying. "I can only wear one outfit at a time, you know."

He shrugged. "I wanted you to have a choice."

"We *could* have gotten something from my condo."

"This way we can hit the ground running. And I wanted to whisk you out of here before Homeland Security could make an appearance this morning. That head nurse was bristling with disapproval when we decided to return to the hospital last night."

"Well, thank you. Good old Lynch. High impact as always."

"I wouldn't want to disappoint you. Though your referring to me as old does not please me." He motioned toward the doors. "Shall we go? I take it that you've been officially dismissed, and they won't put a bounty on us? Want to go see if the techs at the FBI garage have found anything?"

"Maybe later."

He raised a brow. "Got a better idea?"

"I just got my phone back, and there was an interesting text waiting for me." She went ahead of him through the doors. "We need to go see Jessie Mercado."

Lynch pulled into the beach parking lot in Carlsbad just twenty minutes north of the city. Kendra climbed out of the car and glanced around.

"Any sign of her?" Lynch said.

Kendra pointed to the Harley-Davidson parked at the end of the lot. "Well, that's her motorcycle. And if I know Jessie, she'd try not to park it anywhere she couldn't keep an eye on it."

Lynch grimaced. "I still don't know why we had to meet her here."

"She said she had a special reason." Kendra pointed to a beachside café where Jessie, seated at an outdoor table, was waving at them.

They walked across a strip of sand to the café where Jessie motioned for them to sit. Her short dark hair was windblown and she wore a pair of John Lennon-style sunglasses with small round lenses.

"Why did it take you so long to answer my messages and texts?" she asked, annoyed.

"Long story," Kendra said.

"I like long stories."

"Another time. But I will tell you that we both spent the night in the hospital and that my phone was being disinfected. Hopefully that passes for a decent excuse."

Jessie slid her sunglasses down to the end of her nose and peered over them. "You aren't joking."

"Nope."

"Intriguing." She slid her sunglasses back up. "I guess that works. I still want that story sometime."

"You'll get it. Right now I want *your* story."

Jessie nodded. "I'm much more interested in me now anyway. I find everything I am and do riveting. Has the name Schuyler Hagstrom come up in your investigation?"

"As a possible suspect?"

"Or even just as a person of interest. Anything."

Kendra thought. "No, I'm sure I would have remembered that name."

"And I'm positive I didn't see that name in any of the case files," Lynch said.

Kendra leaned forward. "Who is he?"

"He may be your killer." She waved at the waitress. "Would you guys like to order something?"

Kendra stared at her in disbelief. "No. I believe I'd rather hear about our killer."

"Suit yourself." Jessie asked for a refill of her

iced tea and turned back to Kendra and Lynch. "Remember, it was totally your idea, Kendra, looking at military personnel who happened to be in each of those cities while the murders took place."

"You told me there weren't any."

"There aren't. But I had my source broaden the net to look at civilian support personnel. A fair amount of people who work on these bases aren't military at all. It took a lot more digging, but he came up with a name."

"Schuyler Hagstrom," Kendra said.

"Yes. He's a data network specialist. Civilian contractor. He's worked in each of those bases you asked me to check at time spans that matched each of the murder cases."

Kendra gave Lynch a hopeful glance before turning back to Jessie. "So what do we know about him?"

"Not a lot. I haven't had time to do an in-depth background check. I didn't even know the guy existed until late last night." She reached inside her leather jacket and pulled out a sheaf of papers folded length-wise. "But here's some general background: Schuyler Keith Hagstrom, age thirty-eight. He was born in Kennett Square, Pennsylvania. His parents never married, and his mother died when he was in his late teens. He went to a vocational school in Cherry Hill, New Jersey. Soon after that, he started working for

Allied Systems, which is one of several companies charged with upgrading and maintaining network infrastructure in U.S. military bases. His job took him to Connecticut, Florida, Virginia, Ventura County, Northern California, and finally here."

Lynch picked up the sheaf of papers and scanned them. "Impressive for just a few hours' work."

Jessie shrugged. "It's what I do."

"Does he have a wife? Kids?"

"No, never married."

"I don't suppose you can tell us what kind of car he drives."

"A Chevy Suburban."

Kendra took a deep breath. "What color?"

"White."

Lynch leaned back. "Promising."

"Is it?" Jessie asked.

Kendra nodded. "We've had some indication that Zachary may drive a white SUV."

Jessie nodded toward the street. "Like that one over there?"

Kendra and Lynch turned. A white Chevy Suburban was parked about half a block down from the café.

Kendra turned back. "Are you telling me . . . ?"

"It's his. I've already checked the license plate. He lives in that tan stucco condo at the end of the block." She nodded at the sheaf of papers. "You're holding the address in your hands." Her dark eyes glinted with mischief. "Does it feel hot to the touch?"

"Maybe." Kendra smiled. "So *that's* why we're here."

"He's home now. I'm not sure what you want to do with that information."

Lynch glanced over at the apartment building. "Even if that is his car, how are you sure that he's home?"

"Because I've seen him."

"When?" Kendra asked.

Jessie took a swig of her iced tea. "He left his condo about forty-five minutes ago. He bought some pastry from that bakery on the corner, got a manual of some kind from his car, then went back into his condo. He looked like he was dressed for work, so I'd expect him to be on the move soon."

Kendra consulted the papers in front of her. "On the move to NAB Coronado?"

"That's where he works. But if he's who we think he is, I'm not comfortable letting him out of my sight for even a minute."

Kendra nodded. "That makes two of us."

"I'll tail him and make sure he goes to his job. That'll give you and the Feds time to figure out how you want to handle him. I don't have a lot experience with this sort of thing, but I imagine there is some advantage to just watching him for a while."

"Especially since we can't hold him," Kendra

said. "It's not enough that he lived in close proximity to these murders, but it does give us a good start."

"True," Jessie said. "And a reasonable judge might consider it probable cause for a search warrant."

Kendra lifted her phone. "I'll call Griffin and see how he wants to play it."

Jessie suddenly slouched in her seat. "Am I right to believe this killer knows you?"

"I know he does."

"Then don't turn around for the next minute or so. That goes for you too, pretty boy. We don't want to tip him off."

"Pretty boy?" Lynch murmured distastefully.

Kendra froze. "He's outside?"

"Yep. And heading for his car. He's almost there." Jessie kept her head low as she watched him. "He doesn't seem jittery. He's not looking over his shoulder, not checking to see if he's being watched."

"That's common," Kendra said. "Serial killers often think they're too good to be caught."

Jessie reached under her chair for her helmet. "Okay, I'm going after him. I'll call when he gets where he's going. Maybe by then you guys can figure out what you want to do with him."

Jessie sprinted across the sand to her motorcycle and started it up. She revved it and hit the street a couple of blocks behind Hagstrom's

251

SUV. After a hundred yards or so, she abruptly turned at a cross street.

"She's good," Lynch said. "She's mixing it up, tailing him from parallel streets so he doesn't catch on."

"Not good. She's the best. There's no way she'll lose him." Kendra punched Griffin's number and he answered immediately.

"You're supposed to be resting, Kendra."

"That's over. The hospital cut us loose. We're golden."

"I'll call and confirm that, you know."

"Go ahead. But first I need you to tell me what you can find out about Schuyler Hagstrom. He lives in Carlsbad."

"Who is he?"

"A possible suspect. His residential history lines up with the time and place of each series of murders."

"How in the hell did you find that out before we did?"

"A friend in low places. She's on his tail as we speak, following him to his job at NAB Coronado. After that, she's out. You'd better figure out how you want to handle this."

"Hmm. I'll see. Let me do some digging."

"Would his social security number help?"

He chuckled. "Maybe a little. Give it to me."

She read the number from a page Jessie had given her.

"Okay, I'll run this and see what turns up. We'll probably pay him a visit and talk to him."

Probably? The casualness of the answer annoyed the hell out of her. "When?"

"Depends what we find out. I'll keep you posted."

"Yeah, you do that." Kendra cut the connection.

"Wishing you were on the back of Jessie's Harley?" Lynch asked.

"It's looking very attractive at this particular moment." She grimaced. "Jessie doesn't know the meaning of the words 'probably' or 'depends.' She just goes for it."

"And that appeals to you."

"Does that surprise you?"

"No, it's part of the Kendra I'm trying to encourage at all cost. I enjoy every aspect of you, but I'm much more likely to end up in bed with that Kendra." He smiled. "And that's exactly where I want to be. So by all means, go for it."

She could feel the heat move through her, the tingle of the pulse throbbing at her wrists, the faint vibration of Lynch's breathing as he sat watching her.

An erotic sensation out of nowhere.

She pulled her gaze away from him. "But the reasonable Kendra tends to get more things done in situations like this." She pushed back her chair. "And Jessie has run off and left me so I'd better just let her have her fun and go back to the FBI office and nag Griffin into getting us what we need."

"As you like." He got to his feet and left some bills on the table. "But I detect a thread of envy in your tone. Do you really think Jessie is having that much fun?"

Kendra had a vision of that last moment when she'd seen Jessie tearing down the street, her hair flying, the sunlight on her bike. Kendra was remembering those times when she'd experienced that same heady feeling of being one with her bike, one with life itself. "Yes, I really do think Jessie is having that much fun." She sighed. "And I'd just as soon you not remind me, Lynch."

Shit-shit-shit-shit-shit!

Jessie swung her motorcycle hard right and jumped onto the sidewalk.

A road construction crew coupled with a dumber-than-hell UPS driver had thrown a serious wrench into her efforts to tail Hagstrom. She needed to cross back to Cassidy Road in time to make sure that he was veering onto the I-5 South as expected.

Time was running out. And so was this damned sidewalk.

She veered around an elderly man and turned down what she hoped was an alley.

Yes!

She roared down the narrow alley, her

motorcycle engine deafening as it echoed against the brick and plaster walls.

Her back wheel spun out as she turned onto Cassidy Road.

Was Hagstrom still . . . ?

There he was, blinker flashing, about to turn onto the I-5 entrance ramp.

As expected.

She eased off the throttle, keeping her distance as he took the onramp. She followed thirty seconds later.

Traffic on the I-5 was heavy. No surprise there. Normally she'd zip between the cars in a way that always terrified her out-of-state friends, but she hung back, keeping an eye on Hagstrom's white Suburban as it poked along.

Hmm. Was this how serial killers drove?

She'd long ago given up trying to equate driving styles with what she knew about the people she tailed. As far as she could tell, corporate embezzlers, cheating spouses, and bail jumpers drove no differently than abusive assholes who beat their wives.

Or, apparently, serial killers. The guy had already politely let two cars merge in front of him.

A well-mannered psychopath. Wonderful.

She followed him downtown past the airport, keeping about a half mile between them. In another few yards, he would take the interchange toward the Coronado Bridge, and then—

What in the hell?

He'd abruptly moved into the fast lane, away from the turnoff.

Had he spotted her? Was this a test to see if she'd follow his last-minute maneuver?

She slowed and stayed in her lane, watching as he sped around the freeway's bend.

He sure as hell wasn't watching her.

She swerved left and put on speed until he was once again within sight.

His head was now bobbing and his mouth was moving. Was he singing along to a favorite song? Cursing a caller on talk radio?

Neither, she decided. He was talking on the phone.

He exited onto Division Street, and she followed him through an industrial neighborhood that she remembered was called Shelltown, named for an abundance of shells in the area's soft, sandy soil.

Not that there was any soil to be seen in this concrete jungle. Where was he going?

The traffic thinned to almost nothing, making it difficult for her to follow without being spotted. She put more distance between them.

Hagstrom drove past a machine shop and turned onto a street populated by narrow one-story houses.

Jessie pulled behind a stopped truck and watched as he parked on the street and climbed out of his car. For the first time, he looked nervous. Edgy. He glanced around.

She leaned behind the truck to avoid being seen.

He walked between two of the houses and opened a rusty metal gate and walked through to the backyard.

Shit. Jessie hit the kickstand and jumped off her bike. She ran to a gate two houses down and tried it. Locked. She gripped the top of the fence and swung her legs over. She crouched and moved along the yard's tall bushes until she could see, two yards over, Hagstrom on the elevated porch. He was still casting furtive glances around.

Afraid of something, buddy?

The back door opened a crack. But only a crack. Hagstrom slid inside and closed the door behind him.

Jessie stood up straight. Okay, that was weird, but not necessarily murderous. She pulled out her phone and snapped a photo of the back of the house.

What now? Just wait around and see if he notched another victim on his knife handle?

It wasn't like she could just barge inside, especially without any proof of wrongdoing. And any such attempt would only tip him off to the fact that he was now under scrutiny.

Well, if she couldn't go inside, at least she could get closer.

She hopped the two fences that separated her from the house Hagstrom was visiting. She moved from window to window, trying to see around the blinds that covered each opening.

Sealed up tight.

She rounded the corner and moved down the side, checking more windows until she found one with an out-of-skew vertical blind. She leaned close and peered inside.

It was dark inside. She appeared to be looking at a small bedroom, furnished with an unmade bed, a small table, and two straight-backed chairs.

The wooden door was open, but she saw nothing beyond.

Wait. There *was* something . . .

Movement.

Was that . . . ?

"Hey!" A strong voice yelled from behind her.

She spun around. It was a large man, late-thirties, wearing a threadbare black tee shirt that read, in fiery letters, hell is where i bury you.

He was coming from the backyard, and he was holding a club.

Jessie was still staring at the shirt's lettering. "A little obvious, don't you think?"

He raised the club menacingly. "Keep your hands where I can see 'em."

She raised her hands and wiggled her fingers.

The guy was getting closer by the second. If

she was going to make a break for it, she needed to—

"Got her covered, Eddie?"

Oh shit. Another voice, this one from the street side. She turned and saw another man even bigger than the first. He had tattoos covering both arms.

She was now boxed in.

"Yeah," Eddie said. "And thanks for telling her my name, dickhead."

Jessie cocked her head toward the tattooed guy. "Great. Now I know *his* name. Would that be Mister Dickhead or just plain ol' Dickhead?"

Neither of the men smiled.

She shrugged. "Come on, that was a *little* funny."

Eddie slapped the club into his palm. "You need a warrant to be poking around on private property. I don't suppose you have one of those."

She wrinkled her nose. "A warrant? You think I'm a cop?"

At that moment, a third man appeared from the backyard, pulling Hagstrom along with him. The man wore a scowl and a bushy beard.

Jessie shook her head. This was getting worse by the minute.

The bearded guy shoved Hagstrom against the wall of the house. "Who in the hell is she?"

Hagstrom looked genuinely rattled. "I . . . I don't know."

"Bullshit!"

"I've never seen her before in my life."

"You're lying."

Hagstrom looked pleadingly toward Jessie. "Tell him. We've never met."

Jessie quickly studied Hagstrom. As he stood there trembling, she found it difficult to believe that this could be a psychopathic killer who'd murdered over two dozen people.

"Tell him!" Hagstrom begged.

She nodded. "He's telling the truth. We've never met."

The bearded guy punched Hagstrom in the stomach. "I don't believe you. Either you're narcs or you're here to rip me off."

Hagstrom doubled over in pain. "No," he wheezed. "I promise, I just came here to do some business."

Jessie closed her eyes. Of course. Hagstrom was just here for a drug buy. Shit.

The bearded guy turned toward Jessie. He was clearly the leader; his other two men looked to him for guidance. "You expect me to believe it's a coincidence she turned up at the exact same moment you did?"

She shrugged. "I just came here to try and score some Adam. I wanted to scope the place out and see what I was getting myself into."

The bearded man glared at her. "What makes you think you can get ecstasy here?"

"A guy I met at a club said you could hook me up."

"*What* guy?"

"A tall skinny guy with longish hair. His friends call him Chewie."

"Doesn't sound like anybody I know."

"He said he knew about you. Or at least this house."

Hagstrom tried to stand straight, but he was obviously still reeling from the punch to his midsection. "Look, I don't know why this woman's here. But I'm telling you, she's got nothing to do with me. You three got a problem, take it up with her. I need to get to work."

The bearded guy shook his head. "Oh, we're way beyond that."

Jessie took a moment to try and size up her opponents. Of the three, Eddie looked like the one most likely to run like hell when the shit hit the fan. The other two would be another matter entirely.

He looked over at his tattooed friend. "See anyone else on the street?"

"No. No one. All clear."

"Okay, at least that's something. We'll take them inside and sort this out." He grabbed Hagstrom and pushed him roughly toward the backyard.

Jessie adjusted her jacket. "I won't be going in there with you. That would be really stupid."

The three men looked at each other. The bearded guy chuckled. "The choice isn't yours, little lady."

Jessie flexed her arms and stepped back to keep all three men in her line of vision. But then there was also Hagstrom, who was still a wild card.

Three tough guy drug dealers and a possible psychopathic killer. Oh, what a beautiful morning.

The bearded guy nodded at Eddie and Dickhead.

Jessie half-smiled. "I like the dumb little nod. Was that your clever 'okay boys, grab her!' signal?"

Eddie and Dickhead rushed her and she whirled around with a bullet kick to Dickhead's face.

He went down. Hard. Blood splattered where his face hit the sidewalk.

Eddie leaped over his fallen comrade, but she grabbed his jacket collar and slammed his head onto the pavement.

Both men tried to stand, but she grabbed each by their hair and slammed their heads together.

Lights out.

The bearded guy looped his arm around Hagstrom's neck in a choke hold. "Okay, lady. Come with me or else I'll snap this guy like a twig."

She sighed. "Again. We're not cops and I don't know this guy."

He tightened his grip. "Then you wouldn't mind if I broke his neck."

"Well, that's not something I really want to see happen to anyone." She looked down at the two unconscious men. "Except to these guys. Or you, maybe."

She looked at Hagstrom. His eyes suddenly went cold.

Dead, even.

The tension left his face.

Chilling.

If you have some homicidal skills, buddy, it might be time to break them out.

But Hagstrom did nothing. He stood motionless with that creepy look on his face.

What the hell to do? Just do *something*. In a blur, Jessie grabbed the bearded guy's fingers and wrenched them backwards.

Pop-pop-pop-pop!

She broke four fingers of his right hand.

He howled in pain. As he recoiled, Jesse grabbed Hagstrom and pulled him toward her.

"Move! You're coming with me."

Hagstrom was still in his odd trance. "Who are you?"

"We'll exchange LinkedIn invites later. Come on."

She pulled him down the narrow opening between houses and emerged in the front yard.

BLAMM!

She turned to see that the bearded guy was now unsteadily holding a gun in his left hand.

BLAMM!

He fired again.

She grabbed Hagstrom and pulled him behind a parked jeep. "Where's your car?"

He pointed to his SUV on the other side of the gun-waving drug dealer. "There."

"No good. Shit. Okay, follow me. We're riding out of here on my bike."

"What?"

"Stay behind the cars. My motorcycle is parked about three spots back."

Jessie poked her head up and looked through the car windows at her injured attacker. He was still nursing his bloody and broken fingers even as he held the gun in front of him.

"Now!" Jessie whispered. She ducked and ran for her motorcycle. She cast a quick glance back to make sure Hagstrom was following her. He was.

Was she really about to give a lift to a suspected psychotic killer?

It seemed she was.

BLAMM!

The driver's-side window shattered on a car as they ran past.

Jessie jumped on her motorcycle and Hagstrom hopped on the seat behind her. She started it up and turned hard right to ride away on the sidewalk, using the parked cars to shield them from more gunshots.

BLAMM! BLAMM!

They roared around the corner and Jessie sped away as fast as her bike could take them.

She angled her mirrors to keep a close watch on her passenger. There hadn't been time to frisk him, but if it looked like he was about to go for a weapon, she was ready to send him flying.

But what in the hell was she going to do with him?

Not her call.

She unhooked her helmet from the console and popped it on.

"Do you have a helmet for me?" Hagstrom shouted over the wind and engine noise.

"No. You're a purely unexpected guest. Live with it."

Jessie tapped the switch that turned on the Bluetooth headset built into her helmet.

She voice-dialed the name of someone who she knew wouldn't be happy to hear from her.

"Hi," Kendra answered. "Having fun? Is everything okay?"

"Depends on your definition of 'okay.' Where are you?"

"Lynch and I are heading to the FBI field office. Griffin was not helpful. We're still waiting to see what they want to do with Hagstrom. You haven't lost him, have you?"

Jessie cast a wary glance at the man sharing her motorcycle seat. "No, though you might wish I had."

"What does *that* mean?"

"It means our options have suddenly narrowed quite a bit. Hagstrom and I are on our way to the field office."

"What?" Kendra practically yelled her response.

"Get your ducks in a row. I'm bringing Hagstrom in. We'll meet you in fifteen minutes."

CHAPTER 11

"What am I doing here?" Hagstrom asked as two agents helped him off Jessie's motorcycle and pushed him toward the front entrance where Lynch was holding open the door. "The FBI? I didn't do anything." He jerked his head back at Jessie. "She was the one who was causing all the trouble." He glared at her. "She almost got me killed. You ought to arrest her."

"You were eager enough to jump on the back of my bike," Jessie said as she got off to stand beside Kendra. "That's called a rescue, not an assault."

"You broke that guy's fingers," he shouted back to her. "He'll be looking for me as well as you."

"Then you'd better tell these agents something interesting enough to make them want to protect you." She turned back to Kendra as Hagstrom disappeared inside the building with the agents and Lynch. "Not exactly brimming with gratitude, is he? It got pretty rough toward the end, he could have bought it." She wrinkled her nose. "Though he's right, I was definitely a contributing factor. We were all caught off guard and reacted accordingly."

"And you broke fingers and indulged in other sundry violence?"

"It seemed to be the thing to do at the time." She got back on her motorcycle. "I'll phone and tell you all about it while I'm riding back to my office. I suppose you're going to take over Hagstrom's interrogation?"

"Probably not. He's being taken upstairs to be grilled by one or all of those detectives in Zachary's fan club. I tend to be a bystander while they vie for attention."

"And you don't like it."

"I want Zachary caught."

"But not stand by and wait for someone else to do it." Jessie met her eyes. "Griffin's nuts to let those clowns have center stage. He's going to lose you."

"Zachary has to be caught. Any way that we can make it happen." She shrugged. "And it gives me time to keep my commitments to my kids. I have phone calls to make, therapies to plan. It's not as if I haven't plenty of appointments that aren't just as important as questioning Hagstrom."

Jessie shook her head. "He's going to lose you," she repeated. "Though I agree Hagstrom might not be worth your while. I was going back and forth about Hagstrom's potential while I was with him."

"No?" Her gaze narrowed on Jessie's face. "Why?"

"The drug connection. He didn't seem to be strong or clever enough to be Zachary. Yet his background is really promising. Though he could be one of Zachary's dupes or followers or something. There was something about him . . ."

"What do you mean?"

"Dead eyes."

"What?"

"There was a moment or two when he gave me the creeps. But then it was gone, and he was just an ordinary dirt bag. But maybe you should watch him and see if you see what I saw."

"I will. I just wanted to know your take on him. I'm going up to the interview room after you leave and see if those ace detectives can detect those dead eyes, too."

"Fine. Are you going to need me anymore right now?"

"Not unless you can dredge up anything more on Hagstrom that won't put you in the crosshairs."

"I'll work on it. Call you from the road." She roared out of the parking lot.

Kendra smiled as she watched her disappear from view. Then she turned and headed for the front entrance. The dream team would probably be congregating eagerly and heaven forbid she not be on time for the show. They weren't really her companions of choice, but she was trying to cooperate.

Then her smile faded and then disappeared. It wasn't really all that amusing.

Dead eyes . . .

• • •

"I have rights, you know."

Hagstrom was alone in Interview Room #1, the largest of the eight interview rooms in the FBI field office's third floor. This one featured a one-way glass at the end of the room. The interview area was designed to accommodate a small group, but that spaciousness didn't extend to the observation room, where Kendra, Lynch, Metcalf, Gina, and the four dream team members were cramped together.

Hagstrom called out to them through the glass. "I didn't have anything incriminating on me. Nothing at all. Should I call a lawyer?"

"The 'L' word," Metcalf said. "He's starting to get pissed off."

Kendra studied him. Hagstrom didn't possess the icy cool of most serial killers she'd encountered, but she knew they came in all shapes and sizes. He'd said little since Jessie brought him to the field office and he'd been escorted to the interview room.

"He thinks he's here on a narcotics charge," Kendra said. "Jessie says he was trying to score something when she picked him up."

Richard Gale turned sharply toward her. "I wish to hell your friend had just let him make his buy and let us do our jobs."

"She would have preferred that, believe me. The situation got out of control. He might have gotten killed."

Gale smiled. "Even better."

Roscoe shook his head. "And we wonder why people are suspicious of law enforcement."

Griffin walked into the already crowded observation room holding the sheaf of papers Jessie had provided, along with a few more printouts. "Okay, we ran Hagstrom's police record. He's pretty clean. He and an ex-girlfriend took out restraining orders on each other a few years back, but they were dropped and the complaints never made it to court. Other than that, there's nothing. We'll have a tough time getting any kind of warrant based on what we have now."

"What do we have on the guy who he was visiting?" Lynch asked.

Griffin looked at his printout. "The house belongs to Warren Goyer. Small-time drug dealer. Jessie Mercado says he shot at her and Hagstrom. Just the fact that he had a gun in his hand would be a parole violation that could land him back in prison for another ten years."

Arnold Huston looked at Hagstrom through the glass. "Let me talk to him."

Griffin thought for a moment. "Think you could push him for a vehicle and domicile search?

Huston shrugged. "I can try. In any case, his reaction might be helpful to us."

"He's not restrained. If you push him, he might

271

erupt. You want to take Metcalf in there with you?"

Huston smiled. "Nah, I can take care of myself. And if he manages to sink his teeth into my jugular, you good people are only a few steps away, right?"

Huston took the sheaf of papers from Griffin and left the room.

The group turned toward the window. Huston entered the interview room from a side door a few seconds later, still holding the sheaf of papers. He tossed the papers onto the table and sat down across from Hagstrom.

"Hell of a mornin', huh?" Huston's voice had dropped to a folksy purr.

"You got nothing on me," Hagstrom said belligerently.

"Then I guess that was a social call you were making this morning?"

"Maybe it was."

"Come on, now. We both know why you were there."

"You don't know anything."

Huston shrugged. "I know I'm in a position to help you."

Kendra watched Huston as he slouched slightly in his chair. He used his voice and his entire body as finely-tuned instruments, working to build trust in the man across the table. Every dropped 'g,' every casual lean, was designed to encourage

Hagstrom to relax and lower his defenses. No wonder his interview skills were so highly regarded.

Hagstrom snorted. "How in the hell are you going to help me? I'm not getting a whole lot of help here."

"Sure you are. You'd be dead on the street if we hadn't pulled you out of there when we did."

"It was your agent, or whoever she was, who got me in trouble in the first place."

"No, your trouble started when you visited Warren Goyer."

"Who?"

Huston looked down at the printouts in front of him. "You may know him as Baby G."

Recognition flashed across Hagstrom's face.

"Funny thing is, we don't give a damn about you. Think about it. Do you really think the Federal Bureau of Investigation cares about some two-bit user?"

"Then why am I here?"

"You were in the wrong place at the wrong time, my friend."

"Tell me about it."

Huston smiled. "Some of the people on the other side of that glass think maybe you're working for Baby G."

Hagstrom's eyes bulged. *"What?"*

"That's not a denial."

"Here's your denial." Hagstrom turned toward

the window. "I've never sold drugs. Never in my life, ever. I don't work for that guy. That's not what I do. I have a good job."

"Then why in the hell were you on that street?"

"You don't have anything on me."

Huston stared at him. "Maybe not yet, but your association with a known drug dealer will give us grounds for a search warrant. What if we search your home? Or your car? We can have a warrant in hand by early afternoon."

Hagstrom's face fell. "Shit."

"My associates think we're going to find something that proves you're dealing. And you're not doing much to convince me otherwise."

"You won't find anything."

"If you're right about that, by the end of the day you won't be our problem."

"Go ahead and look."

Huston cocked an eyebrow. "Are you granting us permission to search your home and car?"

"If it'll get me out of here faster, sure."

On the other side of the glass, Lynch spoke quietly. "Huston is making him think we're only interested in a drug charge. Good tactic."

Kendra shot Lynch a look. "High praise from the Puppetmaster."

"I told you I don't like that name."

"I guess that's why I enjoy saying it so much," she murmured.

They turned back toward the interview room,

where Hagstrom was now projecting greater confidence. "I'm telling you, you won't find weed, pills, powder, or anything else."

Huston turned back toward the window. "You're being recorded. Do we have your express permission to search your home and car?"

"Knock yourselves out."

"Yes or no, please."

"You have my permission to search my home and car. But I'd appreciate it if you could tow my car from the street where I parked it. It's on Baby G's block, and the last time I saw him, he was trying to kill me."

"Trust me, we'll make life very difficult for your drug dealer. And we'll bring your car in." Huston stood. "Sit tight. I'll check back with you."

Huston exited the room and reentered the observation area.

Griffin gave him a respectful nod. "You got permission for a search. Well done."

Huston bit his lip. "Yeah."

"What's wrong?" Kendra said.

"Didn't feel right."

"Why not?"

Huston thought for a moment. "Anyone else think he consented to that search too easily?"

"You were convincing," Lynch said. "You made him think we're only interested in drug crimes."

"Even so. Shouldn't there have been a little more hesitancy? A few seconds' pause?"

"Not necessarily," Trey Suber said. "If this is Zachary, he's probably been planning for exactly such an incursion for years. He thinks he's taken every precaution. He may be thrilled it's finally happening."

A flash of annoyance crossed Huston's usually kindly face. "I don't need your Serial Killer 101 tutorial, Suber. I'm well aware of the narcissistic serial killer personality profile."

Suber didn't look bothered by Huston's cutting remark—to the contrary, Kendra noticed that he seemed pleased to have provoked such a strong response. Suber was smirking as he stepped toward Huston.

Griffin cut in before Suber could say anything. "The point is, we got the okay to search Hagstrom's house and car. Let's do it and see where we stand. Okay?"

Suber nodded. "Sounds like a plan."

Metcalf nodded toward Hagstrom. "In the meantime, what do we do with him?"

"He stays here," Griffin said. "At least until our search is finished." He turned to Kendra. "I'd like you to be there with us when we look his place over."

She nodded. "Sure."

Griffin addressed the other occupants of the cramped room. "I don't want to give him a chance to change his mind. We're going in as soon as we can. I'm bringing in an evidence response team to lift prints, swab for DNA, and pick up whatever else they can." He checked his watch. "Okay, we'll meet downstairs in five. Let's move."

In forty minutes, the group was assembled in front of Hagstrom's condo in Carlsbad, accompanied by two ERT vans. They waited on the sidewalk outside while Griffin allowed the videographer and forensic specialists to make their initial sweep.

Trey Suber walked up to Kendra and Lynch. "These situations always remind me of the Aurora theater shooter."

"I'm almost afraid to ask," Lynch said.

Suber pushed up his glasses. "He was the shooter who mowed down those people in that movie theater. He booby-trapped his house with explosives rigged to detonate in case law enforcement caught on to him and raided his place."

"Charming thought," Kendra said. "Surely the people going in here are being cautious."

"I wouldn't bet on it. You've been part of several serial killer investigations, Dr. Michaels. How many agents have you seen taking time to look for door triggers or tripwires?"

"Somewhere around . . . none."

"Exactly. A booby-trapped home is still an incredibly rare serial killer phenomenon, of course." He smiled cheerfully. "But it would only take one to ruin your day."

"I can see that. Thanks for putting yet another terrifying thought into my head, Suber."

"Happy to help."

She spotted Metcalf standing alone a few yards away. She turned back to Suber. "I need to talk to Metcalf for a minute. Tell you what, why don't you fill Mr. Lynch in on the details of the bomb-making theater killer. Would you do that?"

His smile became even wider. "Sure. Delighted."

Lynch gave her a desperate glance. "Uh, are you sure you don't need me with you over there . . . ?"

She smiled. "Not in the slightest. Have fun."

While Suber reeled off facts and figures, Kendra approached Metcalf.

"What's going on, Metcalf?"

He tensed. "What's *that* supposed to mean?"

"Jeez, touchy much?"

"Whenever Kendra Michaels asks me what's going on, it usually means she knows *exactly* what's going on. And it's almost always something that will cause me a great deal of discomfort."

"You're being silly."

"Am I?"

"Yes." Kendra lowered her voice. "Unless you feel awkward about sleeping with your fellow FBI agent."

"Dammit."

Her lips turned up at the corners. "I told you that you and Gina would make a good couple."

He glanced around to make sure no one could hear them. "How in the hell did you know?"

"You're wearing the same clothes you wore yesterday."

"So? I've often worn the same suit two days in a row."

"But today, for the first time I can recall, you smell of 50:50 shampoo, moisturizing body wash, and bar soap, all made by Giovanni. Either you've suddenly become incredibly brand loyal or you got ready for work at a hotel this morning. Gina's hotel. I told you I've known people who've stayed there. I know Giovanni is their house toiletry brand."

"Shit."

Kendra smiled. "And how's it going?"

Metcalf sighed. He still looked uncomfortable discussing it, but he continued. "Good. You were right about her. She's not as tough as she seemed at first. We have fun together."

"I'm glad. I'm happy for you, Metcalf."

"Hey, it's not like we're getting married or anything."

"I know. But it's still nice to see you make a connection with someone."

Gina Carson walked toward them. "Griffin says the ERT is almost finished with their sweep.

We'll be inside within the next couple of minutes."

Kendra nodded. "That's good." She glanced at her watch. "Because I have to be out of here in another forty. I have an appointment."

Gina looked at her, shocked. "Can't you cancel it? This is a very strong lead. It may change the entire direction of the case. Griffin thinks he needs you."

"And he's got me. For the next forty minutes. But unless we find either a body or Zachary inside that house, I'm going to keep my appointment. I've committed too much of my time as it is to this hunt. I told you when I began that it's not the only thing that's important to me. Griffin has an entire dream team to analyze any evidence he finds hidden in there." She grimaced. "Or not. And I've put a child on hold too long who doesn't have a team to tell him whether I'm doing the right thing for him. He just has to trust me."

She frowned. "I still think you could postpone—"

"You're not too certain that Hagstrom is our man, are you?" Metcalf interrupted, his gaze narrowed on Kendra's face. "You agree with Huston?"

"I'm not certain about anything without firm evidence. Maybe we'll find it in that house." She shrugged. "I do believe that Zachary is capable of setting up a scenario to lead us away from him or just to make fools of us. Could Hagstrom be a key figure? We'll have to find out. Is he Zachary? He could be. Merely because I'd judge Zachary to be a master actor and Hagstrom isn't projecting any of the chilling vibes you'd expect from a totally merciless serial killer."

"What do you think?" Metcalf asked softly. "Guess."

"I've told you what I think. Stop pushing me." She turned to Gina and smiled. "You'll learn he can be a real pain in the ass. But most of the time he's worth it. Just hang in there."

Gina flushed. "I've always found Agent Metcalf to be thorough and competent at whatever he does."

"I'm sure you have," Kendra said solemnly. "And I'm sure with time and experience your confidence in him will continue to grow. That should make it very exciting for you." She turned away and headed for the house. "See you inside."

"She *knows,*" Gina hissed to Metcalf behind her. "Dammit, you told her. I can tell. How could you do that?"

"I didn't tell her. Exactly. It was the hotel shampoo and body wash. Besides, she's not going to tell anyone. I can't even guess how many secrets Kendra must learn just from strolling through a room at a cocktail party."

"Not *my* secrets. Not until now. It was just little

things before, but I hate having anyone with that much power over me. And you just accept it. How can you—"

Kendra was glad that she was out of range now. It was far from the first time she had been exposed to the indignation and anger of people when she had seen or heard too much for them to be comfortable around her. But she genuinely liked Gina and she should have resisted the temptation to make any teasing comment at all. There was no telling where sensitivity began and sense of humor ended with some individuals. Evidently Gina's ended in the bedroom in both cases.

"What did you do to Gina?" Lynch murmured. He was suddenly standing beside her, his gaze on Gina and Metcalf across the yard. "She's staring daggers at you, and Metcalf is cowering like a whipped dog."

"He isn't cowering," Kendra said curtly. "He's just trying to explain why . . . actually he's defending me. And it's probably making her even angrier. So stop taking shots at him."

"Whatever you say." His gaze was on her face. "I'd hate to go to battle when Metcalf is obviously doing such a good job. Am I allowed to ask why Metcalf is having to defend you?"

"Because I'm being me," she said flatly. "And sometimes people have trouble with it. I probably would if I had a sensitive bone in my body. I just blurt out things that people would prefer to keep secret."

"I find that part of your charm."

She made a rude sound. "That's because you don't have a sensitive bone in your body, either. I just amuse you."

"Yes, you do. And if you didn't have a modicum of sensitivity, it wouldn't bother you that evidently Gina took offense that you found out she was sleeping with Metcalf."

She looked away from him. "I didn't say that."

"Please." He looked pained. "I was aware of the signs of intimacy fifteen minutes after we walked into the FBI office today. I would have known before if I hadn't been absorbed with watching Hagstrom. I might not have your in-depth ability in that area, but I can see what's in front of me. And so can any number of other detectives and agents. It's what we do for a living. You're only on the hot spot because everyone knows that you're damn good."

"And I tend to open my mouth when I shouldn't."

"That's due to the fact that you're honest and believe everyone else should be honest as well." His lips quirked. "And you have a mischievous sense of humor that surfaces occasionally. I take it that Gina didn't appreciate it."

"She has a right to her privacy."

"That I just told you I'd breached before you

got around to it. If she's lucky enough to live in your world, she'd better get used to accepting who you are." His smile faded. "Or you can send her to me for counseling. I'd be a hell of a lot better at it than Metcalf. Though I'm feeling a good deal more cordial toward him right now than I usually do." His eyes were suddenly twinkling. "I'm not sure if it's because he's jumping Gina and it takes him out of the running, or if it's because he's nobly defending you."

"I don't think how you feel about him would make any difference to Metcalf," she said dryly. "You persist in believing it's all about you. It's my opinion that matters; you just kind of dropped into this conversation."

"I agree, it's your opinion that matters. And I find it's interesting that I discovered that you do have a few random moments of doubt that you're not perfect."

"Only a few." She smiled. "And only when I like the person inspiring those doubts. Usually, I revert to how I felt years ago when I first realized that there were so many ways to identify what was going on around me."

"After your operation? Now that interests me. How did you feel then?"

"At first, I was full of wonder," she said softly, remembering that heady, exultant sensation of discovery. "Every day, every hour, was a new adventure. It wasn't that I hadn't known before how to compensate for that lack of vision by using my other senses. I just took it for granted. Then, when I could suddenly see, everything came together and it was like . . ." she searched for the right word ". . . kind of like a symphony. All the world around me was open and singing, telling me what was happening. All I had to do was reach out and study and observe and listen, and it would all come to me."

"And no one can say you didn't reach out," he said gently.

"I thought anyone would be insane not to take what was offered. I devoured it." She grimaced. "Which brought me to phase two. Because no one else seemed to understand how important it was to see everything, to hear every sound, to know what you were touching, to be *complete*. All those people who'd been given those same gifts the day they were born and had never bothered to use them in the way they should have. Too lazy? I don't know. I only know, it made me angry. I wanted to shake them."

He chuckled. "Now that's the Kendra I know."

"And then I went to phase three. Impatience." She shrugged. "I guess that's where I am right now. And why sometimes I don't care if I'm a little rude to some of Griffin's agents who drift around and just don't get it." She glanced at Gina. "And why it's hard for me to care if someone is intimidated by me because they think

I have some kind of power over them just because I pay attention."

"It's not that hard for you to care," Lynch said quietly. "That's what this is all about. I like all three phases of Kendra Michaels, and they all care. Though I'd really like to meet phase one Kendra just to compare the differences. Do you suppose you could pull her out of the mothballs and let me see all the wonder she saw?"

"Maybe someday. I think it would amuse you a little too much for me to tolerate."

"You're wrong. I'm not looking for amusement value. I think I might want to keep her around for the perfect balance."

"Haven't you been listening? The last thing I am is perfect. Ask Gina Carson."

"I've been listening. But I don't think I'll ask Gina. I'll look for someone less biased. Maybe I'll take a poll."

"Well, I can tell you at least two people who don't believe I'm perfect. One is my patient, Ryan Walker, who I'm going to see this afternoon. Most of the time I'm not sure if he's even aware I'm in the room."

"And the other?"

"Zachary." She was no longer smiling as she headed toward the front door now being opened for Griffin by a forensic tech. "Zachary wouldn't believe I'd even come close to being perfect . . . unless I was dead."

• • •

Griffin spoke to the tech at the door and then motioned to the assembled investigators. "Okay, we're on. Put on evidence gloves on the way in and try not to destroy the place, okay?"

Kendra and Lynch entered the building behind Griffin, Metcalf, Gina, and the dream team, filing past a young FBI agent whose only job seemed to consist of handing out plastic evidence gloves.

Kendra glanced around the sparsely-furnished condo, which featured hardwood floors in the kitchen and dining area and slightly outdated tan carpeting in the living room. There were no pictures on the walls.

"Not much to it," Lynch said to Kendra. "Does this tell you anything?"

She scanned the walls from floor to ceiling. "Well, it does look like the home of someone who moves around a lot and isn't in the habit of putting down roots in the places he does live."

"How brilliantly perceptive." Agent Gale smirked sarcastically. "Now I can see why you were brought in to give us a hand."

Lynch strolled over to Gale and leaned into his face. "You've done nothing on this investigation since you got here except talk trash and take up space. Unless you have something useful to contribute, try keeping your mouth shut."

Gale didn't give an inch. He smiled. "Is that an

order? Because I don't see where you fit in the chain of command around here."

"Consider it friendly advice," Lynch said softly. "Which might get considerably less friendly if you don't do as I suggest."

"Enough," Kendra said. She didn't need Lynch to defend her, and Gale had no idea who he was up against. "If you're through flinging testosterone at each other, we should take a closer look around."

Lynch stepped back toward her and murmured, "You weren't impressed by my protective instincts?"

"No, I can protect myself."

"That goes without saying. But I thought you might appreciate having someone around who's willing to beat the hell out of a patronizing dirt bag for you when the occasion demands."

"That's a little too caveman for me."

"Just putting it out there. He annoyed me."

"Obviously." Kendra walked through the tiny kitchen before circling back to the living room. "Okay, Hagstrom comes home from work every night, cooks a frozen dinner in that microwave, then eats and watches TV alone on the couch."

"I'm sure you can smell all kinds of processed foods that I could never pick up," Lynch said. "But how about the couch?"

She pointed toward the living room. "Only one side of that couch is depressed. On the arm is a faint impression of the size and shape of a dinner plate. Also on the arm are stains from about a dozen different meals. It's probably where he eats dinner every night, right in front of the TV."

Gina motioned toward the dinette set. "But the chair looks worn."

"Only on the edge. He does something else there, something that requires focus and concentration on the table." She ran her gloved fingers across the tabletop. "Something that leaves this fine metallic powder."

Metcalf stared at the dark residue. "Metallic shavings . . . Some kind of sculptor?"

"Possibly." She looked closer and smelled the shavings. "But could also come from . . ." She glanced around. "Are there guns here?"

Griffin called out from the hallway. "The advance team found four guns under the bed, plus an assortment of scopes and replacement parts. They're now on the floor of the bedroom, if you'd like to see them."

"Guns?" Roscoe said. "Zachary has never used guns before. Anywhere."

Suber nodded. "Although there is some indication he may have used a gun in Florida in the initial abduction stage of one of his killings."

Kendra was still staring at the table top. "These are barrel filings, perhaps to fit a scope. Hagstrom is a gun enthusiast."

"Like half of the other people in America,"

Lynch said. "Still, nothing to connect him to any of your killings."

Kendra and the other investigators were moving to the bedroom, where the guns and parts where displayed on a small tarp.

Roscoe crouched and inspected them. "Nothing unusual here. Barrels haven't been tampered with to disguise ballistic signatures."

Kendra glanced around. "Any knives here?"

Griffin shook his head. "Just a few in the kitchen drawer. Nothing even close to the type that would have caused the victims' stab wounds."

"Let's take a look anyway," she said.

They filed out of the room. Metcalf closed the door behind them and Kendra froze in her tracks. "Wait."

The other investigators stopped and looked at her quizzically.

Kendra pointed to Metcalf. "Open that door and close it again."

He swung open the door and pulled it shut.

"Again."

Close your eyes.

Concentrate.

Once again, he opened the door and closed it.

She looked at the others. "Did you hear that?"

"Hear what?" Griffin said.

Kendra rapped on the wall next to the hinge side of the door. She then did the same to the wall on the doorknob side. "Listen. There's a metallic sound over here. That's what I was hearing." She closed her eyes as she ran her fingers over the wall. "Let's go back into the bedroom."

They followed her back into the bedroom where she ran her hands over the wall. "The drywall texture is slightly different here. It's probably newer with fewer coats of paint. It may have been recently replaced." She rapped on the wall again where the slight metallic sound was obviously more perceptible to the others.

"Maybe an HVAC duct?" Gina said.

"No, that's a different sound," Kendra said. "Usually more of a rattle. This sounds more like . . ." Kendra pushed on the drywall and it suddenly clicked and swung open slightly.

"Whoa," Metcalf said. "If that leads to a hidden dungeon, I'm gonna freak out."

"No dungeon." Kendra pulled on the drywall panel to reveal a tall, slender metal cabinet.

"A gun safe," Griffin said. "That's what you were hearing."

"Kind of an elaborate setup for a place like this," Gina said.

Roscoe inspected the hidden drywall door. "Interior hinges and spring-loaded latch. I've known people to put these in their homes. You can do it in an afternoon if you know what you're doing."

Kendra tried the safe door. Locked. She turned

to Griffin. "Do we need a warrant to get inside here?"

"Nope. We have Hagstrom's permission for a full-premises search though he probably didn't think we'd find this." Griffin examined the key-lock. "I have a guy in the next room who can get us inside in under a minute."

Lynch stepped forward with two L-shaped picks he'd pulled from his jacket pocket. "You have a guy in here who can do that even faster."

In less than thirty seconds, Lynch opened the cabinet door.

The group crowded closer, and Lynch stepped aside to reveal several more guns, each suspended on metal hooks.

Gale let out a low whistle. "A Zoli, a K-80, a modified AR-15 . . . probably $40,000 worth of guns here. No wonder he wanted to hide them."

Kendra knelt in front of the cabinet. "There's something else here. Can someone give me light?"

Metcalf and Gina aimed their flashlights downward where a length of rolled-up black felt lined the cabinet's base. Kendra unrolled the felt to reveal several small objects.

Yes. She ignored the exclamations from the agents and detectives around her as she carefully examined them.

Keys.

A hearing aid.

A monogrammed handkerchief.

A prescription pill bottle.

A bag filled with a clear gelatinous material.

Kendra looked down at the pill bottle and read that name aloud. "Shelley Waldrop."

"She's one of mine," Gale said eagerly. "Murdered in Fairfield."

In short order the detectives linked the remaining items to each of the other cases, ending with the gruesome realization that the gelatinous bag was a breast implant cut from Los Angeles resident Ann-Marie Tepper, the first victim from Roscoe's case. A quick call to the manufacturer confirmed that the serial number was a match.

"We've *got* the son of a bitch," Griffin said. "I'll get the photographer back in here to document everything, then we'll take these back to the office and shove them down Hagstrom's throat until he talks."

"Give me the chance to do the verification first," Gina said eagerly. "Then he won't be able to deny anything."

"That seems to be the thing to do." Kendra took one last look around and then she nodded at Griffin. "Good luck."

"Aren't you coming back with us?" Griffin asked. "You should be there when the son of a bitch goes down."

She shook her head. "No. Grilling suspects is

your thing, not mine. I have somewhere to go. We'll talk later." She headed for the door.

Suber was suddenly beside her, blocking her way. "We really need you there during this final stage of the case." His eyes were shining with eagerness. "Can't you see that it's a historic moment in crime solving? I was planning on featuring you prominently in my paper. Our efforts here will be taught in universities all over the world."

"No." She was trying to be patient. "I'm not going back to the field office, Suber."

"All right, then give me a statement I can quote in my paper."

She'd had enough. "A quote? Here's a quote. Stop concentrating every minute on death, Suber. In short, get a life."

She pushed past him and left the house.

"Dear me," Lynch said mildly as he caught up with her as she reached the street. "I believe that you've hurt poor Suber's feelings." He clicked his tongue reprovingly. "You're definitely not behaving as the star of Griffin's august team."

"I didn't volunteer for the assignment of being either their therapist or a member of the team itself." She was already in the passenger seat of his car. "And he kept talking and he was making me late." She checked her watch. "Which he probably managed to do. I should have left ten minutes ago."

"Only ten minutes?" He started the Ferrari with a low roar. "I can get you there on time."

"I prefer it to also be in one piece," she said dryly. "I won't do Ryan Walker any good from the ICU."

"Have a little faith." He was already halfway to the freeway. "I wouldn't risk you. It's all a question of regulating the traffic lights. I have a gadget I ordered from Rome that—"

"I don't want to hear about it."

"I wasn't going to really describe it. There's such a thing as plausible deniability. Besides, Jessie would appreciate it far more than you would. You might occasionally be envious of Jessie, but it's obviously pretty much all talk. I've noticed that you've grown a little stodgy of late."

"Stodgy?" She shot him an outraged look. "Because I don't want to end up in jail or the hospital? Just because I don't drive a Ferrari or smuggle hackers out of foreign—" She stopped as she met his eyes, which were gleaming with sly satisfaction.

"Gotcha," he said softly.

Yes he had, she realized. She had risen to the bait. "You're right, I wouldn't want to be thought boring. Pull over. I bet I can get back to the studio with time to spare. Just let me get behind the wheel and see what I can get out of this—"

He lost his smile. "Hell, no."

"Chicken."

"Merely possessive. Haven't you noticed?" He held up his hand. "And no, you're not stodgy. I still shudder when I remember you and Jessie on that motorcycle on the freeway a few months ago. I just thought that I'd distract you from a mood that appears to be on the stormy side."

"By pissing me off?"

"By making you feel superior. You can't deny that making a man such as me back down is a real victory for anyone."

"So you did it on purpose?"

"Why, of course."

"Liar."

He grinned. "Also, of course." He glanced at the sign on the freeway. "But I did make the time go by at lightning speed, didn't I? We're halfway to your studio. You have just enough time to tell me why you were being curt to Suber. You practically stomped out of there."

"No, I didn't. I just . . . left. I was late."

"And you think all those brilliant, eager detectives are full of shit."

"No."

"But you do think they're wrong."

"Maybe not." She looked straight ahead. "It just seemed . . . too easy. Zachary is brilliant. It shouldn't be that easy. And then there were all those guns . . . But I could be wrong. Those other wonderfully convenient clues back there seemed to be panning out." She shrugged. "I just didn't want to spend my time being the one to explore those clues or question Hagstrom right now. If the team comes up with something that's absolutely irrefutable proof, or they get a confession from Hagstrom that he's Zachary, then I'll congratulate them and be the first one to join the party."

"But you don't think that's going to happen."

"I don't know," she said in exasperation. "That's what Metcalf asked me. He wanted to know if I was thinking in the same vein as Huston . . . Zachary is a wild card, he could go in any direction. Did I get the impression that something wasn't quite right with Hagstrom? Yes. But it might not have had anything to do with Zachary. We'll have to wait and see." Her lips tightened. "And I didn't want to get involved in endless discussions about Hagstrom or Zachary with those detectives today. Zachary always seems to be hovering over my shoulder every minute of the day. I wanted to send him packing for a few hours."

"And you headed in the direction of little Ryan Walker," he said. "I can see why you'd want to throw a dash of hope into the mix after dealing with Zachary." His brows rose. "There *is* hope for Ryan, right?"

"Oh, I have plenty of hope. You never let go of hope no matter how many times you get knocked down and have to pick yourself up. But it's not as if it will be a slam dunk. He's been very close to catatonic. It might be a process of years before I'm able to help him." She shrugged. "I think I might have found a way to stage a breakthrough, but it could still go either way."

"But you'll keep searching and fighting," he said quietly. "He's lucky to have you on his side." He pulled into the studio parking lot. "And someday he'll realize it."

"Maybe. If he doesn't, I will. That's what's important." She got out of the car. "I'm on time. You may now say I told you so."

"Not for such a tiny victory. I save that for more stellar triumphs. How long is his session? Do I only have time for coffee, or a couple drinks at the bar down the street while I watch the hockey game?"

"Neither. I can call a Vroom car to take me home."

"A couple drinks and the game," he answered himself. "Call me instead. We've already discussed this. The studio is your home turf and he knows it." He was pulling out of the parking lot. "Good luck with Ryan. See you . . ."

She watched him drive away and then turned to unlock the door. She should have argued with him, but it was always exhausting to argue with Lynch. She was going to need all her strength and stamina to deal with Ryan this afternoon.

The studio is your home turf and he knows it.

She felt her shoulders and neck stiffen as Lynch's words came back to her. Stupid. She almost felt as if she could feel Zachary watching her. Her imagination was working overtime.

Forget him as she had fully intended to do today.

Forget about death and only remember she had a chance to save a young boy, she thought, as she shut the door.

She started down the hall and then stopped and turned around and came back.

She quickly locked the door again.

CHAPTER 12

"There's been no change," Janice Walker said as she looked through the glass windows of the observation room at Ryan huddled in his wheelchair in Kendra's studio. "I know you warned me that tiny response might have been a fluke, but I hoped you were wrong." She moistened her lips. "Oh, how I hoped you were wrong. I wanted it so *badly,* Kendra."

"I know you did," Kendra said gently. "And that's why I warned you. I couldn't have you breaking down. You're too important to us."

"Not to Ryan." Janice's eyes were glittering with tears. "He hardly knows I'm with him anymore."

"He knows you're there. The pain is just too great for him to break through to you. We have to find a way to do that for him. Did you bring what I asked you?"

"Yes." She reached into her bag and pulled out an SD memory card and handed it to her. "It's about two and a half minutes in."

"Good. Thanks. I know it must not have been easy for you."

"What do I care about that? Nothing's easy for Ryan these days. Do you think I don't watch him hurting from the minute he wakes up in the

300

morning?" She paused. "But you failed last time."

"And I might fail this time. Another warning, Janice. But that doesn't mean we should stop trying. We just go on until we find the magic formula."

"Should I go in with you this time?"

"Stay here. It's better if you leave it to me." She looked down at the SD card. "No, if you leave it to *us*." She grabbed her guitar and headed for the door leading to the studio.

The next moment she was crossing the studio to stand before Janice's son. "Hello, Ryan." She smiled, ignoring his lack of response. "It's good to see you. I've been thinking about you." She went around the room making adjustments. "I feel like singing today. How about you?"

No answer.

"Or we could just start playing first and then make up our minds as we go along." She sat down on her regular stool in front of his chair. "I know your mom would like to hear you sing. She says she misses it." She started plucking the strings. "I've always liked 'Forever Young,' don't you? I remember Rod Stewart singing it with that cute, red-haired boy." She started softly playing the melody.

No sign of response.

She went on to play "I Hope You Dance" and then crooned "What a Wonderful World." A slight sign of alertness during that last song . . .

Time to go for it.

"I told your mom that sometimes when everything looks dark, you have to keep trying until you find the magic formula to make the darkness go away." She started strumming softly, beginning to integrate the melody. "Because there *is* magic in the world, isn't there, Ryan? You know it, you've seen it." She let the melody grow. "You've been shown the magic." She started to sing softly, "Puff, the magic dragon . . ."

Ryan's eyes were suddenly riveted on her face, watching her lips move as she sang the tale of magic and love.

Yes.

"You used to sing that song with your daddy," she murmured as she continued to play the melody. "Remember? Your mom said that you loved it. It's a wonderful song about a dragon and a little boy, and love and friendship and memories. You loved that song, but you were always sad that the little boy left Puff in the end, because he grew up. Your daddy knew that, didn't he?" The melody drifted through the studio. "And one night he told you that he'd looked up the poem on which the song was based. He'd found there had been another verse written that had never been put in the song. It told how Puff helped other little boys with the magic after his friend grew up. That way the love would go on

302

and on . . . But that verse somehow disappeared, and maybe that was also magic. Because you and your daddy knew how the song really ended. And your mom said you knowing your daddy had gone out and found it for you made you very, very happy." She smiled and coaxed, "Would you like to sing it now?"

He didn't answer.

But he was listening, she thought. He was *hearing* her.

"Maybe a little later." She looked down at the guitar and pressed a button as she continued to play softly. "Because someone else loved Puff, too. He believed in the magic. He wouldn't want you to forget it."

Suddenly, as she continued to strum the guitar, a man's soft, tenor voice came out of nowhere. "Puff, the magic dragon . . ." Then he continued to sing the entire song as Kendra accompanied the recording on her guitar.

Ryan was sitting bolt upright in his chair. His eyes were wide with shock as he stared at Kendra.

"I told you there was magic," she said. "You just didn't remember. I had to remind you. I *believe* in magic. Because I know blind people can see again. I know kindness can create miracles. I know if you hold on tight to faith and memories, they'll always be with you." She pressed another remote button as she started playing again: "Always."

Two monitors in the studio flickered and an old home video suddenly appeared of Ryan's father playing his guitar and singing to Ryan. Kendra felt her throat tighten. So much love. She could almost feel the strength of the bond between the father and son. "You sang with him then, Ryan."

Tears were running down Ryan's face as he stared at his father's face.

"A song about magic and love and friendship that would never really go away, even if you grew up and had trouble believing, or even if your father had to leave you," Kendra said. "You both believed it then, didn't you? I think your father probably loved to have you sing with him. I know your mother loved to hear the two of you together."

Ryan didn't look away from the image on the screen. He whispered, "Daddy?"

Silence.

Then, softly, only a wisp of sound . . .

"Puff . . . the magic . . . dragon . . ." Ryan's voice was so low and broken Kendra could scarcely hear it as he started to sing. His voice broke again. "Puff—the magic—" He had to stop as sobs shook his body. "Daddy?"

"Always, Ryan," Kendra whispered. She gestured to Janice to come in. "As long as you and your mom remember him and believe in the magic, he'll always be here."

Then Janice was beside Ryan, holding him tightly

in her arms. He was still. Then he slowly reached out and suddenly his head was pressed to her breast as he grabbed her even closer. "Mom . . . she said there's magic if we both . . ."

"Maybe there is," Janice said as the tears ran down her cheeks. "I think maybe she's right. I'm willing to believe in it if you are. How about it?"

He didn't answer, but he held her closer as she rocked him back and forth.

Kendra moved quietly across the room. They didn't need her now. There might be questions later, but what they were sharing now should only be between the two of them. She'd come back later.

But it was somehow filling her with contentment that she was still hearing the strains of "Puff (The Magic Dragon)" as she left the room.

Kendra smiled as she watched Janice settle Ryan into her minivan. "Remember, he should see his primary physician as soon as possible. Maybe not today; you two have a great deal to talk about. But first thing tomorrow."

Janice nodded. "I'll call on the way home. But I'm not worried about waiting a little while to tell him what happened today. He'll think it's the same miracle I do." Her face was radiant as she turned and hugged Kendra. "Thank you. Thank you. I can't tell you—" Her eyes were misting. "Look at me. I can't stop crying. But at least they're happy tears now. We're halfway there, aren't we?"

"We're on our way," Kendra said gently. "But your specialist has to answer those questions. That's why you have to consult with him. Ryan was in bad shape, and we have to make certain his body will heal with his heart and mind."

"It will. He's already using his arms and he—" She stopped. "I'll do whatever you say. What should I do when I get him home?"

"Whatever comes naturally. Play all kinds of music you know he likes. Some that you know your husband also liked, but also music you like. Or get down the photo albums and look at photos of the three of you through the years. This isn't only about his father, it's about you and Ryan and the family as a whole." She smiled and took a step back. "And what the two of you are going to do to work out what comes next. Call me if you need to talk to someone besides Ryan. Somehow I don't believe you will." She leaned closer to the van and said to Ryan, "See you next session. Maybe we'll try a few guitar lessons."

He stared gravely at her. "More songs about magic?"

"I know a few." She smiled. "Maybe you and your mother will be able to find more." She waved at him and stepped back. "Get out of here, Janice. You're both exhausted. You may not be feeling it right now, but it's going to hit soon."

"I know." Janice was getting into the driver's seat. "I'm just . . . flying so high." She looked around the parking lot. "Where's your car? Do you need a lift?"

"No, I called my ride. He'll be here soon."

"Do you want me to wait?"

Kendra chuckled. "No, but I can tell your maternal instincts are also flying sky high. I don't need you to hover. It's broad daylight, and my ride will be here any minute. Lynch is very punctual."

"Whatever you say." Janice lifted her hand. "Thanks, again. I'll call you."

Kendra watched her back out of the parking spot and then head for the exit. She couldn't keep from smiling. She wanted to reach out and hug the entire world. She was feeling as if she was riding as high as Janice at this moment.

Softness. Vitality. Radiance.

Zachary had never seen Kendra Michaels with that expression of exuberant happiness. She was standing there in the parking lot surrounded by sunlight and that glowing look of triumph and supreme satisfaction.

What a magnificent time it would be to take her life now when she at the height of realizing how much she valued every moment of living.

Pity, he thought regretfully. His plans didn't call for her death yet. She was to be the last and best. He'd been very careful about choosing the victims to precede her. Each one to make a statement or cause her pain to accelerate. He mustn't be impatient because this particular moment was close to perfect.

But why not, he thought recklessly. He could change those plans. He was the one in charge. He'd have to move fast, but he was brilliant enough to change his plans and still obtain the extreme pleasure that this opportunity offered.

He reached out to start his car.

He muttered a curse.

Too late.

Lynch was driving into the parking lot in his damn Ferrari and pulling up in front of Kendra.

A bolt of searing rage tore through him. He hadn't realized how much the idea of taking Kendra Michaels today had begun to grip him. Okay. Adjust. Think about it. He refused to give up the idea entirely. How to destroy her in this perfect moment of happiness . . .

"You look . . . extraordinary," Lynch said as Kendra got into the car. He tilted his head. "It reminds me of that phase one that you told me about earlier. You're practically glowing. Everything went well?"

"Everything went splendidly." She still couldn't stop smiling. "Not perfect. We're a long way from perfect. But we're on our way. His mother was over the moon."

"And so are you." His gaze was on her face as he pulled out of the parking lot. "I've never seen you like this."

"I was able to *reach* him. I made a difference. That doesn't happen every day. It's wonderful. Zachary has surrounded me with sadness and horror for too long. But not today, not right now."

"No, not today." He smiled. "Want to go out to dinner to celebrate? What do you feel like? I know a great Mexican restaurant."

"Why not?" She leaned back in the seat. "I don't care where we go. Surprise me."

"You are feeling good. That's very tempting," he said. "Okay, lean back and tell me all about your day. I won't mention the fact that my hockey team lost."

"You just did."

"Only to make your day seem even brighter in contrast. Tell me."

"It was that old Peter, Paul and Mary hit." She leaned back, remembering that moment with Ryan. " 'Puff (The Magic Dragon)' . . ."

She had almost finished relating the last few minutes of conversation with Janice when they pulled into a huge restaurant whose entire roof was shaped like a red and yellow sombrero. It had arched windows lit with flashing colored lights and even a good-sized gift store. She laughed. "Good heavens, a little gaudy?"

"But great food and I thought you might be in

the mood for a touch of flamboyance." He opened the car door for her. "Okay, now it sounds as if you were understating your session today. I didn't hear one thing that was less than spectacular . . ." He glanced up at the sombrero on the roof. "And flamboyant from the moment I left you. Right?"

"I've got to admit that—"

The studio is your home turf and he knows it.

"What's wrong?" Lynch's gaze was on her face.

"Nothing. I just remembered something you said right before you left."

"You're saying I managed to spoil something for you?"

"No, it was just— You didn't spoil anything. My imagination was working overtime. You said something about Zachary knowing the studio was my home turf. It freaked me out. I felt as if he was there staring at me. I forgot about it right away."

After she had gone back and locked the door.

His eyes were narrowed on her face. "What else, Kendra?"

"Nothing." She smiled with an effort. "Not your fault. You were right to remind me."

"Yes, I was right. I'd do it again. But I didn't mean to freak you out." He paused. "I don't like that I was able to do that. You're still freaked out talking about it now. Why?"

She shrugged. "I told you, imagination. Zachary

has me strung out and I—" She stopped as she realized where this was going. "You're saying you don't think it was imagination? You're saying that you think he might really have been there?"

"I'm saying that it might be imagination, but it might have also been instinct. You ought to consider who you are and how sharp those instincts have been shown to be. You shouldn't just take it for granted. It might not be a bad idea for us to reexamine your studio and the grounds around it."

"The studio has state-of-the-art security."

"I know. I checked it out. Let's go look at it again tomorrow."

Instinct.

Kendra felt chilled. The studio, that place of joy and work and accomplishment that had given her one of the happiest days of her career today. The idea that Zachary might have been there, watching, perhaps manipulating, made her almost ill.

"Tomorrow," Lynch said gently. "Come on. Let's go into the restaurant and have dinner."

"It could have been instinct," she said slowly. "I guess I didn't want it to be. I didn't want him to be able to touch this part of my life. Why would he be there, watching me?" She answered herself. "Because it's my turf. He was looking for bigger and better ways to destroy me or hurt me in some way." Her lips twisted bitterly. "If I'm his prime victim, it can't be just an ordinary kill. I have to be special."

"You are special. And I'm a son of a bitch for not keeping my mouth shut until later."

"No, I'm glad you did." She was starting to shake. "Because then I wouldn't have made the connection. I protected Olivia and everyone in my personal life, but I never thought of any of my clients. I thought my professional life was different, that he wouldn't strike at them because he wouldn't realize they could hurt me." She looked at him. "But if he was watching today, he'd know that destroying Ryan and Janice might hurt me. You said I was glowing. He'd *know*, Lynch. Just as you said."

"He might not have been there today, Kendra."

"I realize that, but what if he was? I don't lay claim to any weird psychic talents, but I do believe in instincts. Everyone has moments when they *feel* things. I felt as if he was there." She moistened her lips, "And if he was, he might have found a way to hurt me by hurting that little boy and his mother." She kept seeing Ryan's face when he was singing that song and it was *killing* her. She took out her phone. "But I'm not going to let him do it." She didn't let herself think as she quickly dialed Janice Walker's phone number.

It rang once.

Twice.

Three times.

"Kendra." Janice picked up and Kendra could hear music in the background. "Everything is going fine. You didn't have to worry."

"I wasn't worried." The last thing she wanted to do was panic Janice unnecessarily. "I just had a thought. After Ryan's emotional day today, he really shouldn't have visitors tonight. No company but you, Janice. Lock up and just snuggle together. Okay?"

"Sure. No problem."

"Except for me. If you don't mind, I'll stop by and give you and Ryan a celebration gift. I'll call you so that you'll know when to expect me."

"Great." She sounded a little puzzled. "But I'm the one who should be giving you gifts."

"Not true. It's been a great day for all of us." She pressed the disconnect and turned to Lynch. "Call Griffin and have him send out a couple agents to watch the Walker house. Tell him I want them outside their place within fifteen minutes. Absolutely without fail."

Lynch reached for his phone. "Why me? You're the star of his happy little dream team."

"Because you always manage to make him jump through hoops, and I don't have any time to waste. Besides, he'd argue with me. He already believes he might have his killer." She was heading up the stairs of the restaurant. "Just get it done, okay? I don't want Janice to know that

313

there might be any danger, but I want Zachary to know that the FBI is watching her."

"And where are you going?" he asked as he waited for Griffin to answer.

"To get a bottle of wine for Janice and a sombrero for Ryan. I need an excuse to look around her house when I go check if Griffin's come through for you." She disappeared into the gift store.

She was *cheating* him.

Zachary's hands tightened with fury on the steering wheel as he watched Kendra and Lynch laughing as they said good-bye to Janice Walker at her front door. Then they strolled down the steps and stopped once again at the FBI van down the block.

Not only cheating him, but mocking him? You shouldn't have done that, Kendra. No one does that to me.

She was showing him that she'd not only guessed his intention but had checkmated him.

How had she guessed? He'd only decided to take second best and kill the Walkers after he'd been thwarted today when he knew he'd be forced to wait for Kendra. He'd desperately needed some form of immediate satisfaction. No, not desperate, he was better than those other mindless killers who couldn't control their emotions. He had just wanted and deserved those kills.

And she had guessed because she was more intelligent and intuitive than those other detectives. It was really a compliment to him that he'd been clever enough to choose her.

Very well, he was calmer now. He could recognize that Kendra had kept him from a kill that he wanted. It was not possible now, but he could always go back later and take both the mother and the child.

He could do without that hot surge of pleasure until he could savor it more fully, he told himself. He would just add them to the list that was growing constantly as he continued to discover how to bring down the world of Kendra Michaels.

He watched Kendra and Lynch get into Lynch's car. They were smiling, talking, laughing, as they always did. Friends. Partners. Lovers? He had not seen signs of that connection. But should he be devoting more attention to Lynch?

He had no time to consider it right now. He was too angry and impatient, and he was done with sitting back and plotting. He had all his plans in mind. He had his chosen victims in his sights. It was time to move forward.

He could feel his excitement growing, building.

His gaze returned to the smile on Kendra's face.

By all means, laugh, Kendra.

But make sure you do it tonight. It will be your last chance.

• • •

"What did you have to do to make Griffin send those two agents?" Kendra asked quietly as Lynch drove into her parking garage at her condo. "They were falling over each other to assure us that Janice would be safe."

"The usual." He parked the Ferrari. "Promised him my first-born son." He got out of the car. "You knew there would be a price."

"Yes. If I hadn't been worried about the timing, I would have negotiated with him myself." She glanced at him as they headed for the elevator. "I'll still try to do it, but he might not think my services quite as valuable as yours."

"Bullshit."

She shook her head. "I'm limited. You can help him on a global level. Griffin always goes for the big game."

"Zachary isn't global."

"But he's causing a hell of a lot of unpleasant media coverage with which Griffin doesn't want to be associated." She glanced at him as she punched the button. "You know all that. You wouldn't even be involved if you hadn't come to try to help me."

"Try?" He grimaced. "If you'll notice, I've done more than try. I might value that first-born son someday."

"I can't imagine you with a child. He'd never see you."

"I can." He smiled. "I'd just pack him in my suitcase and take him with me. I'd make sure he enjoyed it."

I bet he would, she thought. A son with Lynch's genes would be brimming with the same intelligence and sense of adventure. She was beginning to picture them together. "I believe you've left out a key element."

"We're speaking hypothetically. I address key elements when hypotheticals fall by the wayside." He tilted his head. "I don't think you want to go there?"

That melting heat was suddenly appearing again, and she had to get away from all intimacy. "No, I don't even know how we got on the subject. I was only trying to thank you. You didn't have to do that for me." She shook her head. "There was no real reason why you should. I had no proof that Janice and Ryan are in danger. Maybe they're not. And I didn't even ask you, I told you."

"And you didn't even give me a sombrero."

"I'll go back and get you one."

"Too late. You screwed up, I'll have to look for other payment."

"Stop joking. I'm trying to tell you I panicked and I'm sorry if I didn't—"

"Be quiet, Kendra." He kissed her. Hard, fast, hot. "I knew exactly what was going on with you. I could see you going through all the stages.

Once you reached the point where there was a possibility of the Walkers being in danger, I wasn't about to try to put anything in your way." He kissed her again. "But now we might have to go into that matter of payment . . . Sombrero or something infinitely more satisfying?"

She couldn't breathe. Her entire body was readying and she wanted to reach out and—

"Damn you." She stepped back and pushed the hair back from her face with a shaking hand. "I won't let you do this to me. You're not being fair. I told you that I won't have Zachary thinking you're another target. You said he knew the studio was my turf, what do you think about this?" She threw her hand out at the parking garage. "He could be here watching right now."

"Good. Let's go hunting." He held up his hand. "I checked it out as I was driving through it to your parking spot. No one lurking."

"But there could be." She punched the elevator button again. "He's clever. You might have missed him." She met his eyes. "Just as I might have missed him at the studio. I'm not going to take any chances. He's been too quiet. That makes me uneasy. But he seems to know things, and I won't let him know that you're important to me."

"Important? Ah, an admission at last." The elevator doors slid open and he gestured to her to precede him. "Not the payment I had in mind, but far better than a sombrero."

"You're not staying in my condo tonight." She entered the elevator and pressed her floor. "So you might as well go home."

He didn't answer.

"I mean it." She didn't look at him. "If you don't, I'll go check into a hotel. Though I'm safer with Olivia and Jessie on the floor below."

"I'll make sure no one knows I'm here."

"I'd know." The elevator stopped and she looked at him. "Want another admission? We both know I want to have sex with you. I'm very vulnerable right now. If you pushed even a little, I'd probably end up doing it."

He went still. "Is that supposed to discourage me?"

"Just an explanation why there's no way I want you here. Because I'm not like you. You're an expert at masking your feelings and pretending. As you told me, I'm too honest. I'm like Gina. Anyone who was the least observant would probably realize that I was sleeping with you. And Zachary would probably be the first to notice." She got off the elevator. "It ain't gonna happen, Lynch."

"I hear you." But he caught the door as it was about to close and got off the elevator. He held up his hand as she opened her lips. "You win. Though I'm having all kinds of erotic fantasies about what a turn-on it would be to watch you try to hide—" He was unlocking her door. "But you're having enough problems at the moment. I'll come in and search the condo. Then I'll go downstairs and bunk with Jessie and Olivia for the night."

"Bad idea. It's too small. Where would you sleep?"

"We'll work it out. And if Zachary hears about it, he'll think I'm sleeping with one or both of them." He was going through the apartment checking the rooms. "Multiples. That should take his mind off any thought that I might have any time left for you. Right?" He stopped at the front door. "Come down for breakfast. Then we'll go to your studio and check it out before we go to the field office and see if they've found out anything more about Hagstrom."

"You have our day planned?"

"I'd cancel it in a heartbeat. We could spend it in bed." He kissed the tip of her nose and added softly, "Ask me."

"Go away." She pushed him out the door. "And tell Olivia and Jessie this wasn't my idea. You do have a home, Lynch."

"Not until Zachary is history." He turned away. "Lock the door. See you at breakfast."

She watched him run down the steps before she closed and locked the door. Then she turned and headed for the bedroom. It had been a frantic and tense day yet there had been a few periods of deep emotional bonding with Ryan. And every hour of the day seemed to bring her closer to Lynch. Both of those exceptions could herald problems. She thought that if Zachary had been planning on targeting the Walkers that she might have stymied it. But Lynch was an entirely different case. He was not about to leave her, and Zachary might—

Don't think about it, she told herself as she got into the shower. She had done what she could and she would continue to do that. She might do a little too much, but that was okay. Zachary was out there, and she would give everything she had until he was caught or killed.

She closed her eyes as the warm water moved over her body.

She could almost feel him out there.

Not as she had earlier today when she'd told herself it was pure imagination. This was . . . different . . . closer. A kind of pressure . . .

Was Zachary thinking about her? Was why she was feeling this sense of impending urgency.

Imagination or instinct, again?

She didn't know which and she didn't care.

She wouldn't let either intimidate her.

If something was coming then she had to accept it and get ready.

And something was coming . . .

• • •

Breakfast the next morning in Olivia's condo was fast, noisy, and generally enjoyable.

It was only after Lynch had gone down to bring his car around to the front that Olivia stopped Kendra as she was heading out the door.

"No," she said firmly. "Lynch is *not* going to stay here, even though it's convenient to your condo. I'll call the building supervisor and get him a place near your place."

"I was going to do that," Kendra said. "I told him your place was too small but he insisted. He said you'd work it out."

"And if he had a couple more nights, I'm sure we'd somehow manage to do exactly what he wanted. The son of a bitch is a spellbinder." She added shrewdly, "But then you evidently know that."

"It's occurred to me a few times. It's not because your condo is too small?"

"It would be a little over-cozy. But we could survive it. He's just too damn disturbing. I didn't realize it until I spent the night with him. I like comfort and so does Jessie. If we want Clooney or Brad Pitt wandering around the place, we'll go knock on their door when we're in the mood." She gave her a peck on the cheek. "I'll call you and tell you when I've found Lynch a new place to roost."

"Do that."

She was still smiling when she got into Lynch's car a few minutes later. "The studio?"

"Yep." He glanced sidewise. "As soon as you tell me why you're grinning like a Cheshire cat."

"I've just been anticipating telling you that you've been evicted. Olivia says she'll find you another home."

"What?" He was frowning. "I camped out on the floor. I fixed that breakfast this morning. What did I do wrong?"

"Too much testosterone," she said solemnly.

"I beg your pardon?" He added warily, "I swear I didn't touch them."

She started to laugh. "Evidently you didn't have to. They thought you might be a disturbing influence. Sometimes no actions are necessary."

He looked disgruntled, and then he shrugged. "Being irresistible isn't all that bad. I've been called worse."

"If you were irresistible, they wouldn't be kicking you out. That's two condos in one night, Lynch."

"You're enjoying this."

"Infinitely."

"So am I." He was gazing at her, his face lit with a gentle smile. "I was a little worried about you yesterday. I'll let you or any of your friends kick both my ego and machismo into the gutter if it will make you smile like that."

Oh, shit. What could she say to that remark?

"You manage to take all the fun out of a perfectly good attack strategy."

"Good. I do my very best." He changed the subject. "Did you get a call from Griffin this morning? I thought it a little odd that he didn't follow up later after I hijacked those two agents from him."

"No call. Maybe grilling Hagstrom didn't prove as productive as he thought, and he's waiting to hit me with everything at one time."

"I could drop you off at the field office and check out the studio myself."

"I'm not in that much of a hurry. I want to see if there are any hints that I could have been right and not just a paranoid nutso." She grimaced. "And I'm not certain that you wouldn't manufacture evidence to make me feel better. I've been noticing suspicious signs of softening in you, Lynch."

He shook his head. "I don't lie when it comes to creeps like Zachary. Honesty is a weapon in itself." He said curtly, "I'll check out the studio itself and then I'll go cruise the neighborhood. You stay there and I'll pick you up when I'm finished."

"I'll go with you."

"Nope, I may be doing a little housebreaking or have unfriendly talks with your neighbors. In the interest of maintaining future peace in the neighborhood, you stay and make client phone calls or whatever else you do when you're not curing catatonic kids."

"I didn't cure, I only set the—"

"Close enough. Then call Janice and check on him." He pulled into the parking lot. "Did I mention having to worry about Zachary getting you in his sights would be a danger to my concentration? You're all into the values of concentration. You wouldn't want me to be scattered, would you?"

"You're never scattered."

"Want to take the chance?"

"No." She scowled as she got out of the car. "Manipulation, Lynch."

"It's important to me, Kendra," he said simply as he gestured to the front entrance. "Now let's check out the studio and get some answers."

No answers to be found in the studio itself. The security was just as tight and incapable of being violated as it had been when Lynch had checked it before. Which caused a myriad of mixed feelings in Kendra.

"Paranoid?" she said as she walked Lynch to the door. "Almost as safe as Fort Knox."

"Safer, I hope." He opened the door. "I've always thought the security there was overrated. I bet I could crack it."

"No bet. You could probably crack the security at the crown jewel room at the Tower of London." She looked out at the sunny parking

325

lot. "But just in case I'm not paranoid, be careful. Okay?"

His brows rose. "What's the fun in that?"

"Lynch."

"Joking."

"Yeah, very funny. I don't know why I'd care anyway."

"Yes, you do." He grinned as he strode toward his car. "Your landlord might make you move if I was slaughtered anywhere on the premises. That kind of thing makes it really hard for a property to survive in the rental market."

Before she could answer, he'd slammed the car door and was driving away.

She watched as he drove out of the parking lot and turned right.

Her phone was ringing.

"Go in and lock the door," Lynch said when she answered. "Now, Kendra."

"You've been gone two minutes." But she went inside and locked the door. "Don't give me orders. And don't talk about slaughter." She hung up.

Make time pass quickly. Make those calls to Janice and her other clients. She shouldn't pay any attention to Lynch's perverted sense of humor. It wasn't as if Zachary would have a chance against him.

But he had killed so many people, and all it would take would be a careless moment.

Lynch didn't have careless moments. He was always on guard.

Always?

Distraction.

She sat down at her desk and started to dial Janice Walker.

An hour and thirty minutes later Lynch called her back. "I'm on my way to you. Griffin just phoned and wants me to bring you to the office. He has something he wants you to see. Lock up and meet me at the front entrance. Three minutes." He ended the call.

He was pulling into the parking lot in exactly three minutes. "Is it urgent?" she said as she got into the car. "Then why didn't Griffin call me instead of you?"

"He didn't say it was urgent. He just said he wanted you there." He added dryly, "Why didn't he call you? I'm guessing that it's part of my servitude for the 'favor' he did me last night. I was to make sure you appeared when and where he wanted you."

"Bastard," she said through her teeth. "I'll talk to him, Lynch."

"No, then I wouldn't be able to negotiate on the same grounds if I have to do it again. He's probably enjoying this. Leave it alone. I'll handle it." He stopped at the parking lot exit before going out on the street. "Turn around and look up at the hill in back of this block. The third street on the hill, fifth house over. Red tile roof. Teal-colored front door."

"Yes, I see it."

"And Zachary could see you," he said grimly. "The house is for sale. It's also vacant. I was looking for something like that. Anyone sitting in a car in that driveway with a scope could see every detail of what went on in this parking lot. All the comings and goings of all your friends and clients." He paused. "And you would be readily accessible to him. Three minutes away. I called you from that driveway."

She was feeling an icy chill as she looked at that pretty little house on the hill. "No proof? Right?"

"No proof. I talked to the neighbors on either side of the house and they said they'd seen a Setzer Real Estate van with the proper logo sitting in the driveway a couple times during the last weeks. Shaded windows. Someone in the driver's seat doing paperwork, but they weren't able to give a description of him."

"Or the van?"

"Dark colored Toyota. No license plate number available. I just called the local Setzer Real Estate office, and they don't know anything about that van."

"Very clever." She couldn't take her gaze off that house. How many times had Zachary been up there watching her? How many times had he been vetting her kids to see if they were worth bothering about? "Not paranoid?" she whispered. "Do we have a chance of catching him?"

"We can be on watch, but if he thinks he tipped his hand about the Walkers, he won't do it again."

She tried to smother the disappointment. "He's very bold. Like most serial killers he probably thinks he's invulnerable." Her lips tightened. "But he's not invulnerable. He didn't get his hands on Janice or Ryan. And I'm still around," she added wryly, "though I've been getting a distinct impression that he might attempt a correction in that area."

"No way," Lynch said flatly. "We've been blocking him, Kendra."

"And that must frustrate the hell out of him. He's arrogant and he's not going to put up with that for long." She wearily shook her head. "And that might be a good thing. Frustration breeds mistakes. Let's go see if Griffin has found any Zachary mistakes that we can use to send him to death row."

CHAPTER 13

San Diego
FBI Field Office

"I've never seen any of this stuff before," Hagstrom shouted. "Never!"

Kendra and Lynch were watching a video recording of Hagstrom being interviewed the previous evening. He was staring in apparent bewilderment at the objects they had recovered from his in-wall safe. The recording was playing on the large wall-mounted monitor at the end of the fifth-floor conference room to which Kendra and Lynch had been whisked by Griffin the moment they had come in the front entrance.

Kendra and Lynch were seated at the table along with Griffin, Metcalf, Gina, and three of the four dream team members. Huston was absent from the room, but he was the one who had conducted the on-camera interview.

"This is bullshit." Hagstrom was glaring at Huston on the video. "You guys planted this stuff because it sure as hell isn't anything I've ever seen."

"Come on, man," Huston replied. Kendra noticed that Huston's folksy demeanor had given away to frustration. "We found this in your place.

In your hidden safe. A roomful of people saw it in there. There was only one way you could have gotten these things and that's if you took them from five different people that you killed in four different cities. Cities where you happened to live when each of these people were murdered."

"You're framing me. I didn't kill *anyone*."

Griffin paused the video. "And that was how it went, over and over again." He added sourly, "As you would have known if you'd deigned to come here with us yesterday, Kendra."

"Which obviously would have been a colossal waste of my time, if you didn't get him to break." Kendra was studying Hagstrom's expression. "And I have to say, he's convincing."

"Very convincing," Gale said. "But then most psychopaths are."

Roscoe leaned toward Kendra. "Griffin said you were a bit uneasy yesterday after you left us. Do you still doubt Hagstrom's our guy?"

No proof. Just a pretty little house in the hills with a red tile roof and a teal door.

"Well, I can't be certain that he's not. But I'm not willing to just lock him up and stop looking for anyone else."

"You can't deny our evidence is pretty compelling," Griffin said.

"Sure it is," Kendra said. "Which is why I have a tough time believing that someone as clever as Zachary would leave it lying around his condo."

"It wasn't exactly 'lying around,'" Roscoe said quickly. "We might have missed it if you hadn't been with us."

Kendra shook her head. "Someone would have caught it, once your people starting popping off vent covers and waving metal detectors around. I'm delighted you give me that much credit, but my feeling is that Zachary keeps his trophy collection someplace where it can't be easily traced back to him."

Suber shrugged. "Throughout history, it's always been the same. The most brilliant criminal in the world is only brilliant until the moment he makes a mistake."

"Not this criminal, not this mistake," Kendra said. "At least I don't think so. And Hagstrom didn't give up a thing, despite some fairly skilled questioning from Huston." She glanced around the room. "By the way, where is he?"

"Back at the hotel," Roscoe said. "He texted us this morning. He said he needed to work on some stuff and that he'd be in later."

Griffin checked his watch. "Well, we're meeting with San Diego PD and the DA in about an hour. Somebody call Huston and tell him that we'll pick him up on our way."

"I'm on it," Trey Suber said as he picked up his phone. He looked at it for a moment. "Wait, I just got an email from him." He frowned, puzzled. "I think he copied it. Did everybody get this?"

There was a general scramble as the rest of the team reached for their phones.

Suber suddenly gasped. *"Shit!"*

Kendra stiffened and then moved swiftly toward him. "What's wrong? What is it?"

Suber's face was ashen. He turned the phone's screen toward her. There, written on a hotel room wall, was a message scrawled in what appeared to be blood . . .

LOOK BEHIND YOU.

Griffin was contacting hotel security and San Diego PD as they rushed toward the vans.

"Come on," Lynch muttered as he grabbed Kendra's arm and they bypassed the vans in favor of Lynch's Ferrari.

"Huston," Kendra murmured numbly. "Why Huston?"

"We don't know anything yet," Lynch said. "Maybe it's a scare tactic. Huston's one sharp operator."

But Kendra could still see those words scrawled in blood on that wall.

Only minutes later they joined Griffin and the team at the door of Huston's ninth-floor room, which security was still trying to access.

"What's the story?" Lynch demanded of him. If Griffin was annoyed that he was superseding his authority, he hid it well.

The security director turned toward the group.

"The card reader is shot to hell. We can't get in."

"Break it down," Griffin said.

The security director raised his hands. "It's not that easy. These locks are built to withstand a force equal to—

"Screw it." Lynch delivered two ferocious kicks to the door, then barreled into it with his right shoulder. The frame splintered apart and the door flew open. "You need to get another locksmith."

The security director's jaw dropped as he watched the team rush past him into the room.

LOOK BEHIND YOU.

The words were scrawled on the far wall just as in the emailed photo.

Kendra stopped, stood still, staring in dread at the words. What was she going to see if she looked behind her?

Do it.

Kendra spun around.

There, between the bed and the wall, was Arnold Huston's horribly mutilated corpse. His blood-soaked torso was in marked contrast to his face, which was remarkably clean and serene beneath a red baseball hat.

Gina knelt beside him. "Shit."

"He's been gutted," Griffin said grimly. "And Zachary took a long time with him."

"He always does," Kendra said. For a moment she couldn't look away from the body. Then she forced herself to shift her gaze to that gentle face. Huston was more than the hideous example Zachary had tried to make of him. Think of the kindness and the humor. "Power. Zachary would want to extend the power trip as long as he could."

As the other investigators gathered around Huston's corpse, Kendra turned away.

"Okay?" Lynch murmured, his gaze on her face.

"No." She swallowed hard. "Yes. I'll be fine."

"Maybe get out of here for a minute or two?"

"I said I'd be *fine*," she said with sudden fierceness. "He wants me to look at Huston, stare up at his damn message, and know that he's beaten me again. I'd never admit that."

He nodded. "Easy. I'm here for you. Whatever you want to do."

She didn't know what she wanted to do yet. All she knew was that she couldn't help Huston now, but maybe she could help get the monster who had killed him.

Put Huston's warm, sweet, grandfatherly face out of her mind.

Detach.

Concentrate.

The firm, short carpeting wouldn't reveal any footprints. There didn't appear to be blood splatter anywhere else in the room, so Huston was probably attacked right where they found him.

"Anything?" Lynch said quietly to Kendra.

"Not much. Further confirmation that the killer is right handed, based on the larger number of stab wounds on the left side of Huston's torso. And there's a good chance that he's about 5 foot 10."

"How do you figure that?"

She nodded toward the grisly lettering on the wall. "When someone writes on a wall or even a chalkboard, they usually begin writing slightly above eye level. Almost even with the top of their head. The top line of that message is about 5 foot 10 inches from the floor."

"Very good."

"And it's the same handwriting as on the message in Todd Wesley's apartment."

"Anything else?"

Her eyes went to the chest of drawers. Sitting on top was a small class ring. Kendra knelt down, her eyes narrowed on it. "Rivermont High School."

Lynch knelt beside her. "It looks like a woman's ring. I don't see any engravings inside."

"There aren't any."

Kendra pulled out her phone and typed furiously into the search bar. After a few seconds, she slowly stood. "This was Charlene Wheeler's ring. She was one of Huston's cases, killed in Arlington, Virginia." She turned to Lynch and the other investigators who were now leaving

Huston's body. "It seems Zachary just left us another souvenir."

"Two," Gale said grimly. "I'm pretty sure that red hat he's wearing belonged to David Schneer, Connecticut."

Nothing new. How many souvenirs had Zachary taken over the years? How many deaths? But these souvenirs were at Huston's death scene. He was mocking Huston, mocking all of them.

She couldn't breathe; she felt suddenly ill. As the others converged around the ring, Kendra backed away. She whispered to Lynch, "Maybe . . . I'm not so fine right now. I've done all I can. I need to get out of here. Now."

"Enough?" He grabbed her arm and nudged her out the door into the hall. "It's about time. You're pale as a sheet. You need some air."

They pushed past policemen and firefighters as they made their way to the elevator and rode down to the lobby. Kendra felt as if she was suffocating as she ran for the glass lobby doors and stumbled onto the sidewalk.

Then Lynch was beside her, holding her close. "Hey . . . It's okay."

"Tell that to Huston."

"He was a cop. It's a dangerous job."

"I know." She clutched him tighter. "But I *liked* him. And you saw what that son of a bitch did to him. It's just that—"

Kendra's phone buzzed.

"That's probably Griffin, wondering why I bolted the way I did."

"Let it go," Lynch said. "Screw him."

Kendra stared at her phone screen.

She froze.

"Kendra?"

She slowly showed the phone to Lynch.

The message read: You aren't wearing the ring I gave you.

Lynch muttered a curse as he instinctively moved between Kendra and the street, using his body as a shield as he looked up and down the busy thoroughfare.

Kendra looked at the message again. The "from" tag was simply: Zachary.

Here? Now?

She whirled and joined Lynch in scanning the pedestrians, the sidewalk vendors, the people in cars . . . Was Zachary one of them?

Lynch pushed her back toward the hotel door. "Move. Get back inside."

"No!" She was still scanning the street. "He's *here*. I have to keep looking."

"The hell you do."

"Wait." She was trying to jerk her arm away from him as she looked over her shoulder. Where are you, you monster . . .

"Get inside. Now!"

Lynch practically pushed her through the door into the lobby.

"But what if he's out there?" Kendra's hands clenched into fists. Her eyes were blazing with anger.

He maintained his grip on her. "Exactly. He could see you and you couldn't see him."

"I might have if you'd let me keep looking."

"Think about it. If Zachary is as clever as you're saying, would he have let you see him? No. And you would be a sitting duck out there."

Her phone buzzed again.

The screen read: **LOOK BEHIND YOU.**

She and Lynch spun around.

There was only the everyday activity of a large hotel lobby. Guests checking in, bellmen handling bags, guests waiting for elevators . . .

Was he playing with them?

Kendra no longer felt fear; pure rage coursed through her veins.

She gripped her phone and began to type feverishly.

"What are you doing?" Lynch asked.

"Typing my response."

"Kendra . . ."

She pushed "send" and stared with fierce satisfaction at her message still on the screen:

Watch your back, Zachary. I'm coming for you.

CHAPTER 14

"Where are you?" Kendra demanded as soon as Griffin answered his phone. "I need to talk to you."

"You're talking to me," Griffin said. "Why the hell did you take off from the crime scene? The team wanted to discuss your findings in—"

"I was having trouble thinking of it as a crime scene. I wanted out of there. Now where are you?"

He was silent. "I'm on my way down to hotel security."

"We'll meet you there." She pressed the disconnect. "Security," she told Lynch. "And we'll be lucky if he doesn't drag the entire team down there so that they can discuss that, too." She added through clenched teeth, "They're driving me crazy. I feel as if I'm being smothered every time they start to analyze and expound."

"Easy," Lynch said. "I know you're on edge, but we need Griffin for the moment. He can smooth the way for us."

She knew that, but it did little to keep her frustration in check. "You're right," she said curtly. "But everyone is treating Huston's death as just another murder. But it's all wrong, he died because Zachary wanted to mock us. He died because Zachary wanted to show me he could do it."

"Entirely possible. But that doesn't make it your fault."

"Then why does it feel like it is?"

"Because you liked Huston, and you're not thinking clearly at the moment. You're angry and feeling a little bewildered. But now the only thing of importance is to find out how Zachary did it." He punched the elevator button. "And that means you have to be moderately civil to Griffin for the next several hours. Don't worry, I'll be there to run interference."

"You don't have the best track record in that area. Not with Griffin."

"Then we'll make it a joint project."

"Maybe," she said skeptically.

Kendra and Lynch caught up with Griffin, Metcalf, and Gina as they walked down the hall toward the second-floor hotel security office. Thank heavens he'd left his precious dream team behind, Kendra thought relieved.

"You can see I'm busy," Griffin said. "What did you want to talk about?"

Kendra held up her phone and showed Griffin the **LOOK BEHIND YOU** text still on her screen.

"What the hell is that?" Griffin asked.

"A text from Zachary, sent to me less than ten minutes ago. He sent me two." Kendra displayed the previous message: **You aren't wearing the ring I gave you.**

Griffin seemed more disturbed by this text.

"Where were you when you received this one?"

"Outside the building." She tried to forget that moment of panic and think logically. "It doesn't mean I was being watched, of course. It wasn't like I was ever going to slip on that class ring we found and go about my day."

"Hmm. But it doesn't mean that he wasn't watching you. We need to find from where that message was sent. Probably a burner phone, but if we determine it was here in a common area, we can check security camera video against the timing to see if someone appears to be sending a text at that exact moment. It could help us. Rendell is upstairs uploading the contents of Huston's phone right now, but you should show him what you just showed me. He'll look into it."

"That photo of the hotel room wall was sent from Huston's phone less than an hour ago," Lynch said. "But I'd say he's been dead quite a bit longer. Did Rendell have anything to say about that?"

"The timestamp embedded in the photo shows it was snapped with Huston's phone at 5:40 A.M. The email with that photo was created at the same time but programmed to be sent over four hours later. According to the M.E.'s initial findings, that lines up with the time of death."

Kendra nodded toward the hotel security office. "Are we here to check security camera footage?"

"Yes. This hotel isn't exactly flooded with

cameras, but there's good coverage in the lobby, most of the exterior entrances, and in the elevator lobbies on each floor. They're giving us copies of all their footage between five and six this morning, but we'll take a quick look while we're here."

Kendra and Lynch joined the group for their "quick look," which ended up taking more than three hours and which yielded, as far as Kendra could tell, absolutely nothing. There was some activity in the lobby and rear loading dock, but otherwise it was fairly quiet.

Gina kept a tally of the departing guests who boarded elevators with their luggage, noting the time and floor number. "I'll compare these with the checkouts," she said.

Metcalf shook his head in frustration. "If he knew what he was doing, and I really think he does, our guy could have come and gone without being spotted by a single camera. There's no coverage on the side garage entrances, and if he took the stairs, he could have avoided surveillance cameras altogether."

"Or if he was a guest," Kendra said. "That would have been easier still. Do we have a copy of the registry?"

"We will as soon as our warrant gets here," Griffin said.

"Good. In the meantime, I'd like to go back up to Huston's room and take another look around. I might have been a little distracted when I did the first examination."

"Sure, no problem. But forensics is still there. They might get in your way. Why don't you wait awhile?" He paused. "The team wants to go back and talk to Hagstrom about those souvenirs. We're not sure how long we'll be able to keep him after Huston's murder. They want you to go with them."

She looked at him in disbelief. "No way. Not now. It would just be a rehash of previous interviews. The only souvenir I'm interested in right now is that ring we found today."

He frowned. "It's a minor request and might yield rewards. After all the team was intimately connected with Huston's work on the cases. They're all exceptional detectives and it's worth—"

"No," she said sharply. She'd had enough. She got to her feet and headed for the door. "I'm done. No more."

Griffin caught up with her as she pressed the button for the elevator. "What's that supposed to mean? All I'm asking for is a little cooperation."

Keep your temper. "I don't believe I can help in this instance. I don't seem to be in sync with your friends on the dream team. We don't appear to even be on the same wave length." She looked him in the eye. "You're absolutely right, I think they're all brilliant. They'd just be better off without me. I'm opting out, Griffin. No more dream team for me."

"What?" Griffin's lips tightened. "Don't be ridiculous. We all have to work together on—"

"This elevator is taking forever." Lynch was suddenly beside them and taking Kendra's arm. "Let's take the stairs." He didn't wait for a reply but was whisking her down the stairs toward the lobby and away from Griffin.

"I wasn't going to deck him," Kendra said.

"Just doing my duty to keep the peace. The minute the word ridiculous appeared in the conversation I thought intercession was called for."

"You might have been right." She grimaced. "I was doing pretty well until then."

"Yeah, you were." He smiled. "Then we go up to Huston's room and you take another look? You don't make mistakes, Kendra."

"I was pretty upset. Everyone makes mistakes." She added wearily, "Except Zachary."

"He makes mistakes, too. We just haven't found them. Where's all that fire I saw just a few hours ago?"

"I'll get it back. He might have made a mistake already. We just have to put together what we know about him." She frowned, trying to examine that list. "He has to be some kind of psychopath, he's extremely smart, he knows a lot about procedural law enforcement, he knew this hotel well enough not to show up on the cameras. That's quite a bit when you think—" She stopped as she started to put it all together.

Could it be?

Perhaps . . .

"Kendra?"

"Maybe I'll wait to do that second check of Huston's room." She reached for her phone. "Maybe I'll go in another direction . . ."

Hilton Hotel
8:20 P.M.

"So you really think they might let Hagstrom go?" Jessie asked as she dropped down into an easy chair in the hotel bar lounge. "I told you I thought the chances of him being Zachary could have gone either way, but I was hoping that we'd gotten lucky."

"We didn't get lucky," Lynch said. "He definitely didn't kill Huston and there are credit card receipts that keep surfacing that might give him alibis at the time of the killings of some of the other victims."

"But I wasn't wrong about him being in every one of those crime locations," Jessie said. "I double-checked and that's pretty damning coincidences."

"We're not accusing you of not being correct," Kendra said. "I'm certain Hagstrom was in the same city as Zachary at the exact same time."

346

"An accomplice?" Jessie asked.

"Possible. But I doubt it. Zachary seems to me to be a loner. He's too egotistical to accept sharing either credit or the pleasure of the kill. It's also possible he could be a dupe. I'm leaning toward that direction. Perhaps he's been setting Hagstrom up all these years and waiting for the right moment to stage the frame."

"Diabolical," Jessie said. "And painstakingly precise." Her lips tightened. "And I'm not fond of the idea of him using me to put all the gears in motion."

She shook her head. "No, he used me. I used you."

"Same thing. When you hired me, we became one partnership. That's the way I work. The son of a bitch tried to manipulate me."

Lynch chuckled. "Interesting business philosophy. But I can see how you might experience difficulties with it."

Kendra grimaced. "Because you're a prime manipulator yourself."

"Guilty," Lynch said. "But I imagine Zachary regards us all as chess pieces."

"Screw him," Jessie said. "And I think that's probably what you intend to do to the bastard." She turned to Kendra. "You didn't invite me to meet you here to buy me a drink. What can I do for you?"

Kendra smiled wryly. "Cut to the chase? I just

had a row with Griffin in which I officially resigned from that dream team he proudly put together. He wasn't pleased. But I can't go on like this. We're not getting anywhere. My first thought after Huston's death was that Zachary might be gathering all those detectives in one place like lambs to be slaughtered."

"You didn't mention that to me," Lynch said.

"Since I would have been the first lamb to be slaughtered, you would have been a trifle upset." She shrugged. "And you probably thought about it yourself."

"It occurred to me."

"So you want protection?" Jessie asked. "Is that why I'm here?"

Kendra shook her head. "No, you're here because I want you to stay here at the hotel and keep those four detectives under surveillance."

"To make sure they're not murdered, too?"

"No." She paused. "To make sure none of them are murderers."

Jessie went still. She gave a low whistle. "That came out of left field. You believe one of them might be Zachary?"

"I believe that there could be a possibility that I don't want to ignore. If Hagstrom isn't guilty, we're left with no one. Zachary has shown an incredibly strong understanding of how law enforcement works. The dream team is staying at the same hotel, so none of them would look out of place to anyone

348

reviewing the lobby cameras. They've all lived and breathed these cases, and there would be no suspicion if they appeared on site at any of them. I want them watched until I can investigate them all in depth." She wrinkled her nose. "In short, I want my own team to watch the dream team."

"And I'm your team of choice?" Jessie was frowning thoughtfully. "I appreciate the compliment, but it won't be easy. Hotels are notoriously simple to escape. Fire exits. Maids with pass keys. Room service deliveries. It didn't surprise me when you said Griffin wasn't finding any clues in Huston's death. There have to be so many people at the scene they're probably stumbling over each other. Police. FBI. Forensics. Plus those guys in the dream team milling around. If anyone knew the hotel, it wouldn't take any effort to slip in and out."

"Is this a refusal?"

"Hell, no. I'm just setting you up to let me call in a couple guys who work with me sometimes. I can't watch all four rooms at one time. And what if one of the guys decides to go pub crawling?"

"Get them. No problem. Just make it happen."

She nodded. "I'll do it. And I'll set up another guard to keep an eye on Olivia while I'm here." She took out her phone and started punching numbers. She gazed at Kendra as she waited for an answer. "You're charged. I can feel it. Huston's death really shook you."

Kendra wasn't surprised she was being this transparent. Every nerve was tense. "Among other things. Every time I turn around Zachary seems to be there . . . waiting for me to make a mistake." She got to her feet. "And he's on the move. We've got to stop him."

"Right." Jessie glanced at Lynch. "So do your job and make certain that you keep the bastard away from her. It appears I'm going to be tied up here." Then her call was answered and she began to talk quickly into her phone.

"I believe we've been dismissed." Lynch took Kendra's elbow and guided her toward the front entrance. "Or at least I have." They were outside and he gave the valet his check. "She evidently thinks there's no reason to urge you to get your ass in gear. You're obviously motivated." He tipped the valet as he got into the driver's seat. "A little too obviously."

"I suppose you mean something by that."

"I mean that you're going to slow down." He started down the driveway. "I'm taking you to dinner and then I'll take you home and you'll get some sleep."

"Bullshit."

"We'll start with dinner and go from there." He tilted his head as he glanced at her. "Unless you have some scheme, some urgent plan, that you have to immediately execute? I don't think so. I think that setting up Jessie with the dream team might have been an act of desperation." He held up his hand. "Not a bad idea. Clever. It might be the way to go. But there might be other solutions and you need to think about what they might be. We'll go to a quiet restaurant that has nothing to do with gaudy sombreros and we'll talk about options. Heaven forbid I try to get you off the subject of Zachary for the length of the meal." He looked her in the eye. "If you have somewhere to go and something to do, forget it. If you don't, you're mine."

He knew her too well. He had read both her desperation and her driving need to get something, *anything* done. Assigning Jessie to the dream team had been the only thing she could think to do that might yield results. But now what else could she do? He was right, she had to think, concentrate, and search for that next step.

"Dinner might not be too bad," she said. "As long as you keep your promise about no sombreros."

What a cozy evening, Zachary thought as he watched Lynch's Ferrari pull into Kendra's parking garage. First a quiet dinner and now they were going to her place to screw and comfort themselves that Kendra was not really in danger.

But there had been no smiles or laughter at that dinner. Kendra had been just as subdued and on edge as he could have wished. She had not given up, but Huston's death had shocked her. She might be having thoughts of her own mortality. She had never faced an enemy of his caliber.

The realization sent a rush of pleasure through him. Even the sex with Lynch might not be so good tonight, Kendra. I've got you on the ropes. He'd had no doubt they were lovers since that moment he'd seen the two of them on the street after they'd seen Huston's body. No question about the intimacy between them. No question either that he'd have to target Lynch before he took Kendra. Seeing a lover die was just too painful not to include it in Kendra's final death agenda.

Lynch.

An important name to add to his growing list . . .

"I suppose I'm not allowed to stay," Lynch said as he handed Kendra her keys. "All this contriving is nonsense you know."

"No, I don't know," she said tightly. "And I won't take any chances. Have you forgotten Huston was gutted this morning?"

"I'm not Huston." He pushed the hair back from her temple. "And it might help to have someone to hold onto tonight."

"Good night, Lynch." She shook her head. "And I don't need someone to hold onto. I need to figure out what's going to happen next, so I can get there ahead of Zachary." She grimaced. "And your quiet, restful dinner did nothing for me. I went blank, dammit. I felt as if there was something I should know, something just out of reach, but I can't *get* there."

"You will. Give yourself a chance. Relax and let it come to you. You know it always does." He kissed the tip of her nose. "I'll be down the hall in that condo Olivia exiled me to. Call me if you need me."

She watched him walk down the hall.

She wanted to call him back. There was no way she wanted to be alone tonight.

But that would be another victory for Zachary and he'd already stolen too many from her.

She closed the door and leaned back against it.

Zachary was getting closer. She could feel it. Body by body, he was making his way toward her. But there had to be a way to stop him.

Think.

Concentrate.

There was only blankness.

She pushed away from the door and headed for the bedroom. Relax, Lynch had said. Let it come to you. It always does.

God, she hoped he was right.

8:45 A.M.

"You're out of luck," Olivia said to Kendra as she threw open her front door. "I thought you might drop by, but I couldn't wait. When you didn't show up by seven, I made a delicious omelet for myself and devoured every morsel. But I can give you a cup of coffee."

"Don't have time." Kendra came into the living room and glanced over at Olivia's desk, which was piled high with papers and devices. "Does that mean you have to work today?"

"Yes." She crossed her arms. "As you can see by that monstrous heap on my desk that you probably checked out the minute you came in the room." She paused. "Okay, say it."

"Jessie called you last night, didn't she? I knew she would."

"Of course she did. She politely told me where she was and that she wouldn't be home for the night. I felt like a house mother at a college sorority. But at least she was smart enough not to say anything else. No warnings. She let the call speak for itself." She shook her head. "But you're not going to be that smart, are you?"

"No. I'm going to plead with you to give me a break," she said quietly. "He's getting too close, Olivia. I have to keep him away. I believe he might have killed Huston to prove that he could strike out at anyone and I couldn't stop him. Huston was hardly more than an acquaintance, but he was a detective and I was working with him. But I think Zachary will try to strike deeper next time." She smiled unsteadily. "And you're very deep, indeed. Please don't make me worry about you for the next couple days."

"Oh, shit." Then she grabbed Kendra into her arms and gave her a bear hug. "There goes all my vaunted independence. Jessie would laugh at me." She took a step back. "I suppose you want me to promise to stay in the condo?" She sighed. "Okay, I have enough to keep me busy for a week much less a couple days." She paused. "But I don't like the idea of you being this scared. Where's Lynch?"

"I told him to wait in the parking garage for me while I talked to you. I didn't want to chance you getting defensive if you thought we were ganging up on you." She smiled. "And you're clearly not worried about Lynch being a threat to my independence."

"That's different. And I bet Jessie feels the same way."

She couldn't deny it after that last remark Jessie had made at the hotel last night. "I don't believe that Lynch has any intention of riding off into the sunset. We'll be too busy."

"Doing what?"

"We're going to the FBI office and check on whether Hagstrom's alibis have been verified. Then we'll probably be spending hours delving into the backgrounds of our four remaining dream team detectives and see if we come up with anything interesting." She gave her another quick hug. "Don't worry. Paperwork, just like you."

"But you're allowing yourself to drop that paperwork and take off to go after monsters." She added fiercely, "Keep in touch, do you hear?"

"Absolutely. Thank you, Olivia."

She closed the door behind her. Olivia was as safe as she could make her under the circumstances. She didn't believe that Zachary would target her yet, but what did she know? She had to protect her own. He was a complete wild card.

And no one was really safe.

"How nice that you decided to drop in to see us," Griffin said silkily, as Kendra and Lynch walked into the office an hour later. "I thought that you might have cut us from your visiting list, when you told me that you were through with working with some of the finest law enforcement officers in the country."

"I told you that I meant no insult to anyone on the team," Kendra said. "It just wasn't for me. I felt . . . hobbled."

"But yet here you are."

"Knock it off, Griffin," Lynch said. "You know you're not going to keep us from seeing Hagstrom or doing any other research just because Kendra isn't going to walk lockstep with your team. It would be hard to explain to the media."

"What kind of research?"

"Anything and everything."

Griffin changed the subject. "And what was Jessie Mercado doing at the hotel last night?

When I asked her, she said that you were upset about Huston and she was there to see that no one else was hurt."

"That seems clear," Kendra said. "What are you asking?"

"Why you hired Mercado when my agents are there to do the job?"

"They didn't help Huston."

"We didn't know there was a threat to him."

"True. But I prefer to have someone answering to me than get it secondhand from you." She added wearily, "Look, I don't blame you for not being able to read Zachary's mind and protect Huston. No one could do that. I just don't want anyone else to die. Let's all work together to keep that from happening."

"Together," he repeated sourly. "As long as you do it alone."

She was losing patience. "Yeah, I guess you might say that's the—"

"What's going on with Hagstrom?" Lynch asked quickly. "He's still here?"

"For the time being. We probably won't have him for long. His lawyer is working nonstop to spring him. All he needs is a couple more pieces of evidence that validate his alibi in the Connecticut murders. If you want to talk to him, it had better be soon." He turned and walked away.

"Well, at least he didn't show us the door," Kendra said. "If you hadn't mentioned the media, he might have had security escort us from his august presence."

"Nah, he likes to keep you around to demonstrate how open-minded he is regarding sharing the spotlight in criminal investigations. Me, he might have tossed." He changed the subject. "Hagstrom or the research?"

"Hagstrom. I just have a few questions . . ."

"Are you trying to get in your final jabs before I blow this place?" Hagstrom growled. "I should sue the FBI, you know. You can't get away with persecuting innocent people. I didn't do anything and you've been harassing me."

"Harassing," Lynch repeated. "Did you get that word from your lawyer? It's very legalese."

"Maybe. But it's the right word, dammit." He leaned back in his chair. "I don't have to talk to you."

"We know you don't," Kendra said. "But we're hoping you'll do your civic duty. You say you don't remember having contact with any of the victims in any of those four cities. You didn't recognize any of the photos?"

"I told you I didn't." He shrugged. "Maybe I might have seen the photos on TV when they found the bodies, but I don't remember. Why should I? How would I know you guys would try to frame me?"

"And you don't recall anyone who might

have been at those cities at the same time as you?"

"Same answer."

She pulled out four photos and slid them across the table to him. "Do you recognize any of these people?"

He glanced at the photos. "What are you trying to do? Trick me? These are those same guys who were sitting there while I was being questioned. Cops, right?"

"Yes. Do you recognize any of them as being in those cities at the same time you were?"

He shook his head.

"Look again."

He looked more closely. "I don't know. Maybe." He tapped one photo. "He looks like someone I might have seen when I was in Jacksonville. But that was a long time ago." He tapped another photo. "And maybe him . . . But I could be wrong. I tell you I can't be sure. Why do you want to know?"

"Just checking your memory."

"The hell you are," he said belligerently. "I have a damn good memory when someone's not trying to trick me. Ask anyone." He pushed back his chair. "I'm not answering any more questions. Talk to my lawyer."

She nodded to the guard. "I hope you'll change your mind. I wasn't trying to trick or hurt you in any way." She got to her feet. "Think about those faces, will you? It might be important." She left the interview room.

"Who did he recognize?" Lynch asked as he joined her in the corridor.

"Trey Suber and Richard Gale." She grimaced. "But you can hardly call it recognition. It was a maybe at best. If he'd allowed himself to look longer at the other photos, he might have said the same thing. Or perhaps given me a valid identification on one of them."

"But a maybe is a maybe," Lynch said. "And it gives us something to work on. Tell me you're a little encouraged."

"Perhaps a little." She smiled. "It could be that I'll feel more than a little after we check backgrounds."

"Then let's go out, get a bite of lunch, and then come back and start research. I don't think you want to go down to the cafeteria and risk running into any of the dream team."

"That could be awkward." Awkward wasn't the word. She could imagine the outrage and incredulity if she was proved wrong. And that was a definite possibility. She was skating on thin and very dangerous ice. "By all means, let's not go down to the cafeteria."

7:40 P.M.

"This is ridiculous." Kendra rubbed her stinging eyes with her fists. "There's always at least one murder that would be impossible to have been committed by any of the dream team. We've gone over every one of the deaths and tried to match them. We keep coming up short."

"It could mean that one of these murders wasn't Zachary's. Or that one of the dream team is more clever in hiding his presence near the kill or better at concocting an alibi." He looked down at the photos. "Suber came up closest."

"And he has a callousness toward death that's very obvious." She gazed down at Suber's face. "And could be phony as hell."

"True. So do we go back through them again?"

"I guess we do. Maybe we missed something." She shook her head. "No, let's go back to talk to Hagstrom again. Maybe we can get him to take another look at those photos. I don't believe it's Suber."

He smiled. "Because you'd rather it be Richard Gale?"

"Maybe. I can't claim any professionalism right now. I'm not thinking straight." She got to her feet. "Let's go talk to Hagstrom. Something's bothering me."

"What?"

"I don't know. Something . . ."

"Well, I'm afraid you'll have to talk to him tomorrow. I saw him going down the hall toward the elevator with his lawyer about two hours ago."

"What?" Her eyes widened with shock. "Why didn't you tell me?"

"You were busy. I thought you were through with him. Why are you this upset?"

She wasn't sure, but she couldn't deny that she was. "You should have told me."

"Sorry. Would you care to tell me why you're acting as if that's a crime?"

"Because he shouldn't be going home, dammit."

"Why not?" He met her eyes. "Talk to me. Because he's Zachary?"

"No." He was right, she was behaving completely erratically, and there was no sense to it. Why had she suddenly been thrown into a tailspin? "He's not Zachary."

"You said something was bothering you. You think he knows who Zachary is?"

Think.

Concentrate.

And then it all came together.

She reached out and grabbed his arm. "No, he doesn't know who Zachary is. Not right now. But Zachary knows who *he* is. And there's a good possibility someday Hagstrom might be able to recognize him if he was shown the right photo. Or if we jogged the right memory of an old co-worker, girlfriend's brother, or personal trainer. Remember earlier today Hagstrom said everyone knew he had a good memory? Even if he's covered his tracks, Zachary wouldn't take a chance on Hagstrom remembering him.

Zachary never leaves loose ends. He used Hagstrom, but now he has to get rid of him. And he can't wait too long to do it. He'll have to guess we'll be showing him photos, examining every person he's ever been in contact with, especially in Washington where the murders began. Every day, every minute, will count."

Lynch's eyes were narrowed on the intentness of her expression, a faint smile on his lips. "And that's what's bothering you?"

"Yes." She could feel excitement heat her cheeks. "Because it's our *chance,* Lynch. Zachary's not going to go after me or anyone I care about next. Not yet. He's going to go after Hagstrom." She got to her feet and headed for the door. "And we know where we can find Hagstrom." Her voice was shaking. "And that means we can find Zachary."

"Yes, it does. And that brings up all kinds of interesting scenarios, doesn't it?" He was grinning recklessly as he caught up with her. "Tell me. Ever been on a stakeout, Kendra?"

CHAPTER 15

10:05 P.M.

"I don't like this," Kendra said flatly. "And it doesn't make sense. I can see sitting out here on the street if we were staking out some criminal, but it would be far more comfortable and efficient going inside Hagstrom's house and camping out there. After all, we're trying to keep him from being butchered. We could explain that to him and get permission to—"

"Very reasonable," Lynch said as he leaned back on his seat. "But may I remind you that Hagstrom didn't appear to be at all reasonable and is belligerent as hell. He would either kick us out or call his lawyer to get a warrant for trespassing."

"Perhaps we could persuade him."

"If you really want this, I'll go and make the attempt." He tilted his head consideringly. "I could always hog-tie him and then we wouldn't have to worry about having to argue with him."

She sighed. It would be dangerous to even keep discussing this. There was no telling where Lynch's twisted humor might take them. "Never mind. I'm just getting restless. You're sure that Hagstrom is inside?"

He nodded. "You watched me go check out the grounds and all the doors and windows forty minutes ago. I saw Hagstrom drinking beer and watching TV in the living room. Porn. Very kinky."

"I didn't have to know that."

"I wanted to give you a complete report. You appear to be a little on edge."

"I wonder why." She drew a deep breath. "I want this to happen, Lynch. He *has* to come."

"I know you do," he said quietly. "Zachary might not show tonight, you know. That's why we decided to wait to contact Griffin until we saw if Hagstrom was actually being targeted."

"But he might show, he'll want to tie up that loose end." She looked at him. "You think so too, don't you?"

"I believe there's a good chance." He suddenly grinned. "Why else would I have left my Ferrari in the garage and taken your Toyota? What a sacrifice."

"Duh," she said. "Even you would have to admit that the Ferrari might be a little ostentatious for this neighborhood. Of course, it would be ostentatious for Buckingham Palace."

"Only because Ferraris have loads more style than any of the Royals' boring vehicles." He reached over and took her hand. "If not tonight, then tomorrow, Kendra. We won't give up. You're really lousy at this stake-out business, but you're great company. And we could think about that hog-tying scenario if we get really bored. Or we could get a DVD player and borrow one of Hagstrom's porn tapes. There are all kinds of—"

"Hush." She stiffened, her gaze on the backyard of the condo. "Something . . ." She leaned forward, her eyes straining. "Dark . . . against that pine fence. Moving . . ." She saw another flicker of movement. "Lynch?"

"I see it. Shadow . . . Might be nothing." But he was out of the car and heading for the back of the condo at top speed. "Better call Griffin."

She was already on the phone. "Hagstrom's, Griffin," she said when he picked up. "Right away. Hurry!" Then she was running after Lynch.

He was standing on the concrete patio in front of the kitchen door.

Dark prints on the concrete . . .

Fresh scratches on the lock of the door . . .

"I don't see the glare from the TV through the windows anymore," Lynch said. "No lights either. The power might have been cut . . ." He tried the kitchen door. "Lock's broke, but it won't budge."

Lynch threw himself into the door, but it gave only slightly. "It's been barricaded." He glanced at a row of side windows. "Over there!"

Kendra followed him as he took off his jacket, wrapped it around his arm, and struck the nearest window. The glass shattered and fell around them. They both climbed inside and scrambled through the dark house.

Silence. Yet that shattered glass would have had to be heard.

"Hagstrom!" Kendra shouted.

Silence.

She flipped a light switch on the wall. Nothing.

"You're right, the power's been cut." She went rigid, her gaze searching the darkness. "Do you hear that?"

There was labored, tortured breathing issuing from the front room.

Evidently Lynch did, because he pulled out his automatic and a pocket flashlight and moved in front of her. "Keep behind me."

Then they rounded the corner, more light here streaming through the window from the glow of a streetlight. But they still couldn't tell where—

And then they saw him.

Hagstrom's body was crumpled in the middle of his living room rug. He was still twitching, blood pooling from his chest and neck. On the far side of the room, a strong breeze was buffeting the room from a broken window, and the curtains billowed outward toward the street.

"Shit!" Lynch fell to his knees beside Hagstrom, grabbed a throw blanket from the couch and pressed it against his chest. Before he could even complete the motion, Hagstrom gave a last gurgle and stopped breathing.

Lynch looked up at Kendra. "There's nothing I can do for him. His throat's been cut."

"I know." She was gazing down at Hagstrom's throat. The cut was clean and the sweep of the incision clear. So clear. Why hadn't she been able to see it before? Why hadn't she been able to see everything before?

Lynch jumped to his feet and ran to the window. "No one out there I can see. Wherever he went—"

"It wasn't a he," Kendra said numbly.

"What?"

"Zachary isn't a man."

Lynch's gaze narrowed on her. "And you know that *how?*"

"Because I know who our killer is. And you know, too." And she knew something else, she realized in sudden cold panic. Zachary would never have executed this kill and then gone out that window. He would know that by showing up here she had signaled the end of the game.

"It's a trap!" She stiffened, her gaze frantically trying to search the dimness. "Lynch, it's—"

Three quick footsteps from the darkness behind her and a cold blade snapped to her throat!

"Very good." The whisper in her ear was icy, and yet there was an element of mockery. "But then you're always exceptionally good. I'm proud of you, Kendra."

The knife was pressed so close to her neck Kendra didn't dare turn around. But she didn't need to. "Hello, Zachary." She moistened her lips. "Or should I still call you . . . Gina?"

Lynch had raised his gun, but Gina Carson angled Kendra toward him. "Drop it," she said. "Now."

"That's not going to happen."

"It needs to, if you want her to live." Gina repositioned her knife. "I've seen your file, and I know what an impressive marksman you are, Mr. Lynch. Your scores were higher than mine or anyone else in the region."

"Then you know how fast I can drop you where you stand."

"Maybe, but you'll notice that I've found Kendra's left common carotid artery. I've already begun to apply pressure. Even if you manage to hit me, one flick of my wrist will make sure Kendra dies long before help arrives. Do either of you doubt me?"

Neither answered.

"Do you doubt me?" she repeated.

"No," Kendra whispered, flinching as her throat moved against the blade.

"No," Lynch finally replied.

"Then put your gun onto the floor. Keep the barrel pointed away from me."

"Lynch . . ." Kendra said. "No."

He slowly put down the gun.

"Now kick it into the next room. You can keep the flashlight. It might prove helpful."

Lynch kicked the gun and it slid into the darkness.

"I do like cooperation. It will make your demise much more efficient," Gina said. "But I've been waiting a long time for this, Kendra. I'm not going to be totally deprived of pleasure because I'm in a hurry. I'm curious, how did you know it was me?"

"That's not important right now, is it?"

Gina applied pressure with her knife. She said softly, "Tell me."

Kendra's gaze was on Lynch standing across the room. His hands were clenched into fists as he stared at that knife. For the first time since she'd known him, he looked helpless.

"Need encouragement?" There was suddenly a trickle of blood running down Kendra's neck as Gina's knife pierced the skin. "I mean it, Kendra. I'm the one in control here."

And Lynch was stiffening, preparing to move.

He mustn't do that, Kendra thought frantically. "No one can doubt you think you're in control," she said jerkily. "Even if you're not as clever as you think you are."

"I'm every bit as clever as I think I am," she said mockingly. "I fooled you, didn't I? The day we met you reeled off all those things about me. Except the one thing that really mattered. I just want to know how you managed to figure out I was the one who broke in here to rid myself of that fool Hagstrom." She added, "*Now,* Kendra. I'm getting impatient."

And Kendra could tell that impatience was growing by the tightening of the muscles of Gina's upper arms, the slight hoarseness of her voice. Play for time. Hope that Griffin would get here before that time ran out. "Have it your own way. There were a few things I noticed after I got in here. We've known that we were dealing with a right-handed killer with a preference for an underhanded stab. I saw the same thing on Hagstrom's body. But between the door and this room, there were signs that the break-in was the work of an ambidextrous person. And you're ambidextrous, Gina."

"What? You knew that?" Gina asked, annoyed. "And you're saying I made a mistake? What signs?"

"When we reached the kitchen door, dew hadn't quite dried from your footprints on the concrete patio. The right shoe print was squarely in front of the door knob, pointed straight ahead. The knob had fresh scratches on the lock, a sign that you used your right hand to try and jigger it with a lockpick gun. But when that didn't work, you used a small pry bar. But you pushed the handle down toward the door frame, as a left-handed person might, tearing up the door itself with the bar's serrated edge."

"Kind of a stretch, isn't it?" Gina asked

defensively. "I didn't really make a mistake. And I always go back and clean up after myself before I leave."

"It's a probability game. And you didn't get a chance to go back and cover your tracks this time, did you? And the more I saw, the more the odds came down on the side of the conclusions I'd drawn. Including what I saw on Hagstrom's face."

"His *face?*"

"He obviously struggled with you before you stabbed him. There's bruising on both sides of his face and neck, but his right side took the brunt of your punches. You led with your left. I'm not sure if it means anything, but it's interesting you favored your left hand for uses of brute force—prying the door, pummeling his face—and you favored your right for more intricate tasks like picking the lock and working him over with this knife. All of it pointed to the attacker being ambidextrous. But like you, I'm curious. As I said, the distribution of tasks is interesting."

"You'll never know, will you?" Gina said defiantly.

"I might not. Just as I didn't realize that we were dealing with a killer who was ambidextrous. It's nothing I picked up from any of the hundreds of crime scene photos we examined, but I definitely got it here. And when I got it, I knew it had to be you. It's very rare. Less than one percent of humans are truly ambidextrous. But, as I said, I already had an idea that you were, Gina."

"Why? How? I'm damn careful, I don't make a big deal of it."

"Because you know how rare it is, and the last thing you want is to stand out."

"How?" she repeated between set teeth. "I *need* to know. For next time."

She was already planning a new spiral of deaths, Kendra realized, chilled. The moment she and Lynch were dead, she'd be off to continue the carnage.

"How?" Gina's voice was suddenly low, gravelly, rough. "Do you think I won't slice your throat, bitch? You might live a few more minutes if you do what I want."

Where the hell are you, Griffin?

Keep stalling. Give her what she wants.

"You didn't need to make a big deal of it," Kendra said. "I didn't think that much about it. It was just interesting. But I noticed you write with your right hand, but shoot with your left."

"You've never seen me hold a gun."

"No, but your shoulder holster is on your right side, indicating that you draw with your left hand. You wear your belts upside down, like many lefties do, but your shoe laces are tied with the first loop formed on the left, like most righties would do it. Callouses on your hands show that you use them both about equally, but for different tasks."

Kendra became aware of a bead of perspiration running from her forehead onto her cheek. She wanted to wipe it away. For some absurd reason, it bothered her that Gina might think it was a tear.

"Go on," Gina said. "I'm enjoying this."

Kendra was beginning to see why that was true. Though it was probably a mixed pleasure for Gina. She hadn't liked the idea that she wasn't as perfect as she'd thought. But the more status Kendra gained in Gina's eyes, the more pleasure she'd get from that final kill. She continued quickly, "I'd already started to suspect that Zachary worked for law enforcement, specifically our investigation. I actually have someone watching the dream team right now. That should amuse you. But there were inconsistencies and I kept feeling something was wrong. But here tonight, it all snapped into place."

"Don't feel bad." Gina's smile was scornful. "You know how many people have spent years and years on these cases . . . I was really rooting for you."

"I doubt that."

"Oh, but I was." She adjusted her grip on the knife. "You've restored my faith, Kendra."

Lynch stepped toward her, and she responded by raising her arm.

He stopped short. "There's no way out of this, Gina."

"Sure there is. This has been a finale years in the making. Zachary has planned everything."

"You mean *you* planned everything," Kendra said.

Gina stiffened. "No, you mustn't think I did it. He doesn't like it." She added quickly, "Don't be stupid. I couldn't do it." For the first time, Kendra sensed anxiety from Gina. What was happening to her? She was beginning to perspire and her breathing became irregular. "You have to respect him," she said, her voice quivering. "He punishes people who don't respect him. He deserves the respect."

"Zachary?" Lynch's eyes narrowed on her face. "*Zachary* deserves the respect?"

What was going on here? Kendra thought in bewilderment. She was speaking as if Zachary was another person but all the signs were indicating otherwise. It was the first sign of weakness she had exhibited and Lynch had seen it, too.

"Yes," Gina said. Her hands shook and the blade vibrated against Kendra's throat. Weird. The moment she had started speaking about Zachary, she had appeared to become weaker. "All the respect. I just do what he wants. I'm nothing compared to him."

But if Gina was displaying any weakness, then maybe they could use that weakness, Kendra thought desperately.

"Where is he now?" Kendra asked. "Where is Zachary?"

"He sees you. He sees what you're trying to do. You're only making him angry."

"Where is he?" Kendra repeated.

"He sees and hears everything we're saying. He's here. He's always here."

Kendra locked eyes with Lynch in total shock. Who could have known? Those few sentences had opened wide the door, and she had made the connection. He gave an imperceptible nod. He thought he understood and she was almost completely sure *she* did.

She spoke in soft, comforting tones, almost as if she was talking to one of her clients. "Of course I respect Zachary. He's the master. He's fooled everyone."

Gina relaxed slightly. "Yes."

"That's why I want to talk to him. No one's ever beaten me before."

Kendra felt Gina shake her head. "Zachary only talks to me."

"And he's talking to you now?"

"Yes."

"What is he saying?"

"You're making him angry. He thinks you're trying to fool him. He's disappointed in you. He's afraid he might have to do the kill before he wanted it to happen."

"And you also do what he tells you?"

"Yes."

"That's how he does all the things he does? The people he hurts? You do it all for him?"

"No. He does things I don't find out about until later. I'm not there for those things. He says I'm not worthy to do them. But I do help him. I do."

"I'm sure you do whatever he wishes." She had to be very careful to avoid any hint of antagonism in Gina. Kendra had never treated a client with what was commonly called split personality, but she knew the basics. She was almost sure that she was dealing with dissociative personality disorder. But it appeared that Zachary was the dominant personality and that meant to avoid him coming to the forefront it was best not to contradict Gina and threaten the constructs she had created.

"You don't have to do everything, Gina. We're here to help you."

"Zachary knows you're lying," she said harshly.

"I'm not."

Gina was trembling again. "He says you are. I told you bad things would happen if you disrespect him."

"So he *is* here."

"I told you, he's always here."

"And you're afraid of him."

"He wants me to be afraid. He says it's a form of respect. He said if I don't do as he says, he'll send me away and never let me come back."

"You think he can do that?"

"Of course he can do it. He's been with me since I was eighteen and he's been getting stronger and stronger." Gina was becoming increasingly agitated. "I know you're some kind of high-priced psychologist. You think you can fix people." She said defiantly, "Well, we don't need fixing."

"No. I only help people who want to be helped."

"Zachary doesn't believe you. He knows what you want to do to us."

Police sirens wailed in the distance!

Gina went rigid, her head lifting, her eyes widening in shock. "*You* did this. You brought them here."

"Let us help you," Kendra said. "We'll keep you and Zachary safe."

"You're *lying*." Her voice was suddenly lower, harsher.

The sirens were closer.

"Then this is where it all ends," Gina said. "After all these years, it ends right here, with you and me, Kendra."

Kendra tensed as she noticed that Gina's voice had now completely changed; her speech was now silky smooth and had dropped to a still lower, almost masculine, register. Was this now Zachary?

Dear God, if Gina was gone, Zachary would strike!

Lynch had obviously also noticed the change. He bent slightly at the knees, tensing, as if ready to pounce.

Gina sounded genuinely regretful. "I'm sorry, Kendra. It's not at all what I planned for you. There's no more time. I have to get out of here. Just know you've lived up to my every hope."

"Wait! There's still something we can—" She broke off as she could feel Gina's muscles tightening, her grasp squeezing the knife . . .

"No!" Lynch flew across the room like a panther springing into action! In a second he was almost there . . .

But in the same instant, Gina grasped the hilt of the knife and hurled it toward him!

The knife buried itself into Lynch's upper chest and he collapsed in a heap onto the floor.

No! No! No!

Kendra didn't know if she screamed the words or if they were just repeating over and over in her mind.

She had to get to him.

She struggled with all her strength, broke free, and tore across the room. She could hear Gina swearing behind her as she fell to her knees beside Lynch.

He was alive, but in pain, his eyes open, struggling to breathe.

"Lynch, hang on," she said frantically. "Listen to me. Please. Stay."

"Waste of time." Gina was reaching into her jacket. "He's a dead man, Kendra. That was only a postponement. Admit it, you're helpless."

Helpless. No weapons. And Gina was reaching for the gun in that holster.

But Lynch was looking up at Kendra, he was trying to tell her something. His gaze left her face and then flicked to the knife protruding from his left pectoral muscle. He looked back at her.

Was he actually suggesting—?

He gave her an almost imperceptible nod.

"I can't do it," she whispered. "I could *kill* you."

"Do . . . it," he said hoarsely. It wasn't just a suggestion, but a command.

Behind her, she saw that Gina was pulling the gun from her holster.

"Now!"

In a blur, Kendra pulled the knife straight up from Lynch's chest and whirled around. Then she was across the room, lifting the blade.

She saw the shock on Gina's face just milliseconds before plunging the knife into the woman's stomach!

But Kendra held onto the knife. She had to be sure. "No more." She pulled it out and stabbed her again. "Never again." The knife came down once more. And again. Then one more time.

She stopped, breathing hard. "Look behind *you,* Zachary. All those people you butchered are waiting for you."

Gina's limbs froze. The only indication that she was still alive came from her bulging eyes, mirroring every painful plunge of the blade.

She finally fell back against the wall and slid down to the floor in a sitting position. In this moment she looked totally masculine, totally Zachary. Her clothes were covered in blood. She looked at Kendra in shock, her lips twitching and blood spurting from her nose. "I . . . still win. Lynch . . ."

"No, you won't." She was already running back across the room to Lynch. "He's tougher than you ever dreamed of being. I won't *let* him die. Believe me, Zachary. You lost big time."

It didn't matter if Gina believed her or not. *She* didn't matter any longer. Gina finally let out one last long breath, her face frozen in that look of pain and bewilderment.

Zachary was dead.

Only Lynch mattered and for an instant as Kendra looked down at him, she was terrified that Zachary had actually won. She couldn't tell if Lynch was still breathing.

And there was so much blood.

She fell to her knees and checked the pulse in his throat. Still beating. But he was unconscious and that blood kept flowing . . .

Was that her fault? Had she damaged him irreparably when she'd pulled out that knife?

She tore open his shirt and gasped as she saw the blood flowing out of the wound in his chest. She reached for her phone and pressed Griffin's quick dial while she started pressure with her other hand.

"What the hell is happening?" Griffin asked. "We're on our way but I need—"

"Shut up. I told you we were at Hagstrom's. I just killed Zachary. But I need an ambulance and blood right away. I don't know Lynch's blood type, but if you can't find out, make sure the EMT's have plenty of universal." Her voice was shaking. "I'm scared, Griffin. He's lost so much blood."

"Lynch?"

"You heard me. Stop asking questions. Get someone here for him." She hung up the cell and immediately used her hand to apply more pressure. "They're coming, Lynch. Don't you dare die. I told Zachary how tough you were and you wouldn't want to make me a liar. He said he'd win, and we can't let him do that."

No answer. Of course there was no answer. He was hurt and in shock. That didn't mean that he was dying. She wouldn't let him die. "You hold on, Lynch. You wouldn't let me die, would you? You're too stubborn to ever let Zachary take anything—" Her voice broke and she had to take a second to steady it. "So you have to do the same for me. Everything's going to be fine. You just do your part, okay? I think I hear the ambulance. Thank God. Griffin must have done something right . . ."

The EMT's were putting Lynch in the ambulance when Griffin pulled up behind it. He and Metcalf jumped out of the car and ran toward Kendra.

"Are you hurt?" Griffin asked. "I thought you said Lynch, but you look awful."

"It was Lynch. What are you talking about? I'm not hurt. He's the one who's hurt and bleeding."

"He's not the only one," Metcalf said gently. "You look like you've been interning in a slaughterhouse. Look at yourself. You're drenched in blood. It's not yours?"

She shook her head. "It's Lynch's." She rubbed her temple trying to think. "And maybe Zachary's. The EMT's were making such a fuss and wasting time trying to check on him. I told them he didn't matter and I'd already killed him." Him. She probably shouldn't be referring to Gina as him. She might be confusing them. But it was how she thought of Zachary. It was as if Gina had never really existed.

"Yes, I'd imagine that would cause a fuss," Griffin said. "How is Lynch?"

"I don't know. They're giving him blood. But I'm going with him to the hospital and find out." She glared at the EMT who had finished hooking up Lynch to the equipment in the ambulance. "He says I can't go. Take care of it, Griffin. It's something about what I did to Zachary."

"She said she killed this Zachary," the EMT said coldly. "And there's a dead man in there. But there's also a woman inside who's sliced full of holes. Either way we have to wait for the police to come and investigate."

"Take care of it," Kendra repeated to Griffin as she got into the ambulance. "I'm going with Lynch."

"No!" The EMT stepped forward, alarmed.

"It's perfectly in order." Griffin stepped in front of him, his tone soothing. He showed him his ID. "FBI. We've been hunting for a serial killer. You might have read about him. You don't want to stand here and argue when you need to get our agent to the hospital. I'll send Metcalf inside to investigate the crime scene."

Metcalf. That pierced the fog of panic enveloping Kendra. "No, go with him. It's going to be a shock for both of you. But it's Zachary," she said. "I don't have time to go into it. Call me later. You'll think it's Gina. But I swear it's Zachary that I killed. Gina was Zachary. I swear."

"Gina? Zachary?" Griffin was staring at her. "Are you crazy?"

"No, I'm telling the truth." She glanced at Metcalf. She'd done what she could to prepare him. "I'm sorry." The EMT slammed the door shut.

Kendra sat down beside Lynch in the ambulance.

Still unconscious. Still pale. But he was hooked up to the IV and maybe he was going to be—

"What the hell—happened to—you."

Her gaze flew to Lynch's face. His eyes were only slits but he'd really spoken. She stifled the flash of wild excitement and hope. "You'd better not talk. You're on the way to the hospital. You've got to save your strength because you've got to get well. I won't have it any other way."

He was frowning. "Happened—to you? Blood all over your face. Tear streaks. What a mess . . ."

"Hush. I guess I kept pushing back my hair." She reached out to hold his hand. "And you're more of a mess than I am. It's your blood, dammit. Now will you please shut up?"

His eyes were closing. "No choice . . . Just so it's—not your—blood."

He was unconscious again. That was all, she told herself, he'd just passed out. She could see the pulse pounding in his throat.

And he'd spoken to her. Only a few words, but they'd been clear and characteristic Lynch. That was a good sign. A dying man wouldn't have told her she looked like a mess, would he?

If it was Lynch, he might. But then he would have had a twinkle in his eye.

Her hand tightened on his hand.

Stay with me. Say anything you want to me. I can always get back at you later.

Just stay with me.

CHAPTER 16

Sharp Memorial Hospital
3:30 A.M.
Waiting Room

"I see they kicked you out of Lynch's room."

Kendra opened her eyes and straightened in her chair as she saw Griffin standing in the doorway. "They sedated him and they wouldn't let me stay. They said they had a family only rule for overnight visitors." She stared at him accusingly. "I tried to get hold of you to make you fix it, but no one could reach you. I left a message."

"Sorry. What a shame." He came toward her and gave her a cup of coffee. "And I do want to make your world run just the way you want it. It's harder for me to change hospital rules than protect you from homicide charges. Though that was a nightmare, particularly when the victim was an FBI agent." He sipped his coffee. "Besides, I thought you might go home if you couldn't be within hovering distance of Lynch. You needed the rest. And Lynch wasn't going to expire on you. That stab wound is serious, but he's had worse."

"Not since I've met him. And he's never taken a wound like that for me. It makes a fairly vital difference. I have to make sure that he's okay and stays that way."

"I thought that was where this was going." He tilted his head. "At least you look like you've managed to shower and change since you got here. By the way, that kangaroo tee shirt is not fetching."

"Gift shop." She smiled faintly. "The shower was a definite necessity. Everyone in this hospital kept wanting to give me treatment. And the first thing Lynch had to say to me was that I was a mess. That's when I had an idea he was really going to live." Her smile faded. "Though I haven't been able to talk to him since then. They were sewing him up, x-rays, and then sedating him. But the surgeon told me the same thing he told you. He has to take care of himself for several weeks but there's nothing that can't be healed."

"Then go home, Kendra."

She shook her head. "Not yet. I have to be sure." She changed the subject. "What did your dream team say when you told them about Zachary?"

"Stunned." His mouth twisted. "Who wasn't stunned? The director wasn't pleased that I had the premier serial killer of the past decade working in my office. I'm a laughing stock. It's going to take a long time to get back in his good graces. The only saving grace is that we caught her."

"Yes, isn't it lucky *we* did. But I asked about the dream team."

"What you'd expect," he said carelessly. "Heartfelt relief expressed in their characteristic manners. A bit of disappointment from Suber. He wanted to be there to document Zachary's death."

"No, he wouldn't. I didn't behave at all like a cool, scientific professional." She moistened her lips. "I was savage, Griffin."

"Self-defense. You were under severe stress."

"Savage," she repeated. "Not like myself at all." She finished her coffee. "What about Metcalf? Is he okay?"

"Why shouldn't he be? Having your partner exposed as a serial killer is a shock, but they weren't working together that long."

"I guess you're right." Evidently Metcalf hadn't told anyone about his intimacy with Gina, and she wasn't about to do it. How he was going to deal with the memory of that bizarre relationship was up to him. She went back to her main objective. "You won't find a way to get me in there to sit with Lynch?"

"Nope. Doze in that chair until visiting hours and then go home and go to bed." He threw his empty cup in the trash bin and turned toward the door. "You did a good job, Kendra. Exceptional."

"No thanks? No gratitude?"

"You cancelled that out when you had Lynch

call and ask for that favor for the Walkers. You owed me."

"Son of a bitch."

"Oh, yes. And you'll owe me another one if I choose to persuade those detectives not to mention you when they're giving interviews to the media." He added softly, "How much is that worth to you, Kendra?"

He didn't wait for an answer but left the waiting room.

She wanted to follow him down the hall and push him down the elevator shaft.

But she was too tired and Griffin would always be Griffin, and she had to accept it. Well, no she didn't, but she had to accept it until she found a way to punish him.

She leaned back and closed her eyes again. Relax. At least, if she was thinking of ways to revenge herself on Griffin, she wouldn't be worrying about Lynch.

She wasn't allowed to see Lynch until after breakfast the next morning. But it seemed the rules didn't apply to Griffin. She saw him coming out of Lynch's room when she was walking down the hall from the elevator.

"Good morning." He smiled. "You look exhausted and a bit like a street kid hanging out in the charity ward."

"There's nothing wrong with that. I give a lot

of my time to street kids. They fight harder. What are you doing here?"

"I got a call from Lynch at the crack of dawn ordering me to come and see him. He objected to hospital garb and wanted his own clothes and the chance to interrogate me. I decided to oblige him. God knows he's useful and I might need him." He held up his hand. "I can't help it if he finds me more interesting than he does you. And he hadn't even seen that tacky tee shirt yet. See you later, Kendra." He strolled toward the elevators.

She opened the door. "Lynch, what did you want with—" She stopped as she saw him propped up in the bed across the room. He was not as pale as he had been the night before and his features looked almost normal. His blue eyes were bright and he was smiling at her. "Lynch?" She cleared her throat. "You look almost . . . You look . . . better."

"Thanks to pain pills and my fantastic stamina." He held out his hand. "But I have an idea I'm not going to last long. You'd better come over here and sit down."

She came slowly across the room. "Yesterday I thought you might be dying."

"Yesterday you might have been right." He grimaced. "But I hear there was an annoyingly persistent woman who kept insisting I stay alive. According to Griffin, she was ready to take anyone down who tried to tell her I wasn't going to make it."

"Rumor. Pure rumor."

"I don't think so. I remember bits and pieces and she was just as hardheaded as Griffin said." He took her hand. "It's a wonder I survived her."

His hand was warm and strong and she felt another rush of relief at that additional sign of recovery. "I don't appreciate you calling Griffin at dawn to discuss me. Particularly when you probably had been told I was already here at the hospital."

"That was a risk I took. Because as soon as the first drugs wore off, I knew I was going to be having trouble."

"I'm not giving anyone trouble. I just thought since you risked your neck taking Zachary's knife thrust for me that I should make sure you were going to be all right." She jerked her hand away from him. "And now that I know you're going to be as healthy and as obnoxious as you usually are, I can leave you on your own."

"No, you can't. I'd immediately fake a total collapse and you'd feel guilty as hell. No, you'll have to stick around for a while." He smiled. "I believe I'm feeling weaker even as I speak about it."

"Blackmail?"

"Why not? Everyone knows that I'll do any-thing to get what I want." He paused. "But this blackmail will have to be very curtailed because I don't have any idea how long I can keep up all this bullshit pretense that you feel so comfortable with. I have to take care of the problem before the pain medication totally wears off."

She was immediately alarmed. "You're hurting? How stupid can you get? I'll go tell the nurse you need to—"

"See?" He was smiling. "You're a pushover. Right now you don't know whether I'm playing you or not."

But she was afraid that he had not been playing her. She knew how strong he was and what he'd gone through over the years. He might be in severe pain and not let her see it. "I'm never sure if you're manipulating me or not," she said quietly. "But I do know you wouldn't be suffering at all if you hadn't stepped in front of that damn knife to keep Zachary from killing me. I don't think it's unusual for me to be concerned."

"No, particularly not for you." His smile faded. "But because of who you are, you tend to go overboard."

"Not true."

"Very true. Griffin said that you were taking this whole thing too hard. So let's deal with that problem first. It could have been serious and it's going to inconvenience me for a few weeks, but it's nowhere near as bad as what I've gone through before."

"That's what Griffin told me. At least, you've both got your stories straight."

"Doubting Thomas? Want proof?" He carefully slid the sheet down and flipped open his shirt. His finger tapped a long scar on his abdomen. "This one was made by a tribal leader in the Congo. A bayonet. Took him two days to get it that wide." He touched a small purple circle beside his rib cage. "Russia. A sniper shot went through the rib cage and out the back. It took a quarter inch of that lower rib with it." He touched a pale pink scar near his shoulder. "Detroit. Goodfella with the mob decided that he'd try to drill a hole through me to impress his boss." He met her eyes. "I'd prefer not to turn over and show you the rest. It might hurt a bit. Most of the attacks are from behind when I've not been aware of the threat. Unless you insist?"

"No," she whispered. She couldn't take her eyes off his body. So much power and strength yet so vulnerable to death and attack. It was no wonder that he'd built a stockade of a house to protect himself and allow him to relax for brief moments. She slowly reached out to touch a small circular scar on his chest. "This one is very old . . ."

"Yes." He took her hand away and put it on the bed. "Cigarette burn. Not a good example. We won't talk about it."

Because he didn't want to talk about that burn. He had revealed more about himself in these few minutes than she had learned in all the months they had worked together, but it seemed that cigarette burn was off limits. "Whatever you say." She reached out and carefully pulled his shirt back over his chest. "What's one more scar?" She stared him in the eye. "Isn't that what you want me to say? That knife wound Zachary gave you will be just one more scar." She took a step closer to the bed. "Wrong. That's *my* scar, Lynch. It will always belong to me. And I'll always know it." Her hands clenched. "Just as I know that Zachary gave me scars I'm going to have to fight like hell to erase. I might never do it."

"You'll do it. You just may need a little friendly therapy," he said. "Which brings us to the second problem. Griffin said that you disposed of Zachary with an enthusiasm that was well deserved but in retrospect upset you."

"I was savage," she said flatly. "I stabbed him five times, Lynch. Again and again. I only knew I had to kill him. You were lying there bleeding, maybe dying. Huston . . . all those others he killed . . ." She was starting to shake. "I don't do that. That's not who I am. Or maybe that's who I am now. If it is, I don't know how I can live with myself."

"Give me your hand. I want to hold you and that's the best I can do right now."

"Comfort? I have to get through this by myself. *Five* times, Lynch."

"Give me your hand!" he said roughly.

She slipped her hand into his grasp.

Strength. Warmth. Comfort.

"That's better, I didn't want to have to jump out of this bed. That would seriously impact my plans of getting out of here in a timely manner." He drew a deep breath. "I'm not the person you should be talking to about this. I know all the words to say but you know damn well I'd probably say anything to get you into bed. Besides the fact that I can only tell you everything from my slightly skewed viewpoint." He stared her directly in the eye. "But I'll always be honest with you. So here it is, Kendra. I don't know if what you did to Zachary changed you. It might have, just as every new experience and emotional trauma can change you. We're all capable of reacting in ways we don't expect when we're brought to the breaking point. You're gentle, you're empathetic, and you're capable of deeper emotional involvement than anyone I've met. That means you'd react accordingly, but it doesn't tarnish what you are. So don't give me any bullshit about what one monster would be able to do to you. Zachary didn't do any permanent damage and neither will anyone else. You're too damn strong." His grasp tightened. "Understand?"

"I guess I do." She could feel his power. She could feel the sheer intensity. She couldn't take her gaze from his face. "You've been pretty verbose on the subject for someone who shouldn't be talking to me about it."

"You know I've never been able to keep from putting my two cents into the pot. But I assure you, it's pure preparation for the main event."

She frowned. "The main event?"

He made a dismissing gesture. "You're smart enough to recognize the main event when you see it." He smiled. "Though you were a little slow identifying what a total prize I am. Now you're getting closer, but I expect to have trouble because of my extraordinary act of heroism."

"Not because of your extraordinary modesty?" she asked dryly. "I thought that wound was nothing in your scheme of things. Remember, I got the whole show."

"Not the whole show, but I was very effective, wasn't I?" His thumb was tracing patterns on her wrist. "But you're very stubborn and you'll still have that thread of ingrained gratitude until it lessens a bit. That's going to get in the way. Not for you, for me. I'm too egotistical to have to wonder if you're going to bed with me because I took that knife for you." His nail was following the life line on her palm. "I wouldn't want to worry that I wasn't as superb as I really am. And what if you talked yourself into that nonsense, too?"

No chance of that, she thought. Just those

fingers on her hand and wrist were causing her pulse to race. And the bastard probably knew it. "What a terrible predicament for you."

"And it gets worse. You didn't like seeing me hurt, it scared you. You're going to shy away from feeling that again. You might panic and run."

"You don't believe you might be flattering yourself?"

"No. I can't afford to do that." He was no longer smiling. "I was almost there. I'm not going to make a mistake and cheat us both. I don't mind taking a step back but only one step."

"You appear to be leaving me out of this decision."

"No way. The decision is all about you . . . wanting me."

"You're making it sound entirely too difficult. I'm surprised you don't want to forget about me and go back to Ashley or one of your other girlfriends."

"The situation isn't that desperate. We can work it out. Shall I tell you how?"

"I can hardly wait."

"I might be stuck in this hospital for a few days. You'll come to visit me every day and enjoy my stunning charisma and vast intelligence. And also reassure yourself that I'm so tough that you don't need to worry about anything happening to me. Then when I'm out of here, I'll go slow and I *might* even let you set the pace."

"Might?"

"I don't want you to believe I'd lie to you."

She shook her head. "How arrogant can you be? You're sure you have me figured out. You even have a damn solution."

"I hope I have you figured out." He laid his head back on his pillow. "I'm wasting a lot of time and energy I don't have if I'm wrong." His smile was weary. "Give it a shot, Kendra?"

He was looking suddenly tired and drained and she wanted to give him anything he wanted to make that exhaustion go away. "We'll see." She turned toward the door. "If I decide you're not using how I feel to manipulate me."

"No promises. It's the nature of the beast. You'll have to make up your own mind." He snapped his fingers. "Oh, and I didn't mean that you have to come back to the hospital today. You have other things to do. Then go home and get some rest."

"I don't *have* to come back today?" Her eyes widened with indignation. "That's the worst thing you could have said to me. And what other things have you decided I have to do?"

"Open the door. She should be waiting in the hall by now."

She jerked the door open and saw Jessie Mercado sitting on the bench a few yards down the hall.

"Jessie?" Her eyes flew back to Lynch. "What the hell?"

"The main event," he said quietly. "She's a woman who had two tours in Afghanistan and was once captured and held prisoner. She knows about rage and sorrow and revenge and how both can change who you are. If you feel like it, you might want to talk to her. If you don't, she'll understand."

But he'd gone to the trouble of getting in touch with Jessie because he'd thought she might need her. She stood there looking at him. He didn't appear either bright-eyed or as strong as when she'd first seen him this morning. He was not invulnerable and he undoubtedly was arrogant and manipulative. But he'd let her see his scars and he'd tried to heal hers. How many men would be strong and caring enough to do that?

"Hi, Kendra." Jessie had gotten to her feet and was strolling toward her. "I heard you were here. Want to go have a cup of coffee with me?"

"That sounds like a great idea." Kendra's smile was brilliant. "If you've got your bike. Let's go take a ride on the beach and find a coffee shop. I need to feel the wind in my hair and maybe jump a few dunes. Someone told me lately I was getting stodgy."

Her smile lost none of its brilliance but there was definitely a hint of sly mischief as she glanced at Lynch. "If we make it back in one piece, I'll see you tomorrow, Lynch."

Center Point Large Print
600 Brooks Road / PO Box 1
Thorndike, ME 04986-0001 USA

(207) 568-3717